THE 9TH PROTOCOL

KEVIN J SIMINGTON

PROLOGUE

They buried the body in the rose garden, along with the others.

Two men dressed in dark clothing dug the hole, taking it in turns with a shovel. The night was dark, with no moon. A spectacular dusting of stars stretched above their heads as they laboured, but the magnificence of the display was completely lost on them as they carried out their grim task.

Finally, the hole was deep enough, and they stepped back, both breathing heavily. Several rose bushes had been dug out and lay on the grass, awaiting replanting. The body was slumped awkwardly across a hover-pallet, arms and legs hanging over the side.

The larger man pushed the pallet to the side of the hole and tipped the body in, grunting with effort as he did so. The body flopped into the hole and landed with a dull thud, face down. They rearranged the arms and legs, then took up their shovels and began covering the body with dirt.

Eventually, the hole was filled in and the rose bushes were replanted on top. The two men stood looking at their handiwork, both sweating and puffing.

"She sure likes her roses," said the smaller man.

They looked along the row of rose bushes, which extended the full length of the building.

"I hope there's not too many more of these," said the larger man. "We're running out of room."

1

The voice seemed to come to him from a great distance. At first, he did not recognise it as a voice at all, for his mind did not identify the sounds as having any particular meaning or structure. All he heard was a dull buzzing, as if someone had trapped a swarm of bees inside a glass bottle. He wondered who had done this to the bees and he considered how he might liberate them. The buzzing became increasingly insistent, and it gradually resolved into recognisable words.

"Wake up. Come on, open your eyes. It's time to wake up."

He vaguely understood the meaning of the words now, even though they sounded as if they were being spoken from inside a vast echo chamber.

"Come on, Mr Newman, open your eyes for me please. Wake up."

Who the hell is Mr Newman, and where did the bees go? Maybe if I ignore the voice, it will go away, and the bees will come back.

He felt a hand grasp his shoulder and gently shake him. "Can you hear me, Mr Newman? I need you to open your eyes. Come on, you can do it."

Now he was getting annoyed. Clearly, this was a case of mistaken identity. *There must be a Mr Newman somewhere else, lying in blissful, undisturbed slumber while I have to suffer this rude interruption! I need to explain that they have the wrong person.* He opened his eyes and told her so, expressing his extreme displeasure and asking her to return the bees. A few moments later he realised that he had managed to neither speak nor open his eyes at all. This was going to be harder than he had anticipated! He tried again to open his eyes and managed a few brief flutters. Someone seemed to have attached heavy weights to his eyelids.

"That's the way, Mr Newman. You nearly did it. Keep trying. Open those eyes."

Who is this Newman guy and how did she get me confused with him? This annoying woman is going to get a piece of my mind, just as soon as I can get my damned eyes open! With a supreme effort he managed to open his eyes a slit and was immediately dazzled by the bright light streaming through the window beside his bed. He grimaced and groaned, pivoting his head away from the source of irritation.

"Oh, I'm sorry. It must seem terribly bright in here. Let me dim the window for you. There. That's better, isn't it?"

It was marginally better, but everything still seemed incandescent and blurry. He blinked rapidly and looked around, trying to make sense of his surroundings. It was a nondescript, small, white room, devoid of furniture apart from the adjustable bed upon which he was lying and a nightstand to his left. A large panel in the ceiling directly above him clearly marked the location of a retractable medibot. He glanced along the length of his body. Several small, circular medpatches on his arms and legs told him that he had recently been attached to medical apparatus of some kind. He looked to his right and gazed out the now-dimmed widow, trying to ascertain his location. A generic scene of hills greeted his gaze, darkened by the window's semi-opacity, as if a solar eclipse were occurring.

He turned his attention back to the room and focused on the source of the annoying voice. An attractive woman in a nurse's uniform stood beside the bed, her hair in a tight bun and a data pad in her hands. She looked to be in her late 30s, and her carefully maintained figure was barely concealed by her nurse's uniform.

"Well done. Welcome back! Here, let me sit you up." She tapped the data pad and his bed tilted him to a sitting position. "That's better. How are you feeling, Mr Newman?"

"I am not Mr Newman!" At least, that is what he attempted to say, but all that came out of his mouth was an inarticulate croak.

"Your throat is probably very dry," she responded. She reached behind him to the nightstand and produced a cup with a straw. "Here, drink this. It's a rejuve formula. Electrolytes, vitamins and nutrients." She placed the straw in his mouth, and he dutifully sucked. The liquid was pleasant tasting, and he quickly consumed the contents, surprising himself with his thirst. The slight movement of his head, however, had drawn his attention to another problem which, prior to this, had remained on the edge of his perception, but which now asserted itself like a schoolyard bully. He had a pounding headache. It throbbed with a regular beat, as if a tiny person with a sledgehammer was trying to break out of his skull.

"Ah ...," he moaned, holding his hand to his head, noticing as he did, the short stubble that covered his scalp.

"Headache?" asked the nurse.

"There's a small rodent trying to eat its way out of my skull," he replied. The words were coming out more clearly now, although his tongue still felt slow and heavy.

"You're due for more pain relief," she replied, moving toward him. "I'll top you up." She pulled a small atomiser from a pocket of her uniform. Before he could comment or give permission, she inserted it into one nostril and pressed the activator. Instantly, he experienced what seemed like an explosion of colour in his visual cortex which quickly resolved into a warm pink glow. The glow faded after a few seconds, leaving him feeling euphoric and completely pain free.

"Wow! That's ... amazing! What is that stuff?"

"It's our own special concoction. Two different pain blockers combined with a stimulant and mood enhancer. You should feel much better now."

"That's an understatement. I feel fantastic!"

"Good. I've sent a message to Dr Blakely, who will be very keen to talk with you. He should be ... Ah! Here he is now."

A panel on the left-hand wall slid open and a man entered the room. He was middle aged, perhaps in his late 40s, with striking, movie-star good looks and silver-streaked dark hair that had been groomed to within an inch of its life. He was meticulously dressed and exuded an air of superiority and easy confidence.

"Ah, Daniel! You're awake at last. I trust nurse Sylvia has been looking after you."

"I've just topped up Mr Newman's meds," Sylvia explained. "He was complaining of a headache." Daniel noticed her nametag, which read, 'Sylvia Stratham. Nursing Administrator.'

Blakely nodded, sagely, and looked at Daniel. "Unfortunately, you will experience some ongoing pain for some time to come. It's unavoidable, considering the nature of your injuries."

"Stop! Both of you!" He held up his hands, as if stopping traffic. "I ... I don't understand. Why are you calling me Mr Newman? Or Daniel? That's ... that's not my name."

A look of concern crossed Dr Blakely's face. "It's not? In that case, can you tell us what you think your name is?"

"It's ... um ... it's ... I don't know." A deep frown furrowed his brow, and he experienced a growing sense of panic. "I can't remember."

"What *can* you remember? Anything at all?" asked Blakely.

He squinted his eyes in concentration, as if by sheer force of willpower he could summon up the necessary memories. He trawled through the recesses of his mind, desperately searching for any clues as to his identity or his history. Shockingly, it was a complete blank. There were no memories at all; no sense of who he was or what he had done, where he had lived or who he had known. He didn't even know what he looked like. He stared into the abyss of his missing memories and a feeling of panic rose up within him. He had nothing with which to define himself: no meaningful sense of self to give his existence any real substance.

He shook his head and said, "I can't remember anything at all. It's a complete blank."

The worried expression that had previously crossed Dr Blakely's face faded and was replaced with a look of relief mixed with compassion. "Do you know who I am?" he asked.

"No."

"I am Dr Nigel Blakely. You work for me."

"I do?"

"Yes. Your name is Daniel Newman, and you are a security officer at one of my research facilities."

"A security officer?"

"That's right. You are part of the security team at Senticorp, based here in Quito, Ecuador. Unfortunately, there was a ... let's call it an incident, and you were seriously injured. You've been in an induced coma for eight weeks."

"Eight weeks?" Daniel's mind was spinning, trying to process the new information. "What happened? What kind of injury?"

"There was an explosion. You suffered significant brain trauma. You required surgery to relieve the pressure on your brain and to remove some blood clots."

Daniel ran his hand over his stubbled scalp once more, feeling for scars.

"There is nothing to see or feel now," explained Blakely. "Biological nanobots have seamlessly knitted your flesh and bone back together, as well as restoring the damaged intercranial tissue. The damage to your neurological pathways, however, isn't as easily fixed. I've ensured that you have had the best possible surgeons and medical specialists working on your case, but their prognosis is that you will almost certainly suffer permanent partial, if not total, memory loss."

Daniel shook his head, trying to make sense of it all. "My name is Daniel Newman?"

"Yes."

"How do I know you're me telling the truth?"

"Why would I lie?"

"I don't know. You tell me."

Blakely sighed and fished a data pad out of his coat pocket. He tapped quickly and efficiently for a few moments and then handed the device to Daniel. "Here, take a look for yourself."

Daniel took the device and saw an image of a company ID tag. At the top was the company name, Senticorp, with a logo featuring a stylised S and C, interwoven with a double helix DNA strand. In the centre of the tag was a photo of a man, and printed underneath was:

NAME: Daniel Newman

EMPLOYEE ID: SC00892

DEPARTMENT: Security

SECURITY CLEARANCE: Blue

COMMENCEMENT DATE: 15th April 2316

He looked more closely at the image on the ID. Shoulder length brown hair with hints of blonde at the tips. Blue eyes, a streamlined nose, firm chin. Not altogether ugly. But it didn't look familiar to him at all. He stared at the image, trying to dredge up a sense of familiarity, but nothing came to him. He looked up at Blakely.

"I don't know what I look like. How do I know that's me?"

Blakely took the data pad and, with a quick swipe, turned its surface into a mirror. He handed it back to Daniel who stared at the reflected image, turning his head slightly to one side and then the other. It was the same face as the ID tag, but with stubble across the top of his head instead of shoulder-length hair.

"Swipe left and right to compare yourself with the photo," suggested Blakely.

Daniel did so, several times, until he could no longer deny the truth. He was Daniel Newman, a security guard at Senticorp. Somehow, it didn't feel right, but he couldn't argue with the evidence that was literally staring him in the face. He handed the device back to Blakely.

"What about my family? Do I have a wife or a partner? Any parents who are still alive? Siblings?"

"Not that we know of. You had only been working for us for two days before the incident, so we don't know a lot about you. Prior to that, you had been working at a mining base on Titan and you transferred back to Earth to take up this position with us. Our records indicate that you are 32 years old. We've tried to track down any family, but we haven't been successful. As far as we know, you aren't married or romantically attached."

"So, no one's been visiting me? No one holding my hand and waiting for me to wake up? Not even any friends?"

"No. I'm sorry. You haven't been back on Earth long enough to make any significant friends."

Daniel shook his head and looked out the window, contemplating his sad state of affairs. "Well, I'm a pretty miserable, lonely sod, aren't I?" He sighed and turned back to Blakely. "What is this place? Some kind of hospital, I presume."

Blakely nodded. "You're currently in the rehabilitation wing of Wellspring Private Hospital, located in the eastern foothills of Quito, Ecuador."

"Dr Blakely owns this hospital," contributed Nurse Sylvia.

"Not me, personally," explained Blakely, "It's owned by my holding company, Blakely Holdings, the parent company which also oversees several of my research facilities, including Senticorp."

"So, you're not a medical doctor?"

"Good heavens, no! I can't stand blood and gore. I'm a research scientist."

"In what field?"

"I dabble in a variety of fields. Speaking of which, I have a meeting to get to, so I'll leave you in Nurse Sylvia's very capable hands." He retrieved the data pad from Daniel and began to walk toward the door but then paused and turned around. "I'm very sorry for your trauma, Daniel. I realise this is not going to be easy for you, but be assured that I will spare no expense to give you the best possible care as you convalesce." He nodded to Sylvia and walked out of the room.

There was silence for a moment, then Daniel turned to Sylvia and asked, "So, what now?"

"Now we get started on your recovery," she replied as she tapped on her data pad.

"Is it going to hurt?" he asked.

She gave him a cold smile. "It won't hurt me a bit."

2

Eight weeks in a coma seemed to have taken their toll on Daniel's body. His primary problem was that he was physically weak. Dr Greer, the attending physician who visited him shortly after Blakely's departure, estimated that he had probably lost up to twenty five percent of his muscle mass, simply from lying immobile in bed.

"You're going to find even simple tasks tiring for a day or so," Greer informed Daniel as he ran a series of scans. The medibot descended on an articulated arm from its hidey-hole in the ceiling and began roving over Daniels body, in response to commands from Greer's data pad. Greer was a short, semi-bald, nondescript man who immediately struck Daniel as someone who needed to convince everyone around him of how important he was. As the doctor stared at the readouts on his data pad, he continued to drone on in a supercilious tone.

"Your tiredness will be partly physical and partly mental. Your brain is still recovering from the trauma you experienced, and you will probably find yourself sleeping more than you usually do."

"I have no idea what I 'usually do', doc. I can't remember a thing."

Greer lifted his gaze from his data pad and glanced briefly at

Daniel before returning his attention to the scans. "Yes, we expected that. Given the extent and location of the brain trauma, you have to face the very real possibility that you may never recover your previous memories."

"Terrific. Have you got any other good news for me?"

"The good news is that we expect a full recovery in all other areas of brain function," responded Greer as he tapped away on his beloved data pad. "Initial scans show no abnormalities in areas associated with cognitive processing, language or any other key areas. You can consider yourself very lucky."

"Oh, I do, doc, I do. I can't believe how lucky I am."

Greer either didn't recognise Daniel's sarcasm or chose to ignore it. He continued to issue his god-like prognostications without even glancing at Daniel. "We will, of course, have to conduct a series of encephalographic scans to confirm the status of your brain function. You will also undergo physiotherapy twice daily to help you regain your strength and balance. We will also be using nanobot technology and stem cell augmentation to assist the reacquisition of muscle mass."

"In other words, you're going to inject me with stuff."

"Correct. The combination of nanobots and stem cells will rebuild your muscles extremely rapidly. I anticipate reacquisition of pre-trauma muscle mass within 72 hours."

"Roger that," said Daniel facetiously.

Greer did not respond verbally but merely raised an eyebrow, as if replying to such flippancy was beneath him. He perused his data pad in silence for a few more moments then nodded his head. "Good. There seems to be nothing particularly amiss."

"Apart from the complete absence of my entire life up to this point," responded Daniel.

Greer ignored him. He tapped a quick command and the medibot retracted smoothly into its ceiling cavity and a panel slid across beneath it. He tucked the data pad neatly under his arm and addressed a vague point in mid-air, about a metre above Daniel's head.

"I've authorised the administration of pain relief, as needed.

Please don't hesitate to ask for me if you want to discuss anything further."

"I will," replied Daniel, with feigned enthusiasm. "In fact, I'll look forward to our next conversation with great anticipation."

Greer looked toward Nurse Sylvia who was standing nearby, and stared directly at her breasts, saying, "And now I'll leave you in Nurse Sylvia's capable hands."

"And her other bits, apparently," muttered Daniel, inaudibly.

Unconsciously licking his lips, and with a final longing glance toward Sylvia's ample bosom, Greer spun on his heels and walked briskly out of the room.

"What a wonderful, warm human being," commented Daniel.

"Dr Greer is extremely competent," Sylvia replied. "You should feel very lucky to have him overseeing your recovery."

"I do, I do. He's like a guardian angel."

Nurse Sylvia shook her head at his sarcasm and followed Greer out the door, leaving Daniel pondering his situation.

Daniel woke up the next morning with a pounding headache. Even moving his head slightly was unbearable and he groaned in pain. He was searching for a buzzer to summon help when Nurse Sylvia strode briskly through the door.

"Good morning, Mr Newman. I've come to administer your pain meds."

"Thank goodness."

"Are you in much pain?"

"It feels like someone is poking red hot wires through my brain."

Sylvia gave him a strange, almost shocked, look, then quickly recovered. She inserted an atomiser into a nostril and activated it. The relief was instantaneous and overwhelming.

"Oh, my goodness!" he exclaimed. "I think I want to marry you."

Ignoring his facetious declaration, she explained, "You will need one dose of this each morning for the next week or so."

She connected an IV bag and set it dripping. He had been given an IV drip yesterday afternoon as well.

"You should be feeling much stronger today," she explained. "The combination of stem cells and nanobots in the infusion works extraordinarily quickly in regenerating muscle fibres and supercharging your vascular system. This will be your final bag."

As she scanned his biochip for his morning observations, she said, "You will start physiotherapy today. You'll have a session at 9:00 am each morning and another one at 4:00 pm each afternoon. In between those two sessions, at 2:00 pm, you will be meeting with Dr Blakely who will be doing encephalographic scans to try to determine the cause of your amnesia."

"Will they be able to fix my memory?"

She gave him a strange glance and said, noncommittally, "We'll see."

At 9:00 am, promptly, a mountain walked into Daniel's room. Nurse Sylvia had returned briefly, prior to that, to remove the IV line from his arm.

"Well, well! What have we got here?" said the mountain, towering over Daniel who was sitting on the edge of his bed. There was a friendly but mischievous glint in his eyes as he cast a critical glance over his new patient. "Looks like a piece of flotsam the tide has washed up, and those skinny white legs look like they could break with a gentle breeze. But don't worry, my man, we'll soon fix that!" He held out a big brown hand. "Carlos."

Daniel shook his hand. "Daniel."

"Dan the man!" exclaimed Carlos enthusiastically. At roughly 190 cm tall, he was built like a tank, but his round face had a constant expression of merriment, as if he found the whole world amusing. Daniel knew, instinctively, that he was going to enjoy working with this man.

An hour later, the word 'enjoy' had completely disappeared from Daniel's vocabulary. As he arrived back in his room, accompanied by the gentle giant, he wasn't sure which part of him hurt the most.

"That was cruel, dude," he complained, easing himself onto the bed and sighing in relief.

Carlos slapped him heartily on the back. "No pain, no gain, my man!"

"Yeh, but you didn't have to be so enthusiastic about the 'pain' part!"

"Ain't nobody gonna say Carlos doesn't do a proper job." The big man began to leave the room, but turned at the doorway to say, "Don't forget, I'll be back to pick you up at 4:00 pm sharp for our fitness session."

"Oh great," feigned Daniel. "By then you might need to literally pick me up. I'm not sure I'll be able to walk."

"You'll walk, my man, you'll walk. No freeloaders allowed on team Carlos!"

At 1:50 pm, Nurse Sylvia arrived to take him to his first encephalographic session. Daniel had spent his lunch hour in miserable solitude, unsuccessfully trying to dredge up even the faintest memory of his past. Despite his whimsical banter with various hospital staff, the complete blankness of his memory weighed heavily upon him. There was a bottomless void in his mind where there should have been a complete history of people, places and events. Without a detailed past to anchor him, he felt adrift and undefined. Who was he? Where had he come from? What kind of man was he? What did he like? Did he have any hobbies? Who were his friends? There were so many questions, and no guarantee that he would ever find the answers. What if his memory never returned? He didn't even want to consider that possibility. He was more than ready to get these scans underway, desperately hoping that the professionals might find the key to unlocking the door to his past.

"My, my. Such a gloomy face," admonished Nurse Sylvia as she walked into his room.

"I was pining for your presence," quipped Daniel, with a deliberate effort to push aside his dark mood. "A minute without your sunny disposition is like an eternity."

She sighed. "Mr Newman," she paused as she considered her next words carefully, "you really are full of it."

He smiled. "I think I know why you don't laugh at my jokes," he said.

"Why is that?" she asked.

"Because you have an irony deficiency."

Sylvia merely shook her head as she moved his lunch tray to the side.

"Let's get you down to Dr Blakely, Mr Newman. I'm sure you're keen to commence therapy."

4

They descended in a lift to the next level down and walked along a short corridor. Sylvia led him through a large doorway marked, 'Pathology and Research'. Daniel found himself in an expansive laboratory filled with impressive technical equipment and staffed by busy-looking people in white lab coats. Various doors led off the central laboratory area, leading to what appeared to be meeting rooms or smaller labs. Sylvia led him across the main laboratory and through one of these doors.

"Ah, Daniel!" said Dr Nigel Blakely from his seat behind a desk. It was a small but well-appointed office, with a timber desk and several comfortable chairs for informal meetings. Blakely was looking as polished and suave as Daniel remembered him from their brief encounter, yesterday. *He looks like a middle-aged heartthrob film star*, thought Daniel.

Blakely rose and greeted Daniel at the door, shaking his hand warmly. "How is your recovery going? I'm hearing good reports from Nurse Sylvia."

"I'm feeling much better today, thanks, apart from the headaches."

"Good. The headaches should improve over time." He nodded at Sylvia. "Thank you, Nurse Sylvia, I'll take it from here."

As Sylvia departed, Blakely explained, "This is my cubby-hole; the office I use when I'm visiting the hospital. I sometimes get more work done here than in my main office at Senticorp." He gave Daniel a movie-star smile and placed a hand in the middle of his back, guiding him back out through the door into the main lab.

"Let's get started. Today we are going to do some encephalographic mapping. We want to see how your brain is functioning."

Blakely led him through the door of an adjacent room. It was dimly lit, and someone in a white lab coat was fiddling with a bank of instruments that lined the left-hand wall.

"This is Dr Marsha Nordstrom. Marsha is the head of this department. She and I will be conducting the scan today."

Marsha turned and nodded at Daniel, not bothering to say anything. She was middle-aged, with grey-streaked blonde hair and obvious Scandinavian features. Blakely led Daniel to a small booth to the right of the room. "This is where you'll spend the next 90 minutes," he explained.

As Daniel sat in the chair, Blakely placed a snug, stretchable cap over his scalp. "This will map your brain activity and send the data to a variety of instruments that we will be monitoring. The screen in front of you will provide prompts and visual input to stimulate the neural pathways in different regions of your brain." He smiled reassuringly. "Just sing out at any point if you need a break."

With that, Blakely closed the door, plunging Daniel into complete darkness. A few moments later the screen in front of him came to life, presenting him with a calming video image of a tropical rainforest.

"Can you hear me, Daniel?" Blakely's voice seemed to emanate from all around him.

"Yes."

"Good. Let's get started."

For the next hour and a half, Daniel was bombarded with a wide variety of images; some serene, some disturbing, some designed to shock and scare, and some simply mystifying. He was asked a variety of questions, told to study certain images and then recall their details, and given a range of mental tasks to perform. Time blurred and Daniel's world shrank to the single, small screen in front of him.

Finally, the screen went blank, and the booth was plunged into darkness. A moment later Blakely opened the booth door and Daniel blinked in the bright light that streamed in.

"How did I go?"

"Brilliant! Wonderful! In fact, better than I dared hope."

"Really? So, is there a chance of me getting my memory back?"

"Your memory?" Blakely seemed momentarily confused. "Ah, yes, your memory. Well, um, it's too early to say, Daniel. We'll need to run a lot more tests. It's still very early days. You'll just need to be patient."

"Speaking of being patient," Daniel replied, "I'm getting bored out of my brain sitting in my room between scheduled appointments. Can I get a device to access Solnet?"

"Yes, certainly. I'll arrange for one immediately. There will be one in your room within the hour."

Blakely escorted Daniel out of the room, leaving Marsha Nordstrom poring over data and graphs displayed on multiple screens. As they reached the door into the corridor outside the main lab, Daniel paused and asked, "Dr Blakely, what was the explosion that injured me? You never explained."

Blakely blinked several times and seemed to consider his response. "There was ... a security breach. We came under attack by several intruders."

"You were attacked?"

"Yes. Several security guards were shot and killed. Several other staff – research scientists, admin assistants and cleaners – were also killed or injured. It was ... horrific."

"And the explosion that injured me?"

"Several explosive devices were set off in key areas. You just happened to be in the wrong place at the wrong time."

"What was the point of the attack? What did they want?"

Blakely paused, and a guarded expression crossed his face. "We think they might belong to a group that opposes one of our lines of research. They were attempting to destroy our research and dissuade us from pursuing it further."

"What are you researching?"

"Senticorp has over a dozen research projects that are ongoing. It's difficult to say which of those has offended someone. We're still investigating." He placed his hand in the middle of Daniel's back and propelled him gently into the corridor. "If you don't mind, I need to get back to my work now. We'll see you at the same time tomorrow, Daniel."

Daniel was left standing in the corridor, looking at the closed door into the lab, wondering if he was just being overly sensitive. He couldn't be sure, but it seemed to him that Blakely wasn't being completely transparent. In fact, the more he thought about it, the more convinced he was that Blakely was hiding something.

5

In a richly furnished executive office in Singapore, a red comm light flashed insistently, an ID screen identifying the caller. The office was in almost complete darkness, the windows having been rendered completely opaque and only a dim desk light issuing a feeble glow from a weak red globe. The sole occupant of the office was dwarfed by the oversized leather chair on which he sat and by the large antique wooden desk in front of him. Soft classical music was playing in the background and the air was filled with the musty scent of ancient leather-bound books that lined one of the walls. A hand that was adorned with multiple jewelled rings calmly placed a crystal glass tumbler of cognac on a coaster and answered the call.

"Speak."

"Sir, we've finished going through all the files that we acquired. What we're looking for isn't there."

"I was assured it would be."

"Our 'archaeologists' apparently weren't digging in the right spot."

"That's extremely disappointing. For the amount of money I paid them, I expected much better service."

"So did I, sir."

"They were also extremely messy and heavy-handed. I detest thuggery. It lacks style and subtlety."

"Yes, sir."

"I want that data."

"The good news is that our analysts believe they know where it is now."

"Good. See that we get it as soon as possible. We can't afford to be left behind: there are literally billions at stake here. If they are on the verge of what I think they are, everything is about to change."

"I'll see that we get it, sir."

"And get rid of the buffoons we used before. Hire some 'archaeologists' with more finesse. And while you're at it, I want comm taps placed on the main man and his offsiders. I don't want to leave anything to chance."

"Yes, sir. I'll get right on it."

6

True to Dr Nigel Blakely's word, a hand-held device was delivered to Daniel shortly after he returned to his room.

"It's already keyed to your retinal scan," explained Nurse Sylvia.

"Really? How did they do that without me knowing?"

"I'm not sure. Perhaps while you were undergoing today's encephalographic scan."

Daniel wasn't convinced, but he let it go. He activated the device, and after a quick retinal scan, the entire far wall of his room came to life.

"You can split the wall into multiple screens, and your room also has inbuilt holographic projection capabilities," Sylvia explained. "You have complete access to Solnet, including all public sources throughout the solar system. Obviously, sources from our furthest bases will be on a significant time delay, so news from those regions will be hours or even days old in some cases. Enjoy!"

She left him to explore the world that he had woken up to, and Daniel soon found himself immersed in fascinating discoveries. There were human colonies scattered throughout the solar system including four on the Moon and two on Mars. Mining bases were located on Saturn's moon, Titan, and Jupiter's moon, Europa. Scientific research facilities were operating at the L1 Lagrange point – the point of gravitational equilibrium – between the Earth and the Sun, as well as a small floating research base in the clouds of Venus, 50 kilometres above the planet's surface. Of course, all of this would have been familiar to Daniel two months ago, but it was a complete revelation to him now.

Just as fascinating was his exploration of his home planet, Earth. The Earth's average temperature was now a whopping five degrees Celsius higher than it had been three centuries earlier, resulting in a planet that was now continually ravaged by fierce, unpredictable weather events. While human atmospheric emissions had fallen dramatically in that latter half of the 21st century due to the advent of much cleaner energy sources, it was the unchecked deforestation of the planet that had turned out to be the main driver of global warming. During the late 21st century, the planet had reached a tipping point that was now irreversible. Global and local mega storms made food production increasingly problematic, and starvation was a growing problem in many parts of the world.

Three centuries of rising sea levels had decimated the coastlines of every continent, and many smaller islands and archipelagos had disappeared altogether. Daniel discovered that metres of water now covered what apparently used to be some kind of launch facility in Houston, Texas, run by a now-defunct space agency called NASA. Earth's space agencies and corporations now utilised tether lifts to lift personnel and light payloads into Earth orbit. A tether lift comprised two large pods that ascended on opposite sides of a tether cable to a space station in geosynchronous orbit, 1000 kilometres above the Earth. A tether cable was five metres in diameter and was constructed of a high-tensile composite of boron nitride nanotubes and maranium, a metal mined on Mars. The cable extended not just to its respective space station, but thousands of kilometres beyond it, anchored to a massive asteroid in higher geosynchronous orbit which stabilised both the tether and the orbiting space station by its greater mass and stable orbit.

Daniel discovered that Earth had two tether lifts. One was located just north of Nairobi, Kenya, and the second was right here in Quito, Ecuador. Both were under the jurisdiction of ANSA, the Alliance of Nations Space Agency. The two tether lifts had accompanying spaceports from which heavy lift rockets were launched, carrying heavier payloads into orbit. The tether lifts and accompanying spaceports were located on the equator, to get the maximum assistance from the Earth's rotation in launching payloads into space. Both locations also had the added advantage of being at a relatively high altitude; 1,800 metres above sea level in the case of Nairobi and 2,800 metres here at Quito.

As Daniel absorbed all this information, he wondered whether the proximity to the tether lift and spaceport was one of the reasons for Senticorp's location in Quito.

He was interested to learn more about ANSA, the Alliance of Nations Space Agency. He discovered that ANSA was heavily involved in exploring nearby star systems via high-speed probes which they had been sending to star systems that looked like promising locations for Earth-like planets. Since the development of the VAR drive (vacuum to antimatter reactor drive), 150 years ago, a series of increasingly sophisticated probes had been sent to the most likely star systems and, so far, one Earth-like planet had been found. It was 37 light-years distant, orbiting a newly discovered K-type main sequence star called Tama. The probe had been sent on its way over 100 years ago and ANSA had been receiving video footage from it for the last 12 years. As a result, they were in the final stages of preparation for mankind's first interstellar manned mission, utilising the newly completed starship, Longshot.

His research was cut short by Carlos's arrival to take him to his 4:00 pm fitness training session. Daniel had completely lost track of time and had even failed to notice the delivery of his afternoon tea, which still sat untouched on his nightstand.

"What's happening, my man?" said the exuberant giant. "Get your skinny white butt off that bed and let's get moving!"

Daniel groaned and closed the multiple screens he had open. "Do we really have to do this?" he complained half-heartedly.

"No, of course not, my friend," responded Carlos, laying a consoling hand on Daniel's shoulder. "We can give these sessions a miss and you can slowly turn into an obese, unfit, wobbly lump of lard with a barely functioning brain if that's what you'd prefer. You're probably part-way there already."

"Ha, ha. Has anyone ever told you you've got the gift of encouragement?"

"Not lately."

"Didn't think so."

It wasn't until later that evening, after having showered and eaten his dinner, that Daniel finally got back to his online research, feeling stiff and sore after his strenuous workout. This time, he wanted to see if he could dig up any details about himself. This had been his primary motivation in asking for a device to access Solnet, but in his earlier session he had been temporarily sidetracked by his discoveries about the world of the 24th century. Now, however, he was determined to drill down into his primary concern.

"Activate system-wide search engine," he instructed the device.

"Certainly, Mr Newman."

A search box appeared on the screen on the far wall.

"Call me Daniel."

"Yes, Daniel."

Daniel knew that he wasn't talking to a true artificial intelligence; it was merely a cleverly designed, sophisticated algorithm. As he reflected on this fact, he wondered how he knew this. There must be some residual, deeply ingrained components of his memory that remained intact. For example, he knew the names of common objects and understood the basic nature and functioning of the world around him. He knew how to open doors and operate devices such as this. What was missing, was all traces of memory that specifically related to his own identity and past: to events and people.

"I'm going to call you 'Sherlock'."

"Any particular reason, Daniel?"

"It's a reference to an ancient fictional detective, named Sherlock Holmes. You're going to help me do some detective work."

"Yes, Daniel."

"Search for 'Daniel Newman'."

"337 results located." A long list of links appeared on the screen.

"Exclude men known to be aged younger than 28 or older than 36."

"119 results."

"Exclude people with dark skin or non-Caucasian appearance."

"75 results. May I ask a question, Daniel?"

"Go ahead."

"Do you wish me to limit my search to people still living?"

"Yes." Then he thought about it for a moment. "On second thoughts, no. Let's not exclude those people just yet. I may have been reported by some sources as being deceased."

"Certainly."

Daniel racked his brain trying to think of further ways of narrowing the search parameters. "Can you read my biochip data?"

"Yes, Daniel."

"How tall am I?"

"178 centimetres"

"Exclude people who are outside the height range of 176 to 180 centimetres."

"61 results."

"Exclude people without blue eyes."

"42 results."

"Can you think of any other refinements?"

"Assuming you are searching for yourself, I suggest excluding people with obvious deformities or missing body parts."

"Do it."

"37 results."

Daniel suddenly had an idea. "Scan my face," he said, holding his device in front of him.

"Done."

"Exclude people whose faces do not bear reasonable similarity to mine." *Idiot,* he thought to himself. *I should have thought of this in the first place!*

"Seven results."

"Are they all listed as still living?"

"There is nothing to indicate that they are deceased."

Now we're getting somewhere, he thought. He opened the first link. It was an entry in a dating website called, 'Lonely No Longer'. His face stared back at him. There was no doubt about it; it was definitely him. To the left of the screen was a list of basic descriptors that had been filled in with minimal detail.

Name: Daniel Newman

Age: 32

Occupation: Security officer

Interests: Music, outdoors, fitness

Relationship Status: Never married

Location: (no information)

Member since: December 2315

In the main body of the page, there was a brief blurb, presumably written by himself:

Hi! I'm Daniel and I'm looking for a down-to-earth, fun-loving girl to share my life with. I don't have any terrible vices or excesses, and I promise I'm completely house trained! I have a generous heart and a vibrant love of life, and I'm looking for someone with those same qualities. Ping me!

Daniel shook his head. *Did I really write that? It's dreadful! I can't believe I was so clichéd and corny!* He considered the date. According to Dr Blakely, he was working on Titan at the time, about 1.4 billion kilometres from Earth. He supposed it was possible that by December 2015 he was already planning to return to Earth and was sowing some seeds in advance.

Daniel moved on to the next link. It was another dating website, this one called 'Love Link'. Same picture, same basic details and exactly the same blurb.

"Not very original, Daniel, you sad excuse for a man," he mumbled to himself.

The next two links had no images but referred to people with his name who were reported as being active during the last eight weeks, while he had been lying in a coma. One had graduated from a university a month ago and the other had gotten married last week.

"Sherlock, how did these two get into the results?" he asked. "They don't have an image that matches my face."

"You said to *exclude* results with an image that didn't match your face. As these links don't have an image at all, they did not match your exclusion criteria."

"I see." He shook his head and moved on.

The final three links were all online news reports of a terrorist attack at Senticorp, with his name listed as one of the casualties who was seriously injured. The deceased were not named. All three news reports were dated 17th April, which was a little over eight weeks ago, and two days after his commencement date at Senticorp. Interestingly, his was the only name mentioned in all three reports. For instance, the first said:

As well as the eight deceased victims, a Senticorp spokesperson reports that up to 20 other employees were injured in the attack, including Daniel Newman, a security officer who remains in a critical condition in hospital.

The other two reports followed a similar line. Why was he the only person named? Daniel didn't understand. Somehow it didn't seem right that he was singled out and none of the other victims were identified. He sat back and stared at the screen. There was something niggling him; something at the edge of his mind, trying to get his attention. He scrolled through all the links again, but nothing jumped out at him.

"Hey, Sherlock."

"Yes, Daniel?"

"Are there any academic records for Daniel Newman? Any club memberships, fines, vehicle registrations, bills?"

"Certainly, but none that match all your criteria. According to your very specific criteria, none of them can possibly be you."

"I see." He scratched his head and let out a long sigh. He had been so optimistic, so hopeful, but it seemed that his prior existence had left barely a ripple in the public records. He was virtually a nobody – a lonely, disconnected man without any apparent history. He closed all the screens, powered down his device and lay back on the bed, thinking about what he had just seen. He couldn't shake the feeling that he had missed something; a tiny detail that was ringing an alarm bell in a dusty corner of his mind. *Maybe something will come to me while I sleep.*

"Lights out."

D aniel came instantly awake. It was still dark and when he looked at his data pad, he saw that it was 3:15 am. He sat up in bed and activated the device and the wall screen. He knew what had been troubling him. In fact, it was so obvious, he couldn't understand how he could have missed it last night. But just to be sure, he had to check it again.

"Sherlock, open the link to my page on the 'Lonely No Longer' dating site."

"Certainly, Daniel." The page came up on the wall screen.

Daniel leaned forward and studied the image carefully. He was right! It was exactly the same image as the one on the Senticorp ID tag that Dr Blakely had shown him. In the image on the ID tag, he had been wearing a light grey shirt with a Senticorp logo on the breast pocket. That meant the photo had to have been taken on or shortly before the day he commenced at Senticorp, on 15th April 2316. But his two dating websites had supposedly been set up in December of the previous year, yet they used the same photo. How was that possible?

"Zoom in on my image."

The image enlarged until it took up a whole section of the wall.

"Enhance for sharpness and zoom in on the bottom of the image."

The image enlarged further. "That is the limit of possible enlargement and enhancement, Daniel. Any further enlargement will result in loss of clarity."

"That's fine. You've done well."

He stood up and walked closer to the image. The image had been cut at the neckline, so the shirt was not visible. But it hadn't been edited carefully enough. At the very bottom of the screen, on the left side of the neck, there was a very thin slice of grey. It was the top of the Senticorp shirt collar – a shirt he would not have owned in December, the year before.

"Sherlock, can you determine when this page was first uploaded to the dating site?"

"Yes. The embedded file information shows that it was uploaded on 22nd December 2315."

"Has the page been updated since then?"

"No, Daniel."

He walked back to the bed and sat down, thinking furiously. How could that be? How could a photo of him wearing a Senticorp shirt have been uploaded four months before he started work at Senticorp, when he was supposedly still on Titan?

"Sherlock, can you determine where this page was uploaded from?"

There was a long pause. "I'm sorry, Daniel. I cannot determine that. It appears that the source utilised an advanced encryption code and multiple proxies. The origin is now untraceable."

Daniel was starting to get a very bad feeling about his situation. Something was not right. He was starting to think that he was not being told the truth. He was fairly sure he had not set up those dating profiles. But what did it all mean? Why would someone go to all that trouble? To what end? And why was there so little evidence of his previous existence?

The use of an encryption code and a trail of proxies worried him the most. If someone had gone to all that trouble, they clearly did not want him to discover that he was being lied to. As he sat on the bed thinking this through, it dawned on him that if his suspicions were correct, there was also a possibility that his online activity was being monitored. If so, whoever was monitoring him would now know that he had been digging into the origin of his dating profiles. They may even be monitoring everything he said.

He furiously thought back over the last few minutes. Had he verbalised his thoughts about it being the same photo? No, he hadn't. All he had done was ask for the image to be enlarged, and then he had stood there looking at it. He hadn't commented aloud. He hadn't said anything to indicate that he thought the dating profile had been set up by anyone other than himself.

The only problem was Sherlock's last pronouncement about an encrypted source and the use of proxies. Damn! He needed to play that down – to make it seem as if he wasn't suspicious. He addressed Sherlock again.

"Wow, I must have been a pretty hot coder. I guess I must have uploaded that stuff from Titan but didn't want anyone to know where I was. Maybe I was embarrassed about going on a dating website."

"Yes, that is certainly possible, Daniel."

"It's not just possible, it's exactly what must have happened. Thanks for your help, Sherlock. I guess I'll just have to stop trying to uncover the past and focus on moving forward."

"That sounds like a sensible plan, Daniel."

"It is. That'll be all for now, Sherlock."

"Thank you, Daniel."

He closed the screen down and lay back on the bed. He wondered if he had laid it on too thick. Hopefully, whoever was monitoring him was satisfied that he was still on the hook. But Daniel was on full alert now. And he was absolutely determined to get to the bottom of this mystery.

A beep sounded on a private comm line in Dr Nigel Blakely's penthouse suite.

"Yes?" he answered, noting the time. It was 6:15 am.

A female voice responded. "Sir, there was some search activity overnight that you might be interested in."

"I'm listening."

"He did a system-wide search for his name."

"That shouldn't be a problem, surely. In fact, we expected that. There's nothing of consequence for him to find."

"No sir, he only found what we left there for him to find."

"So, what's the problem?"

"Well, he dug a little deeper and discovered that the dating profiles had an untraceable upload origin. He discovered the use of encoding and multiple proxies."

"Damn it! That was a mistake. We should have provided a fake upload server ID from Titan. Is he suspicious?"

"I was starting to think so, but then he seemed to change his mind and accept it. I'll play you his final exchange with the search engine."

After the recording concluded, Blakely asked, "So, do you think he's still on board?"

"I'm ninety percent certain, sir."

"Mm. It's that ten percent I'm worried about."

"He's certainly a lot more curious than the last one," the female voice said.

"Yes. But that's what makes this so exciting." Blakely paused for a moment. "Keep monitoring and let me know if there is anything further we should be concerned about."

"Yes, sir. If things get bad, we've always got the failsafe."

"Yes. But let's hope we don't have to use it."

9

Daniel's third day in hospital began with a familiar pattern: a pounding headache and instant relief after Nurse Sylvia's administration of pain blockers. He noted again that she entered his room almost immediately after he awoke; a sure sign that he was being meticulously monitored. His bio chip readouts were probably being constantly displayed on a screen in the nurses' station and he strongly suspected that his room was also being monitored with hidden cameras and microphones. From this point forward, he would simply have to assume that everything he said and did was being recorded.

"You're looking particularly beautiful this morning, Nurse Sylvia," he said as she disposed of the atomiser she had just used to administer his morning pain relief.

"That's probably just the drugs talking, Mr Newman."

"Love is the only drug that's influencing me. My simple heart is smitten, and I've fallen under the influence of your spell."

"Humph!" was her only response as she departed the room.

Breakfast arrived shortly afterward, and Daniel spent some more time searching unsuccessfully for any clues of his past as he ate his muesli and drank his coffee.

"Dan the man!" exclaimed Carlos as he walked into the room. "What's the story, dude? You aren't even dressed yet!"

Daniel glanced at the time on his device and saw that it was already 8:57 am, almost time for his morning physiotherapy session. He groaned. He suspected that all physiotherapists had an innate sadistic streak.

"You inflicted enough pain on me yesterday to last a week. I'll make you a deal; I'll tell everyone we had our session, and you can slip down to the café and enjoy a quiet hour off."

"I'll make you a better deal," said the big man with a mischievous glint in his eyes. "You get dressed in two and a half minutes and I promise I won't whoop your butt."

Daniel smiled and walked to his clothing locker. "That's a very kind offer. Seeing you put it so nicely, how could I possibly refuse?"

An hour later, as Daniel sat on the edge of the physio bench with a towel draped over his shoulder, he decided to fish for some more information.

"So, how long have you worked for Senticorp?"

"Not Senticorp," corrected Carlos. "Wellspring Private Hospital. Not long."

"Aren't the hospital and Senticorp both owned by Nigel Blakely?"

"Yes – or more correctly, by his holding company, Blakely Holdings. So, I suppose he's my ultimate boss."

"Do you have much to do with him?"

"I don't think I've ever spoken to him. Maybe just once or twice to say hello as we passed in a corridor."

"What's your impression of him?"

Carlos shrugged. "He's a very busy man. He's a research scientist, not a medical doctor, but he seems nice enough."

"Do you have any idea what he's researching?"

"Man, I don't even *pretend* to know what he's into – something to do with genetics, I think. It's all probably way over my head. I just stick to stretching muscles and making people cry."

"You do it well, dude."

"I like to think so."

"What about Nurse Sylvia?"

"The ice lady! Man, she's a scary lady, that one."

"Not so scary, I think," replied Daniel. "What's the bet I can get her to laugh out loud by the time I leave here?"

"Serious? No way, man. You're dreaming."

"I'll bet you two rounds of drinks at your favourite pub," said Daniel.

"You're on, dude!" Carlos reached out and they bumped fists. He shook his head. "Easiest drinks I've ever won!"

10

After lunch, Daniel watched a newsfeed which was giving a special report into the final preparations for mankind's first interstellar mission which was about to launch. The starship, Longshot, had been built on the Moon and, for the last month, had been undergoing final pre-flight checks. 200 colonists and 40 crew had been training for the mission for years on Earth, and were now doing final training at Longshot Base, on the Moon. The starship was due to launch in another three weeks and, using its newly developed VAR (vacuum to antimatter reactor) drive, would take 38 Earth years to make the journey to the new world.

"That's definitely a one-way trip," muttered Daniel as he sipped a cup of coffee. The newsfeed explained that because of the relativistic effects of the starship's final velocity of 99.9 percent of the speed of light, only 7 years would pass on board the vessel and the colonists would be in cryogenic stasis for most of the trip anyway.

"Just as well," said Daniel to himself. "They'd go bonkers otherwise."

"Who would go bonkers?" asked a nurse as she walked into his room.

"The colonists on board that new starship, Longshot," he answered.

"Oh, yes. You couldn't pay me enough to go up there. I'm keeping my feet firmly on the ground." She glanced down at the data pad in her hand and looked back at him.

"You must be Mr Newman. I'm Rita Jones."

"I haven't seen you before," he commented. By now, Daniel was familiar with all the nurses on the ward, although Sylvia was the only one who ever came into his room.

"I'm new here. My first day actually." She gave him a reassuring smile. "I'm just doing the rounds, doing the obs."

Daniel raised his eyebrows, "Obs?" he asked sleepily.

"Observations. Checking your vital statistics from your bio chip readings." She tapped efficiently on her data pad for a few moments and began to frown. "That can't be right." She glanced at him with a look of concern. "How are you feeling?"

"Sleepy," he mumbled, with eyes half closed.

She stepped closer and took hold of his arm, placing her fingers on his wrist to check his pulse. A look of alarm crossed her face. Her eyes registered panic and a moment later she punched the emergency call button on the wall behind the bed, at the same time yelling, "Code blue! Room 8! Code blue!"

Daniel sat up, fully alert. "What's wrong? What's happening?"

Footsteps could be heard running down the corridor. The panel in the ceiling slid back and the medibot quickly descended on its articulated arm and began moving over him, scanning for problems.

Medical staff burst through the door; three nurses with a crash cart, followed closely by Dr Greer, the unpleasant physician who had examined Daniel when he first woke up.

"There's no pulse!" yelled Nurse Jones, clearly in a panic.

"Activate resus mode!" said one of the other nurses.

Daniel was freaking out now. "What's ... what's happening? I .. I feel okay."

His bed had reverted to the prone position and the medibot had produced two defibrillation paddles which it was trying to position on Daniel's chest. Everyone was talking at once and giving conflicting instructions when a strident voice cut through the melee.

"Everyone, stop this at once! What's going on here?" Nurse Sylvia had arrived and had a face like thunder. "Why are you all in my patient's room?"

Nurse Jones looked stricken and explained timidly, "There's no pulse."

"Don't be ridiculous! Get out! All of you! This is my patient, and none of you are authorised to be in here!"

Nurse Jones tried one more time. "But ..."

"LEAVE NOW!" Sylvia's eyes drilled holes into the young nurse as the others all hastily departed. "I'll deal with you later, Nurse Jones."

The medibot retracted into its ceiling space and Daniel was left with just Nurse Sylvia and Dr Greer in the room.

"What the hell just happened?" Daniel asked.

Sylvia gave Dr Greer a conspirational glance, then said, "There must be some kind of glitch – either in our software system or a fault in your biochip." As she spoke, she held her own data pad close to his left breast, where his subcutaneous biochip was located. "Hmmm. It's not picking up your heartbeat. I'll report it and we'll look into it." She and Dr Greer began to leave the room, but Daniel called out to them.

"Wait!"

They stopped and turned back to face him.

"You're not telling me the truth. There's something not right here." He reached down and placed his fingers along the veins in his wrist. He frowned as he concentrated.

"She's right, isn't she? Nurse Jones? There's no pulse!" He felt sick in his stomach. He moved his hand to his neck and felt for a pulse in his carotid artery. Nothing.

"What the hell have you done to me!"

Sylvia and Dr Greer glanced at each other uneasily.

"Tell me! What am I? Why don't I have a pulse?"

Dr Greer took a step toward him. "Mr Newman, you're obviously distressed ..."

"Don't bullshit me, Greer! Tell me the truth!"

Greer froze, clearly uncertain how to proceed.

"Tell him," said Sylvia.

Greer pursed his lips and then explained simply, in his cold, efficient voice. "You have an artificial heart."

"What?!" Daniel shook his head, as if trying to dislodge an unpleasant dream. He unbuttoned his shirt front and examined his sternum which was completely scar-free.

"There is no scar tissue," explained Greer. "As you probably know, bioplas therapy and nanobot technology ensure that tissue and bones heal perfectly within a few days of surgery or injury, leaving no scars."

Daniel rubbed his sternum with his hand and looked at Greer.

"Why? Why do I have an artificial heart?"

Greer seemed uncertain about what to say and glanced at Sylvia, who took over the explanation.

"You suffered irreparable damage to your heart during the attack at Senticorp. The explosion that rendered you unconscious and traumatised your brain also resulted in a piece of shrapnel piercing your chest and rupturing your heart. The surgeons deemed it irreparable."

Daniel shook his head. "That doesn't make sense. If my heart was ruptured like that, I would have died instantly. I wouldn't have lived long enough to make it to surgery."

Sylvia continued, "Your heart was still beating but it was pumping a lot of blood into your chest cavity. It was only the quick thinking of the medical staff at Senticorp that saved you. They ran an IV line and started blood transfusion while they waited for the ambulance to arrive."

"So, Senticorp has a ready supply of blood and IV lines, just handily lying around? I thought it was a research facility, not a hospital."

Sylvia took a step closer as she explained. "There's a whole department that specialises in medical research, including a section that is investigating the enhancement of blood chemistry. Your swift recovery in these last few days is a direct result of advances in the augmentation of blood chemistry that Dr Blakely's team has pioneered. You were in the best possible hands from the moment of your injury."

"And what about the artificial heart? The hospital just happened to have a spare one lying around?"

"Yes, as a matter of fact, they did. This is the 24th century, Daniel. We aren't in the dark ages anymore. Artificial hearts are quite common now."

Daniel felt his wrist again. "Why don't I have a pulse?"

"You have been given the latest model. It generates a continuous flow that doesn't pulse like a normal heart. It's powered by a nuclear isotope and adjusts the rate of flow instantly to the changing demands of the body."

Daniel was stunned, not only by the revelation that he had an artificial heart, but also by the fact that they had not told him.

"Why didn't anyone tell me? Why did you hide it from me?"

"Dr Blakely was going to tell you in due course. It was decided that you had enough to worry about at the moment, with your memory loss."

"What else aren't you telling me? What else have you done to me? What other bits have been replaced?"

"There's nothing else, Mr Newman," Sylvia assured him.

"How do I know you're telling me the truth? If you've been secretive about one thing, there could be others."

Sylvia sighed. "Very well. Let me show you." She activated the medibot, which slid smoothly out of its ceiling cavity again. "Lie down please, Mr Newman."

Daniel hesitated for a moment and then complied. Sylvia then activated voice command mode. "Initiate full body scan. Display results on the wall screen." The wall screen came to life as the medibot moved across Daniel's body. "It's a multi-wavelength scan that provides a detailed image of all the organs of your body."

As the medibot moved across Daniel's body, a corresponding image appeared on the screen. The medibot finished its scan and retracted into the ceiling again, leaving the completed image on the screen.

"You can sit up now, Mr Newman."

Daniel sat up and stared at the image. He could see every organ of his body in vivid 3D, as if his skin and flesh had been peeled back. Apart from his heart, everything else looked completely normal: bones, muscles, ligaments, lungs, brain and all his other soft organs. His new heart was egg-shaped and clearly metallic. He stared at it, still trying to come to terms with this new reality.

Sylvia's officious tone softened slightly. "You see, you are completely normal. We aren't hiding anything from you."

"Anything else, you mean."

"I'm sorry, Mr Newman. You weren't supposed to find out like this. We would have told you in due course."

"Sure you would have," Daniel replied sarcastically. He thought about the kerfuffle that had just taken place in his room. "None of the other nursing staff knew, did they? That's why you made sure you were the only person allowed to interact with me."

Sylvia just stared at him, saying nothing.

"I'm guessing my biochip data was only being streamed to you, so that no one else had access to it."

"There was no particular need for anyone else to know. I am the Nursing Administrator, and I chose to oversee your care personally."

Daniel shook his head and sighed. "I'd like to be left alone now please."

Sylvia nodded. "As you wish." She switched off the wall screen. "Don't forget, you have a scheduled session with Dr Blakely in 15 minutes." She turned and walked briskly out the door, leaving Greer standing alone in the room. He nodded awkwardly at Daniel and then scurried after the departing nurse.

"Humph," said Daniel aloud. "It's obvious who wears the pants around here."

As he sat on the edge of his bed, shock gradually turned to anger. *How dare they! How dare they keep me in the dark about my own body!* This was the final straw. Someone had faked his online profiles and now they had deceived him by withholding vital information. He came to a decision. He wasn't going to wait 15 minutes. He was going to confront Dr Blakely right now.

With grim determination, he strode out the door.

11

—————

Daniel walked purposefully down the hall, on his way to confront Dr Blakely. Over the last 24 hours he had grown increasingly uneasy about his mysteriously absent memories and what appeared to be the creation of a phony online profile. Now, the discovery that he had been given an artificial heart and had not been told about it had tipped him over the edge. He was going to demand a full explanation from the man who seemed to be behind it all.

He walked past the nurses' station and noted the furtive glances he received from the nurses behind the desk. The new nurse, Rita Jones, was nowhere to be seen. Daniel suspected he wouldn't be seeing her again. As he approached the bank of lifts, he noticed that the door to Nurse Sylva's office directly opposite the lifts was slightly ajar. The sign on the door read,

Nursing Administrator
Sylvia Stratham

He was about to press the lift button when he heard Sylvia's muffled voice coming through the small gap in the door. He looked up and down the hall and saw that there was no one else in sight. On an impulse, he moved closer to listen. The gap in the door was just wide enough for him to see a vase with a magnificent bunch of roses on a small table in the corner of the office. Sylvia's desk was out of sight, behind the door.

Daniel bent down and pretended to be doing up his shoelace and placed his ear close to the gap in the door. He heard one side of a comm call and realised that she must be using an ear pod.

"Yes. It was unavoidable."

Pause.

"I've dealt with her. She won't be back again."

Pause.

"No. I only told him what he needed to hear."

Pause.

"Of course not. I'm not stupid, Nigel."

Pause.

"No. I don't think he suspects. He's angry, of course, which is understandable. I did tell you we should have told him about his heart from the start."

Pause.

"Yes. He's certainly feistier than the others."

Pause.

"Well, we've always got the failsafe if things get badly out of hand. It would be a shame, of course, because he's the most promising so far."

Pause.

"The headaches are still pretty severe, the same as the others. But so far, there's no sign of rejection. I think he could be the one. How close do you think are we to full initialisation?"

Pause.

"That's exciting. We have to stay focused, my darling. We are on the brink of possibly the most important scientific breakthrough of all time. We're so close, I can almost taste it."

Pause.

"Alright. I'll see you tonight."

Daniel heard the click of a comm button being pressed and then the sounds of footsteps approaching the door. In a mad panic he straightened up and ran to the visitor's toilet immediately next door, pushing the door open and leaping inside. Did he make it in time? Had she heard his footsteps? He waited a few moments then opened the door a crack and peeked out. Nurse Sylvia was striding up the hall, back toward the nurses' station, without giving any indication that she had noticed anything untoward.

He breathed a sigh of relief. He walked to the hand basin and splashed some water on his face as he processed what he had just heard. He had been right to be suspicious. They were hiding something from him. Something big. Somehow, he was part of some important experiment. How had Sylvia described it? A 'scientific breakthrough'. What kind of breakthrough? And could it have something to do with his lack of memory? What if his memory loss was not the result of his injury, but an integral part of their experiment? What did his headaches have to do with it? What was the 'initialisation' Sylvia had referred to? And who were the 'others' she had mentioned? Were they in the hospital, too? And what was the 'failsafe' Sylvia had spoken about? It sounded ominous. It was also interesting to learn of Sylvia's romantic relationship with Dr Blakely. He wondered whether anyone else knew about it.

He had so many questions, and no clear answers. But one thing was increasingly clear: he could not trust these people. In fact, far from having his welfare at heart, he was beginning to sense that he might actually be in danger in this hospital. As he thought through his predicament, he decided that confronting Nigel Blakely would probably not be the wisest course of action. In particular, he mustn't let them know his suspicions about the false online profiles or that he doubted the backstory that they had told him. He needed to be smart. He would express anger at not being told about his artificial heart, because they would be expecting that. But he would not express doubt about the overall scenario that they had fed him. He would play along. He would be careful and circumspect.

He sensed that his life depended on it.

12

Daniel walked through the door marked 'Pathology and Research'. The large lab was once again a hive of activity, filled with people in white lab coats engaged in all kinds of tasks involving a variety of equipment. Daniel walked through the lab toward the line of smaller rooms on the far side, with no one paying him any attention at all. He paused outside Blakely's office. He needed to display the right level of anger without taking it too far or giving the impression that he was not buying the story he had been fed.

He opened the door without knocking and found Dr Blakely at his desk, tapping on a data pad.

"Daniel? You're a little early."

"I'm also a little angry."

Blakely sat back in his chair and clasped his hands together on the desk. "Yes. Nurse Sylvia informed me of the incident in your room a short time ago. I'm sorry you had to find out like that. It must have been a shock."

"You could say that. It's not every day you get told you've had a heart transplant. Why did you hide it from me?"

"In retrospect, I can see that we should have told you from the beginning. In fact, Sylvia recommended that we do so. It was my decision to delay that conversation. I take full blame here. I was concerned that you already had enough to deal with during the first few days after waking from a coma. I didn't want to add to your mental anguish until you were mentally and physically stronger. I apologise. I can see now that it was a mistake."

"You bet it was! Is there anything else you're keeping from me?" Daniel wondered if he had pushed too hard with that comment, but it was out now.

"Of course not, Daniel. We are totally committed to helping you get better. I feel deeply responsible for what happened to you at Senticorp, and I am doing everything I can to make it right."

Daniel decided to back off from his anger. He didn't want to overplay his hand or make it appear that he was going to be uncooperative. He let out a sigh. "I guess I can see that you had good intentions."

"Of course I did," said Blakely, sounding and looking relieved. "We all do. We only want what's best for you."

Daniel sat down in a comfortable chair on the other side of Blakely's desk. He ran a hand across the growing stubble of his scalp. "It's just that I'm finding it so frustrating not being able to remember anything."

"I'm sure you are. It must be very difficult."

"It's like being adrift on an ocean without any reference point. I keep hoping that I might see or hear something that might trigger a memory or open a mental door to my past, but so far I've got nothing."

"Well, we're going to try to help you with that."

"Speaking of helping me, can I have another look at my Senticorp ID tag? Maybe it might trigger a memory."

"Certainly." Blakely tapped a few commands on his data pad and handed it across the desk. Daniel stared closely at the photo. There was no doubt in his mind now. It was the same photo as the ones on his dating profiles, except more of the shirt was visible in this one, including the Senticorp logo on the breast pocket. He needed to ask a crucial question now, and it was important that he didn't seem suspicious.

"I wish I could remember. I assume this was taken when I first started at Senticorp?"

"Yes. The morning of your induction, on your first day. The attack and your injury happened the very next day."

There it was! It confirmed what he already suspected. The photo was taken in April this year, but it had been used to create a false dating profile, supposedly opened in December last year. They must have fudged the date on the fake page when they set it up and somehow backdated it to December to give him a credible past. Given the sophistication of the coding that Sherlock had discovered, it was probably a relatively simple thing to access the website's data base and change an upload date.

Daniel pushed the data pad back to Blakely and shook his head. "It doesn't ring any bells for me. Do you think I'll ever remember anything?"

"That's exactly what we're trying to find out. In fact, it's what I'm hoping to find out in these sessions. I know you must be wondering what good it will do, but all these tests are helping to build a picture of your neural pathways to see if there are any areas that are obviously damaged." Blakely stood to his feet. "Come on Daniel, let's get started with today's session. I'm as keen as you are to get to the bottom of this."

Daniel doubted that very much, but he played along.

For the next two hours Daniel was bombarded with images and asked to respond to a variety of questions and stimuli. He was given puzzles and problems to solve as well as various memory exercises. Throughout the session, his brain activity was recorded via the wireless encephalographic cap that he wore. By the end of the session, he was mentally exhausted, and his head was spinning. Blakely assured him that they were making progress and that he just needed to be patient.

As they walked through the central lab toward the main door into the corridor, Daniel asked the question that had been forming in his mind over the last two hours.

"How much longer do I need to be in hospital? I'm feeling strong and healthy, apart from the headaches."

"Let's see how the next day or so goes, shall we?" replied Blakely. "I don't want to discharge you until we can be sure there won't be any setbacks. Recovery from a long coma shouldn't be rushed."

It was only as he walked away that Daniel realised something: he had no idea where home was.

~

As he ate his afternoon tea back in his room, Daniel decided to do a little more digging. But he would have to be careful not to arouse suspicion, as he was almost certainly being closely monitored.

"Sherlock, do a search for Senticorp."

"Certainly Daniel. 15 primary sources and 11,344 secondary references."

Daniel found Senticorp's official site and began to browse through it. The landing pages were filled with the typical waffle of organisations that were trying to present a wholesome image to the world. There was lots of verbiage about respect, inclusion, equal opportunity, values, employee empowerment, community mindedness, environmental sensitivity and a whole lot more feel-good fluff that declared, 'Aren't we a wonderful organisation?'

"Blah, blah, blah," muttered Daniel. "Why does everyone think that by typing words on a page they've actually achieved something tangible." He didn't care whether Blakely was listening or not; he had a highly sensitive crap detector. *Have I always been like this? Is this cynicism part of my old persona or is it something new?* He shook his head. Maybe he would never know.

What Daniel was mostly interested in, was finding out about Senticorp's research projects. What were they trying to develop? And what was the link to himself? Because, by now, he was convinced that he was some kind of test subject in one of their experiments.

The mission statement on the home page painted with a very broad brush:

"Senticorp is a scientific research organisation dedicated to the advancement of humanity."

Not much help there. He scrolled through their site menu and opened the page entitled, "Research".

"Senticorp is one of the most respected scientific research organisations within the Alliance of Nations. Our research focuses on some of the biggest challenges facing humanity as we seek to improve the quality and quantity of life for all people. Research projects are currently being conducted in a wide variety of fields, including Biomedicine, Biotechnology, Diagnostics, Vaccines, Genetics, Artificial Intelligence and Robotics."

The rest of the page was just photos of smiling scientists and shiny lab equipment. Daniel spent several more minutes digging through the remainder of the site but could find no specific information about any individual projects. He gave up and went back to the other primary links that Sherlock had identified. They were all merely regurgitations of the same fluffy propaganda. After 30 minutes of laborious reading, he was no closer to discovering what kind of experiment he was apparently caught up in. He closed all the windows and sat rubbing his eyes, not sure what his next step was.

13

"Ow! What are you trying to do, rip the muscles off my bones?"

"You know what they say, dude, no pain, no gain." Carlos the physio produced what Daniel interpreted to be a masochistic grin and pushed even harder.

It was the afternoon of his fifth day in the rehab ward and Daniel was undergoing his regular stretches before his fitness training session. He swore and sweat broke out on his forehead as his right leg was pushed further upright, stretching his hamstring even tighter.

"That's the trouble with you white boys," said Carlos calmly, a cheeky glint in his eyes. "You're all too soft. No staying power."

"Oh, my giddy aunt!" moaned Daniel. "You're just plain cruel, dude!"

"No, I'm just very good at my job."

"Let's make a deal," said Daniel, breathing a sigh of relief as Carlos eased his leg back down. "How about you decide to be not so good at your job and I promise I won't tell anyone."

"Not gonna happen, my man. I've got a rep to maintain. Ain't no one gonna say Carlos didn't do a proper job." He handed Daniel a towel and declared, "That's the stretching all done."

"All done for today, and all done forever," Daniel replied. "They're letting me out of here tomorrow morning."

"So I heard. Congrats, man!"

"Thanks. I'm gonna miss you, Carlos. You're literally the only friend I have in the whole world."

"You're not gonna get rid of me that easily, dude. You still owe me two beers, remember? Unless you've managed to crack the ice queen?"

Daniel shook his head. "No chance of that. I admit defeat. Nurse Sylvia is definitely made of granite. Not even the hint of a smile." He wiped some sweat from his forehead, thinking back over the last couple of days. To be honest, after the discovery of the deception regarding his artificial heart, Daniel's relationship with Sylvia had changed. He could no longer bring himself to engage in playful banter with her, and in return, Sylvia had become even more brusque and business-like.

"So, where is home for you?" asked Carlos.

"Apparently, I had only arrived the day before I started at Senticorp, and I had taken up residence in an apartment block owned by Senticorp."

"Blue Dolphin Apartments," said Carlos.

"You know it?"

"Sure. A lot of hospital staff and Senticorp employees live there because they get discounted rates."

"You too?"

"No. I like my privacy. I've got a little cabin up in the hills. No high-rise for me." Carlos slapped him on the back. "Come on. Up you get. Time to hit the treadmill."

Daniel groaned, but it was all show. This was the part he liked. For the past few days, he had been pushing himself hard on the treadmill and was making surprisingly rapid progress. The IV infusions of nanobots and stem cells that he'd been given over the first two days had successfully rebuilt his muscles. The infusions had also contained biogenic supplements which had stimulated his blood chemistry and vascular system, resulting in a noticeable improvement in his aerobic fitness. The result was that Daniel was now feeling supremely fit and healthy. "Are you gonna run with me again, dude?" he asked Carlos.

"Of course, my man."

"Are you sure you'll be able to keep up with me? After all, you've got a much larger carcass to lug around."

Carlos patted his stomach and said, "It's all pure muscle, my friend. Don't worry about me. Ain't no white boy gonna outrun Carlos."

Daniel smiled at the big man and thought to himself, *we'll see about that*. At nearly 190 centimetres tall, Carlos was built like a line backer and appeared to be a solid wall of muscle, but Daniel suspected that he was carrying some excess weight.

They selected adjacent treadmills and the machines beeped as they paired with each of their biochips. A complete set of biometric graphs and readouts appeared on the front panels in front of them both.

Carlos frowned. "These machines still aren't registering your heart rate. I've logged the fault with the tech department. It's probably just a calibration glitch."

It was clear that Carlos knew nothing about his artificial heart, proving to Daniel that the big man wasn't involved in whatever Blakely and Sylvia were doing to him. He wasn't sure why, but he had decided not to tell Carlos about what they had done to him.

Carlos scrolled through a preference screen on his own machine and asked, "What scene do you want today?"

"How about Newport Beach, California?"

"Nice!" replied Carlos. "Not that we'll ever see that again – at least not in the real world." Like much of the world's coastlines, that part of California was now under several metres of water, the result of over three centuries of rising sea levels. "We're going back exactly 300 years, to 2016," said Carlos as he selected the immersive visual display. Instantly the walls, floor and ceiling of the gym disappeared, and their treadmills were resting on the golden sands of Newport Beach. The sky was a deep blue, a colour unfamiliar to humanity in 2316 who had become accustomed to a dirty grey/brown canopy. The golden sand stretched endlessly ahead of them and to their left, the crystal-clear water sparkled in the sunlight as perfect waves formed and broke in peeling lines. To their right, waterfront condos lined the dunes, interspersed with shopping malls and waterfront parks – all of which was now, in the 24th century, home to fish.

"I'll slave your machine to mine," Carlos said as he tapped his screen. "I'll set the pace."

"Go as hard as you like, big fella. I'm ready."

"Humph. We'll see about that."

They started off at a steady pace and the golden sand started flowing past their machines on either side as they pounded away on their treadmills. Small magnofans hidden in tiny recesses of the front wall produced a slight breeze, simulating their apparent movement through the air, and the rhythmic rolling swish and rumble of the waves to their left added to the immersive experience. Daniel felt exhilarated as he ran, and he was relishing his newly acquired fitness.

At the one-kilometre mark, Carlos increased the speed to 16 kph and glanced at Daniel as he did so. "Are you comfortable with that?"

"It's a stroll in the park, dude. I've barely warmed up."

They ran on together, occasionally swapping friendly banter as they admired the idyllic scenery that flowed past. At the five-kilometre mark, Daniel was still feeling good but thought he could detect Carlos starting to labour in his breathing. "How about we step it up another notch?" he suggested. "Let's really push it for one more K."

"I don't think your skinny white legs are ready for it yet," said Carlos between heavy breaths.

"Let me be the judge of that," responded Daniel. He activated the voice command setting on his machine. "Transfer master control to this machine. Increase speed to 18 kilometres per hour." The soft whine of both machines increased in intensity and the sand started flowing past them faster. All conversation ceased as both men concentrated on keeping pace with the machines, their legs pounding furiously and their breathing coming in louder gasps. Daniel glanced across at Carlos and saw that he was frowning and gasping and perspiring profusely. At the 5.5-kilo-metre mark, Daniel spoke again. "Increase speed to 20 kilometres per hour." The machines responded instantly and both men were forced to increase their intensity again.

They were both gasping heavily now, and Daniel wasn't sure he could keep it up much longer. His lungs were burning, and his legs felt like jello. His eyes were glued to the instrument panel, as he willed the distance to tick over. His body was screaming at him to stop, and he was having trouble feeling his legs altogether as the odometer slowly ticked over: 5.6 ... 5.7 ... 5.8. He was about to give up and jump his feet to the side stabilisers when he saw Carlos do exactly that. Carlos straddled the treadmill now, his legs station-ary, his arms holding the stabiliser bars, while he gasped for breath. That was all the encouragement Daniel needed. He spurred himself on and finished the final 200 metres, punching the stop button as the odometer finally ticked over to 6.0 kilometres.

Both men stood hunched over, their breath coming in huge lungful's and sweat pouring off them. As their breathing gradually slowed, Carlos muttered, "Nice work, my man."

"Nice work, yourself. I must confess, was about to give up just before I saw you stop. I couldn't have gone on any longer, myself."

Carlos nodded and held out his closed fist, and they fist-bumped in mutual admiration. "I think your recovery is complete, dude. My work here is done."

"I couldn't have done it without you, Carlos. Thanks for all your help."

"Don't mention it."

"I just did."

"Well, don't mention it again."

"I couldn't have done it without you, Carlos."

"I told you not to mention it again."

"I know, but I don't like being told what to do."

14

Daniel stood outside the main entrance to the hospital. He was holding a small carry bag that contained a few clothes, some pain relief tablets and his Solnet-linked data pad. He was a free man! It was a strange feeling. His only memories consisted of the five days he had spent in this hospital, and now, standing outside its doors, he was seeing the world for the first time. It was as if he were being born anew.

For a few moments, he stood breathing in the warm air, his face lifted toward the sun and his eyes closed. Despite Quito's altitude of nearly three kilometres, it was a warm, humid day of 34 degrees Celsius. Daniel pitied people who lived in lower altitudes – it must be stifling closer to sea level.

He opened his eyes again and gazed through the haze toward the city, five kilometres to the west. From the hospital's elevated position in the eastern foothills, he had a scenic view of the needle-like high-rise buildings that dominated the city skyline. Due to the location of the tether lift, Quito had become one of the two most important cities among the Allied Nations, the other being Nairobi, Kenya, where the second tether lift was located.

Daniel looked toward the north and saw the tether lift itself, rising from a hilltop several kilometres beyond the city outskirts. The spaceport with its heavy lift launch facilities was not visible, being a further 20 kilometres north. The tether lift was a strange sight: a cable that rose from the hilltop and disappeared into the sky above. From this distance it looked flimsy and insubstantial, a mere filament, but he knew from his research that it was five metres in diameter and rose to Hubble Station, 1000 kilometres above. The two pods that ascended and descended the cable would probably not be visible at this distance, but Daniel couldn't help wondering what it must be like to ride in one. Presumably he had done so. If it was true that he had worked on Titan, his return journey to Earth would have involved a long-haul transport ship from Titan to the Moon, a shuttle from the Moon to Hubble Station, and a pod down the tether lift to the terminal here at Quito. It would have been an exciting journey, if only he could remember it!

A robocab pulled up in front of him, a driverless vehicle with a clear domed roof. The central door slid open, revealing two inward facing bench seats. His name appeared on a screen above the door and the cab announced, "Daniel Newman, please scan your ID chip and enter."

He held his left wrist to the external scanner and entered the cab, seating himself facing forward.

"Welcome Daniel Newman. Your destination is Blue Dolphin Apartments. Please confirm."

"Confirm."

The door closed and the cab smoothly accelerated.

"Estimated time to arrival, eight minutes. Enjoy the journey."

Daniel breathed a sigh of relief as he left the hospital behind. Given his troubling suspicions, he found it difficult to believe that they had let him go. Yesterday afternoon he had met with Dr Nigel Blakely and Nurse Sylvia in her office and had been informed that he was being discharged today.

"Your physical recovery is complete, and the ongoing encephalographic tests and any resulting treatment can easily be continued at our facilities at Senticorp," Blakely had informed him. "There is no need for you to be cooped up in a hospital any longer."

Daniel had been surprised. In his darkest moments he had envisaged being trapped here indefinitely, the victim of some kind of insidious, Frankenstein-like experiment. Their willingness to release him made him question whether he had misjudged the whole situation. In fact, Dr Blakely had been extremely accommodating and helpful, explaining that his apartment had been freshly cleaned and stocked with food, ready for his arrival. They had updated his ID chip with an access code to his apartment and explained how to access his money which had been accumulating during his stay in hospital. Dr Blakely had offered to have a Senticorp employee accompany him on his journey from the hospital to his apartment, but Daniel had declined, wanting to enjoy his new-found freedom alone.

Now, as he was driven away from the confines of the hospital, he felt a sense of elation. Even though a seemingly impenetrable wall still separated him from his past, he was determined to face the world with optimism and make the best of his life. Dr Blakely had assured him that his job at Senticorp was still there for him, but Daniel had already decided that he would quit as soon as he found other employment. Whatever he might have enjoyed doing in the past, the new Daniel wasn't interested in being a security guard.

The cab pulled up in front of a surprisingly attractive, modern building. With a name like Blue Dolphin Apartments, Daniel had expected something slightly down-market, but that was certainly not the case. As the cab drove away Daniel craned his neck upward. It was a glittering skyscraper amongst a forest of skyscrapers. Holding his pathetically small carry bag, he approached the entrance to the building, scanned his wrist ID chip and walked in as the large transparent door slid aside. The lobby was huge and luxuriously appointed, with ambient music playing softly in the background. There was a small, automated reception desk against the left wall, presumably presided over by an artificial intelligence. Daniel ignored it and walked to his right, toward the lifts, but was stopped by two beefy security guards in Senticorp uniforms. They wore the same uniforms that Daniel had seen in his own photo: black trousers and grey shirts with the Senticorp logo on the breast pocket. He noted that their belts featured sidearms, a spray can of some kind, and a retractable stick.

One of them held out a portable scanner and said, rather bluntly, "ID scan, please."

Daniel wondered whether either of them might recognise him. After all, he was apparently a Senticorp security guard, too. He held out his wrist and the scanner gave a beep and immediately showed a green light. The guard nodded and said, "You're okay to proceed, Mr Newman."

"Do you recognise me, by any chance?" Daniel asked, looking at both of them.

They both looked him up and down and shook their heads. The guy who had scanned him said, "No. Should we?"

"I guess not. It doesn't matter. Thanks. Have a good day."

"You too, buddy."

Daniel entered an already open lift, scanned his wrist and spoke his apartment number. A few moments later he stepped out onto the 44th floor, walked along a softly lit hallway and located his door. Another quick scan of his wrist, and the door slid smoothly aside and just as smoothly closed behind him again as he stepped through.

He was home.

Only it didn't feel like home. Not even slightly. It felt like a temporary apartment – the kind you would rent for four or five nights while visiting another city for a business trip or a brief holiday. Not that there was anything particularly wrong with the apartment. In fact, it seemed very new and modern, and it was surprisingly spacious. A separate bedroom, adequate bathroom, large open-plan lounge and dining area with a shiny, functional kitchen. There was nothing wrong with the place. And the view was amazing. But Daniel had no cosy 'welcome home' feeling.

Maybe he had expected too much, too soon. Perhaps, if he gave it time, he would feel more at home here. Then again, maybe he wouldn't stay long enough to put down emotional roots.

He spent a few minutes wandering around, opening cupboards and doors, checking out the food pantry and turning on taps. Finally, he took a beer out of the pantry, popped it into the insta-chiller for a few seconds and then cracked it open.

"Here's to you, Dr Blakely," he said, taking his first gulp. He sat down on a lounge chair and gazed out at the city skyline.

"Now what the hell am I supposed to do?"

15

The weekend stretched out interminably before Daniel. With nothing to do and without knowing anyone, he spent his time watching vids, going for walks and, sometimes, just staring out the window of his apartment. On Saturday night, he spent an hour having a couple of drinks at a local bar called Cascades, which was two blocks from his apartment, but was home again by 10 pm.

Daniel's headaches continued to plague him, although he wondered if they were improving slightly. The tablets they had given him at the hospital weren't as effective as the nasal atomiser, and he had to take them twice a day to keep the pain at bay.

By Monday morning, he was more than ready to go to work. At 7:30 am he was standing on the sidewalk outside the apartment block wearing his security uniform with a growing crowd of people who were waiting for the Senticorp shuttle bus. The driverless shuttle arrived and they all piled on, scanning themselves as they did so. The shuttle had only one or two spare seats by the time it departed.

"Good morning," said the woman who had seated herself beside him. She was about his age, with shoulder length brown hair and a pleasant face.

"Morning."

"You're new. I haven't seen you before. Just moved in?"

"Yes. First day." He didn't feel like explaining his supposed first two days of work, nine weeks ago.

"What were you doing before this?" she asked.

"I was working on a mining base on Titan."

A strange look came over her, and she seemed about to say or ask something and then changed her mind. A moment later she changed the topic.

"Well, your first day is certainly going to be interesting. Have you been watching the news feeds?"

"No."

"There was another break-in on Saturday night. This time they got into a lot of offices as well as the labs on B2."

"B2?"

"Basement 2. It's our most secure area. Home to Senticorp's most cutting-edge research."

"What sort of research?"

She smiled. "I'm not allowed to say. Not even to you."

"You work down there?"

"Yes. Senior researcher. Not that we'll be doing much research today. We'll probably be spending our time trying to work out what was interfered with and what data systems have been compromised." She shook her head. "Loads of fun."

He glanced at her Senticorp ID tag and saw that she had "Dr" in front of her name. "What are you a doctor of? If you don't mind me asking."

"I have a doctorate in microbiology." She smiled. "Not everyone's cup of tea, but I love it."

"What are they after – these people who broke in?"

"Whatever they can get. Scientific research is a highly competitive field. It's a frantic race. The first organisation to develop new technology stands to make billions of credits. Some people will do anything to get their hands on their competitor's research."

She took a data pad out of her carry bag and as she started tapping, said, "Anyway. Enjoy your first day."

The first half of Daniel's day turned out to be more boring than his weekend. He was taken to Personnel Department where he waited for over an hour to be processed. Finally, he was seen by a harried-looking woman who issued him with a new ID tag and took him to a small cinema room.

"Dr Blakely asked that you go through orientation again," she explained as she ushered him into the room.

"Do you remember me?" he asked hopefully.

"No, love. Sorry. A lot of people come through these doors. But the records show you started here a couple of months ago. So, I guess you must have been through this, once already."

There were four other people present, two wearing cleaners' uniforms and two in smart casual clothing. As soon as Daniel was seated, the lights dimmed and they sat through two hours of orientation videos, broken by light refreshments in the middle. At lunchtime the group was taken to the cafeteria where they lined up and selected a buffet-style meal. The large dining area was bustling and noisy, with at least 100 staff from various departments eating and chatting at round tables.

Daniel ate his lunch in silence, sitting at a table with people who all seemed to know each other and who weren't interested in talking to a security guard. After lunch, Daniel was taken to the Security Department where he underwent further orientation specific to his job, once again having to sit through a boring video presentation – this time in a small room by himself. Finally, he was taken to the office of the Head of Security, a gruff bald man named Doug Reed.

He waited patiently while his boss finished tapping out a message on a data pad and finally looked up at Daniel.

"Damned admin. It's the bane of my existence." He looked at Daniel with a frown. "And you are?"

"Daniel Newman."

"Ah, yes. Newman. Any previous experience in security?"

"Not really. I was here for two days about nine weeks ago, and was injured during the previous break in."

"Is that so?" He scanned his device and tapped a few commands. "Ah, yes. Here it is."

"You don't recognise me?"

"I've only been here six weeks, myself. A lot of staff were transferred out after that last fiasco."

Reed leant back in his chair and rubbed the back of his neck. "I've assigned you to the ground-level foyer security detail. You'll be buddied up with Lee Chen. He'll show you the ropes. You aren't licensed to carry a gun, of course. You'll have to get your gun license and do some training if you want to qualify for that."

"That's OK. I'm not planning on shooting anyone just yet."

"You'll be working the 8:00 am to 2:00 pm shift, starting tomorrow. Make sure you're on time. The guys on the night shift don't like their relief showing up late. Any questions?"

Daniel shook his head. "No." He was completely over his orientation day and just wanted to get home and have a cold beer.

"Good." He looked at his data pad with a slight frown. "Now, it seems you've been requested to see Dr Blakely before you leave. What have you done to piss off the big boss?"

"Nothing. I think it's just a follow-up to see how my recovery is going."

"You were injured?"

"Yes, nothing major," Daniel lied. There was no point going into detail with his new work colleagues.

"Alright. You'd better not keep him waiting. Head to reception on the ground floor and they'll point you in the right direction."

Reluctantly, Daniel made his way toward the main reception desk. All he wanted to do was go home, but he was also curious to get to the bottom of Blakely's ongoing interest in him. Over the last few days, the boredom of his circumstances had dulled his suspicions, but now they came to the fore again. Why was the head of a scientific research facility taking such a personal interest in him? And what was the truth about his past?

Daniel wasn't to know it, but his boring life was about to be shattered, and the answers he would soon discover were more shocking than anything he could have imagined.

16

Daniel walked into the plush outer office of Nigel Blakely's personal assistant, located on the top floor of the building. The door to Blakely's inner sanctum was slightly ajar and Daniel could hear his frustrated comments as he spoke to someone on a comm call.

"I want to know how they accessed that lab, damn it! You've had nearly two days to figure it out! The tech guys should be all over it by now!"

There was a pause and then Blakely spoke again.

"I don't care! I want retinal scans as the only means of access from now on. And contact Reed in security. I want two guards outside that door 24/7 from now on!"

Daniel heard the click of a disconnected comm and then a frustrated expletive. The personal assistant noted Daniel's ID tag and calmly pressed an intercom button.

"Dr Blakely, Daniel Newman is here now."

"Good. Send him in."

Daniel walked through the door into what could only be described as pure opulence. The huge office reeked of ostentatious wealth: plush lounges, expensive furnishings, a fully stocked bar, and the biggest desk Daniel had ever seen. Two floor-to-ceiling transparent walls looked out onto the Eastern foothills of Quito, and a partially opened door led to what appeared to be a private bathroom.

"Daniel! Come in. Sit down. How are you settling in?"

"Pretty well, thanks."

"How is your apartment? Is everything satisfactory?"

"Yes. Thank you."

"How was your first day on the job? Or should I say, your third?"

"It was OK, I guess. A bit boring with all the orientation stuff."

"Yes. Boring but necessary, unfortunately." He paused and looked more intently at Daniel. "How are your headaches? Are they improving?"

"Yes, actually. They're getting a little better every day."

"Wonderful! That's wonderful news!" Blakely seemed relieved, almost to the point of exuberance. Daniel wondered why his diminishing headaches mattered so much to the scientist, and felt like asking him, but something held him back.

"In that case, I want to continue with your scans. Once you've finished your shift each day, I want you to come down to our lab on B2. It will only take less than an hour each day."

"Can I ask what the purpose of these scans is? Will they help to restore my memory?"

"Scanning your brain every day allows us to map your neural pathways and monitor your brain's gradual recovery. Your headaches are a product of your brain establishing new synapses and new pathways. Once the headaches cease, we will be in a position to implement a highly-effective treatment."

"What kind of treatment?"

"It's something we've been developing for years and we've finally perfected it. The loss of memory is the result of a breakdown of transmission between axon terminals and dendrites, often caused by an excess of the GABA inhibitor and a deficiency in the major excitatory neurotransmitter, glutamate. We have developed the technology to identify the individual neurons that are underperforming or not performing at all and recalibrate the neurotransmitters at each specific site. In this way, whole networks of neural pathways can be brought back online. It's very exciting."

"I see." Actually, he didn't see at all, but it sounded very impressive.

Blakely continued. "The reason we need to map your brain every day, is that it takes considerable time to produce a neural map down to the level of individual synapses. You just need to be patient and trust us, Daniel."

"I'll try. As you can imagine, I'm very keen to recover my memories."

"I'm sure you are." Blakely stood up. "Come and I'll show you where you need to go."

He walked Daniel out of his office and through his PA's reception area.

"Janine, I'll be down in B2 for a while."

"Yes, sir."

"Hand me a chip updater, please."

Janine opened a drawer and handed Blakely a small hand-held device. He tapped its screen several times then held it against Daniel's left wrist. It gave a satisfied, soft ping.

"There. You're authorised for B2. Come this way."

He led Daniel to the lift directly outside his reception area. The door opened almost immediately, and they entered.

"Test your chip out," encouraged Blakely. "Scan it and then ask for B2."

Daniel did so and the lift responded with a verbal confirmation. "Access to level B2 granted." The doors closed and they descended swiftly.

"There is a dedicated lift that only goes to levels B1 and B2. Your chip will give you access to level B2, but you won't have access to any of the labs down there. You will have to scan your chip and then wait to be identified by the personnel in the lab. That's why I'm taking you down there now – so they can meet you and identify you."

The lift doors opened, and Daniel found himself in a large, circular central foyer, with wide hallways leading off in different directions, like spokes branching out from the centre of a wheel. Blakely selected one of them and after only 20 metres they came to a large set of double doors. The doors were currently open, and a team of technicians was working on them, with equipment strewn across the floor and a variety of cables scattered around. A sign above the door read, QEBS.

"We are currently beefing up our security here," explained Blakely. "These doors will normally be locked. You will need to scan your chip here and someone will come to ID you through the plexiglass window."

"What does QEBS stand for?" asked Daniel.

"It's highly technical. It would take me too long to explain it."

They stepped around the workmen and continued into the lab. It looked very similar to the lab at the hospital, only much bigger. White-coated scientists and lab assistants were busily working at benches which contained an impressive array of equipment. A few heads popped up and regarded them curiously for a moment before returning their attention to their various tasks.

Blakely guided him through to an inner office.

"Daniel, you remember Dr Marsha Nordstrom. She will be continuing your daily scans."

The taciturn scientist was seated at a desk, scanning data on a large screen. She looked up and merely nodded. Daniel had barely heard her utter more than a few words in each of their sessions at the hospital.

"Dr Nordstrom will let you in when you scan at the door." Addressing her, he said, "Daniel will be here by about 2:30 each afternoon."

"Good. I will be ready for him then."

Turning to Daniel, Blakely continued. "I won't be at these next sessions. Dr Nordstrom will conduct them herself. But once we are ready to initiate our final treatment, I will definitely be here."

He nodded at Nordstrom and guided Daniel back out though the laboratory. As they neared the main entrance doors, Daniel glanced to his left and recognised the woman he had sat next to on the shuttle bus that morning. She was in a white lab coat at a bench in a far corner of the room and was staring at him with a look of deep concern. As their eyes met, she quickly looked away and turned her back on him, busying herself with something on another bench.

Why did she look so worried? What does she know that I don't? Daniel continued to ponder that all the way home on the afternoon shuttle bus but was no closer to an answer by the time he walked through the door of his apartment. He cracked a beer and sat in a lounge chair looking out of his 44th floor window. One part of him wanted to cut and run. There were some things that still weren't adding up; too many warning bells, not the least of which was that very disturbing conversation he had overheard between Nurse Sylvia and Dr Blakely at the hospital. They'd spoken about him being more feisty but more promising than 'the others'. They'd spoken of being very close to 'full initialisation', whatever that meant, and more alarmingly, had referred to some kind of 'failsafe' which they could implement 'if things turned bad'. Daniel didn't like the sound of any of that. Perhaps he should just pack his bags and leave.

On the other hand, his conversation with Dr Blakely this afternoon had given him hope, even though the technical details were beyond his understanding. Perhaps they really could restore his memory. And maybe it was this new restorative process that Sylvia and Blakely had been discussing in the phone call he had overheard. Maybe he was just being paranoid and was attributing sinister motives where none actually existed.

He took another long swig of his beer and pondered his situation. He decided to wait it out a little longer and see what happened.

17

The red light on the private com channel was flashing again, its soft glow intermittently lighting up the almost pitch-black room. Ice clinked as the crystal tumbler of vintage cognac was placed delicately on an ornately carved ivory coaster. A richly jewelled hand reached out to the flashing light and answered the call.

"Speak."

"Sir, we've struck gold. Our new archaeologists have successfully obtained the hidden treasure."

"No mess this time?"

"No, sir."

"Good. Continue."

"They're further advanced than we thought. They've progressed to the biological testing phase."

"To what extent?"

"Living test subjects."

"My God! Have they been successful?"

"Not completely. Not yet, anyway. The first eight subjects all died. But each subject survived a little longer than the previous one as they refined their protocols. The last two made it to full consciousness. Number seven lasted only two hours. Number eight lasted nearly two days."

"So, they haven't yet achieved complete success."

"We think they have. There is a ninth. I've had some of our own scientists examine the ninth protocol. It looks flawless. After the death of number eight, they were finally able to identify the problem. Their newly designed long-chain molecule was short-circuiting neurons in the brain. They've now been able to synthesise an enzyme that acts as a bridge between neurons and the new molecule. We believe they are about to achieve complete integration."

"My God!" The man in the dark room was breathing heavily now, his excitement adding a tremor to his raspy voice when he spoke again. "Did our archaeologists get the formula for the molecule and the enzyme?"

"No, sir. We don't believe that the formulae are kept anywhere onsite. They're simply too valuable to leave lying around, even in a heavily guarded facility such as his. We think he has either committed them to memory or he has locked them away somewhere else, safely offsite."

The raspy voice swore. He thought furiously, taking a large gulp of cognac as he did so. The caller waited patiently, knowing his boss would reach the inevitable conclusion regarding their only viable course of action.

"But we don't actually need the two formulae, do we."

"No, sir. We don't."

"We just need to obtain the living specimen of the ninth protocol."

"That's correct, sir."

"Don't patronise me! I know it's correct! I don't need you to tell me what I already know!" He took another gulp of cognac as he savoured the plan that was starting to take shape in his mind. "Do we know the location of number nine?"

"Yes, sir. They've set him up in his own apartment while they are waiting for the new molecules to finish replicating and binding to the neurons. Once that is complete, they will initialise the system."

"What level of security do they have surrounding him? How difficult will access be?"

"Just two standard security guards in the ground floor lobby. It will be ridiculously easy to get at him. Plus, there is always the possibility of grabbing him when he is out of the building, so we may not even have to deal with the guards."

"I don't care how you do it, just do it."

"Does it matter what condition the target is in when we deliver him to you, sir?"

"No. All we need is viable copies of those long-chain molecules and enzymes. He doesn't even need to be alive for us to extract those, as long as his demise wasn't more than 72 hours previously."

"Good to know. That will make it even easier."

"Get it done."

"Yes, sir."

18

Daniel's second day at Senticorp wasn't quite as tedious as his first. He looked for the woman from B2 on the morning shuttle bus, hoping to speak with her again, but she wasn't there. Perhaps she was working a different shift today. Lee Chen, his security buddy, proved to be a friendly, affable person, unlike most of the surly, barely articulate characters who seemed to proliferate within the security department. Lee was more than happy to coach Daniel through his first shift, which didn't require an over-exertion of brain cells anyway. Their job was simply to stand in the foyer and ensure that all employees 'scanned on' as they entered the building and 'scanned off' as they left. Visitors were directed to the reception desk, where they were given temporary scan tokens if appropriate. And that was it! Nothing to it.

At the end of his shift, Daniel made his way down to B2 where Dr Marsha Nordstrom ushered him to a room that was strikingly similar to the one at the hospital. She continued to exhibit the warmth and interpersonal skills of a rock, and Daniel began to wonder if there was a reason underlying her detachment. It almost seemed that she was deliberately treating him as a project rather than as a person. He tried unsuccessfully to engage her in meaningful conversation but soon gave up. The scan took about 45 minutes and, once again, was tedious but painless.

As Daniel stepped off the shuttle bus outside his apartment building later that afternoon, he felt a tap on his shoulder. Turning around, he saw a teenage boy with multiple facial piercings and brightly coloured hair.

"Are you Daniel Newman?"

"Yes."

"Some guy paid me 50 credits to give you this. He said you should open it here and not in your apartment." The boy handed him a fire note and then took off at a run before Daniel could question him any further. Daniel stood on the sidewalk, slowly turning in a circle, scanning his immediate surroundings. Whoever had paid the boy was probably watching him right now. It was late afternoon and there were crowds of people making their way home from their places of employment. There was virtually no chance of spotting someone watching him.

He examined the small, folded note. It was only half the size of the palm of his hand. It looked too small to be a bomb, but who knew these days? He considered dumping it in a bin but couldn't bring himself to do it. Finally throwing caution to the wind, he broke the seal and unfolded it. The message was brief.

"Meet me at Cascades tonight at 7:30. Your life is in grave danger. A friend."

He had barely finished reading the message when the note began turning to grey ash in his hand. The ash continued to degrade further until there was nothing left of it at all; it had simply dissolved into the air.

Daniel looked around him once more but saw no one acting suspiciously. He walked into his apartment building, trying to decide what he should do.

∽

A little before 7:30 pm, Daniel walked into Cascades. All afternoon he had debated with himself whether he should turn up, changing his mind on several occasions, but in the end, he didn't really have a choice. If there was even the slightest chance that someone had information that could help him, he knew he had to find out.

He stood inside the doorway and looked around. It was an attractive bar, dimly lit with predominantly green and blue subtle lighting, cascading down the walls. The service bar was situated in the middle of the room, like a four-sided island, decorated in fake palm trees and a thatch roof. Daniel bought a beer, took it to a table and settled down to wait.

He didn't have to wait long.

"Don't turn around." The voice came from directly behind him. "Before we can proceed, I need to ask you a question."

Daniel took a sip of his beer and asked, "What question?"

"What's the square root of 81?"

"What? What kind of a question is...?"

"Just answer the question!"

Daniel shrugged. "Nine."

"Good. Now, what's the square root of 1,081?"

"This is ridiculous! Why do you want me to ...?"

"Answer the damned question!"

"Um ... Ok ... I don't know what the square root is."

"Are you sure?"

"Yes, I'm sure. I'm not that good at math."

"Good. It's safe to proceed."

The chair beside him was dragged back and a man sat down beside him. He was medium height, medium build, medium complexion, medium everything. If Daniel had seen him in a crowd, his eyes would have passed right over him.

"What the hell was the math test for?"

"I'll get to that, eventually. But if you'd been able to answer the second question, we wouldn't be having this conversation now – I would have left."

"You got something against math nerds?"

The man ignored the sarcasm and got straight to the point. "Daniel your life is in grave danger. I'm part of an organisation that wants to help you."

"What organisation?"

"I'll explain about that in a moment. But first, order me a beer. A craft brew of some kind. It's your shout."

"You tell me my life is in danger and the first thing on your mind is beer?"

"A man is not a camel, Daniel. Now be a good boy and order me a beer."

"Unbelievable," Daniel muttered, but he pressed the order button in the centre of the table and ordered the beer. "OK," he said. "I'm listening."

"I work for JUDAN: the Justice Department of the Alliance of Nations. I'm a Senior investigator."

"Prove it."

The man pulled a portable ID scanner from his pocket and held it to his wrist. The scanner read his ID chip and revealed his identity on its tiny screen: George Mallard, Senior Investigator, JUDAN.

"Okay, George," said Daniel. "What's all this about?"

"Senticorp was attacked recently by a competing research company: Blackstar Industries, based out of Singapore and headed up by a character called Eli Tang. Tang is also a Colonel in RISC, the Republic of Independent States Commissariat, the secret service of the Republic."

"And you're saying they are the ones responsible for my injuries?"

The George's beer arrived, and he took a long pull on it. He licked his lips and said, "No. They didn't injure you. You weren't even here when the attack happened."

"Really?" Daniel responded, letting his disbelief show. "Where was I?"

"This is the part you're not going to like." He gave Daniel a piercing gaze. "Your name is Daniel Mendez and until two and a half weeks ago, you were in the maximum-security section of a Federal Correctional Facility, awaiting execution."

19

"I don't believe you," Daniel said.

"You'd better start believing me," said George. "Your life depends on it."

"You're telling me I was in prison a couple of weeks ago? Prove it!"

George handed Daniel a palm-sized device and said, "Do a search for Daniel Mendez."

Daniel hesitated, then took the device and typed the name in. He clicked the first link that contained an image, then stared at the screen with mounting shock. It was his face. There was no doubt. He closed that link and chose another. Different photo, same face. His face. He was absolutely stunned. He looked closer.

"The photos show a scar down the side of my ... of his face. Am I a clone?"

"No. You really are Daniel Mendez. Senticorp removed the scar when they messed with you."

Daniel started to read the text on the screen. It was a news report dated several years ago, describing the handing down of his death sentence and his subsequent incarceration in a federal prison in Bogota, Columbia. The article went on to list his crimes. He was a multiple murderer: a hit man for a drug cartel.

A thought suddenly occurred to him. "How do I know you haven't pre-loaded all this false information on your data pad?"

"Call in to a data café on your way home and do another search. But don't use the device Senticorp has given you, because they're watching you. I assure you, Daniel, what you are seeing on that screen is the truth."

Daniel felt sick. "I'm ... I'm a murderer." He shook his head and his face drained of colour. It looked like he was about to throw up.

"Hold it together, Daniel. Don't lose it. You're going to have to come to terms with all of this very quickly if you want to live." George gave Daniel a searching look. "You do want to live, don't you?"

Daniel nodded.

"Good. Have a sip of beer and pay attention." George took a sip of his own beer and continued. "Senticorp paid the prison to fake your execution. It was easily done; it's still the wild west in that part of Colombia. They brought you here to Quito a little over two weeks ago and used you as a test subject in their experiment."

"What kind of experiment?"

"I'll get to that. But first, let me clarify something. Did they tell you that you were in a coma for eight weeks?"

"Yes. They said I was injured in an explosion during the attack. And I even found some online news articles about the attack that mention me as a casualty."

"They lied to you, and they uploaded those fake news reports for you to find. You were operated on as soon as you arrived here, and you were probably only in an induced coma for about a week. They would have had to shave your head for the procedure, so when you woke up you would have had about a week's worth of stubble on your head. Is that about right?"

Daniel though about it. "Yes. I hadn't thought of that. If I'd been unconscious for eight weeks my hair would have been much longer."

"Exactly. Are you starting to believe me now?"

Daniel nodded, the shock evident in his features.

"They simply used the story of the attack at Senticorp as a

convenient way to explain your supposed brain injury and your loss of memory."

"So, how did I lose my memory?"

"They wiped it. They took it from you, Daniel. The very people who claim to be trying to help you regain your memory are the ones who took it away from you in the first place. And they aren't going to help you get it back. They've lied to you all along, and they're still lying to you."

Daniel shook his head in confusion. "I don't understand. What do they want with me?"

"It's complicated, but I'll try to explain it in simple terms. Have you heard of QEBS?"

"I've seen those initials outside the door of a laboratory at Senticorp, but I don't know what it stands for."

"Quantum Enhanced Biological Sentience. Does that ring any bells?"

"Not really. I'm guessing it has something to do with artificial intelligence."

"Yes, it does. Mankind has been attempting unsuccessfully to create true artificial intelligence for hundreds of years. So far, all we've managed to do is create very sophisticated programs that can mimic humans, but they aren't truly self-aware; they're not sentient in the true sense of the word. When quantum computers arrived on the scene in the mid 21st century, they were hailed as the solution. It was believed that the faster processing power and greater flexibility of quantum computers would enable true self-aware sentience to develop. They were wrong. All it did was make our artificial intelligence algorithms faster, but they didn't achieve true self-awareness. It's now widely acknowledged that self-aware sentience has a non-physical component that simply can't be recreated in a laboratory."

"A soul," Daniel suggested.

"Something like that, although some scientists are uncomfortable with that term. The other problem that has remained unsolved until this time is the extreme conditions required for a quantum computer to operate. The essential sub-atomic elements of a quantum computer, qubits, can only survive and operate at an extremely cold temperature of minus 273 degrees Celsius. That means that they aren't exactly portable. Quantum computers can only be housed in specially built facilities with freezers that can achieve that kind of extremely low temperature. That's why we don't have quantum computers in our portable devices. We are still limited to our old-fashioned binary processors, which are literally millions of times slower than quantum processors."

"The upshot of all this is that scientists have been desperately searching for a way to make qubits function effectively at room temperature. The theory is that it might be possible to manufacture a molecule inside which qubits could operate at normal temperatures. Senticorp have developed such a molecule."

"What's all this got to do with me?"

"The quantum-friendly molecule is a living molecule that needs a living host. It cannot exist outside a biological organism. The quantum molecule that Senticorp has developed has been specifically designed to reside within the human brain. Guided by nanobot technology, the molecules grow into micron-thin filaments, thousands of times thinner than a human hair, that spread throughout the brain, making connections to individual neurons, which are the electrical transmitters and receivers that are at the core of the brain's functionality. Your brain was initially injected with a mixture of these quantum molecules and pre-programmed nanobots. You were then given several supplemental IV infusions to speed up the process."

"You're saying I'm a quantum computer?"

"No. At least, not yet. You're still completely human, Daniel. Flesh and blood, with a real human brain. But these microscopic quantum-molecule filaments are now insinuating themselves throughout your brain. It's why you are getting severe headaches. When the infiltration process is complete, Senticorp will initialise the quantum computer system. They believe you will become the world's first fully sentient, quantum computer."

Daniel was stunned. "That's why you asked me for the square root of 1,081."

"Yes. If the system had already been initialised, you would have been able to compute the answer. And that would mean that Senticorp would be able to see and hear everything you do, because built into the technology that is growing inside your brain is a micro transmitter that will provide a wireless link to their mainframe computer. Once the quantum system in your brain is initialised, the stimuli received via your eyes and ears and other senses will be broadcast directly to the mainframe server at Senticorp. If you had already been initialised, I would not be sitting here talking with you, because my life would be in danger."

Daniel shook his head, trying to process everything he had been told. "How do you know all this?"

"My first degree was in microbiology. That's why I took an interest in your case. Plus, we have someone on the inside. Someone working in Senticorp's highest security lab."

"The woman in B2," said Daniel. "The scientist who sat next to me in the shuttle bus on my first day."

"Yes."

"How did you get her into Senticorp?"

"We didn't. She was there legitimately, working as a research scientist. She began to have serious moral concerns when she saw what they were doing. She approached us after the deaths of the first couple of subjects. She was going to resign, but we convinced her to stay on."

"There have been deaths?"

"Yes. Eight previous test subjects. Six died during the initial infiltration and growth stage during the week of their induced coma. Subjects are kept unconscious during the first week because it is the most painful stage. The seventh test subject made it through that stage but died within a few moments of regaining consciousness. Number eight lasted a couple of days. You're the only one who's made it out of hospital alive."

"My God! They're murdering people! They're monsters!"

"I agree. But they don't see it that way, of course. They regard themselves as innovators; as saviours who will elevate mankind from our primitive condition to a new state of existence. Plus, they only use criminals who have been given the death penalty. They figure their test subjects are going to die anyway, so their deaths may as well serve some purpose."

Daniel's face grew pale. "So, I'm going to die too?"

"No. At least, we don't think so. Our contact informs us that after the eighth death, the scientists at Senticorp finally figured out what was going wrong. The quantum molecule was not binding properly with the synapses in the brain and was causing the neurons to short circuit. They have now developed an enzyme which effectively binds the quantum molecules to the synapses and creates a perfect electrical pathway. Our contact says they are confident that the new protocol will be completely effective."

"So, I'm number nine?"

"Yes. You're the ninth protocol."

20

"So, what you're telling me is that I've got a quantum computer growing inside my brain?" asked Daniel.

"Basically. Yes."

"And when they switch it on ..."

"Initialise it," George corrected.

"Whatever. When they flick the switch, I will become some kind of zombie computer? The real me will be gone?"

"We don't think so. All the research seems to indicate that the quantum interface will simply augment your mental capabilities, rather than wiping out your consciousness. You will still be you. You'll just be a hell of a lot smarter."

"But you don't know that for sure. It could also fry my brain, couldn't it?"

"Well ... it's never been done before, so no one knows for sure what will happen."

"Exactly!" Daniel thought for a few moments, then looked directly at George.

"I want to get the hell out of here."

"That's why I'm here, Daniel. We want to get you out, too."

"Good. Let's go!" Daniel started to stand.

"Sit down. It's not that simple."

"Why not?"

George sighed and considered his next words carefully. "You have a tracking device implanted inside you, along with a failsafe device."

"What does that mean?"

"It means they can track you wherever you go. In fact, they know where you are right now."

"What's the problem with the tracking device?"

"The problem is the failsafe device that's attached to it. Senticorp doesn't want their ninth protocol falling into the hands of a competitor. After all, the technology growing inside your head is worth billions of credits to whoever possesses it. The failsafe device is a tiny explosive device attached to the tracker which is located at the back of your brain stem, just under the base of the cerebellum. It's programmed to detonate if you ever go beyond the range of their tracking signal, which our contact tells us extends to a radius of about 30 kilometres from the Senticorp complex. They can also detonate it manually if they believe you have been compromised in some way."

"There's a bomb in my head?" Daniel asked incredulously.

"Yes. I'm sorry. The explosion would be tiny; not big enough to be heard or seen by anyone else. But it would turn your brain to mush. To anyone looking on, it would simply appear that you had suffered a catastrophic stroke."

"Bloody hell! This just keeps on getting better and better." Daniel reached for his glass of beer and took a long gulp, his hand shaking so badly that he spilt some beer down his shirt. "I'm stuffed, then! There's no way out for me, is there?"

"That's not true," assured George. "We have a plan. We're flying in a surgeon. He'll arrive here tomorrow. We're going to get that device out of you and then take you to safety. They won't be able to hurt you anymore after that."

"Why are you doing this? What's in it for you?"

"Isn't it enough that we want to help another human being?"

"So, there's nothing in it for you at all?"

George smiled. "Fair enough, I won't deny it. JUDAN is

building a case against Senticorp, and we want you to testify. When we rescue you, we will also be pulling out our contact at Senticorp and placing her in protective custody. With both of your testimonies, we will have enough evidence to put Nigel Blakely and several others behind bars for life."

"And then what? What happens to me after that? Back to my cell to await execution?"

"No. I'm hopeful that we can get clemency for you; get your previous convictions quashed."

"Hopeful? What does that mean? You're not certain?"

"Well ... this is uncharted territory here. I am going to argue that the person you once were, is gone – wiped clean by Senticorp. Not only did they erase your memories, but the process they use to implant the quantum molecule filaments also irrevocably alters a person's character and personality. Your obvious revulsion at your past actions is evidence of that. The old Daniel Mendez is dead. You truly are a new man, hence why Senticorp gave you that surname; Newman."

"But you still can't guarantee me clemency?"

"I'm working on it, Daniel. As I said, this is uncharted territory. The courts will need to be convinced, but I plan on making a strong case for your complete pardon. It's going to take a little time, but I'm hopeful."

Daniel took another sip of beer as he thought through his options. "I guess I don't have a choice. I want this thing out of my head, and I want to get the hell out of here." He looked directly at George. "So, what's the plan?"

"Meet me back here, tomorrow night, same time. I'll take you to a secure facility where the tracker and explosive device will be removed. It will be a relatively quick procedure. After that, the rest will be easy. There will be a skipjet on standby at the airport. Both you and our Senticorp contact will be safely in Pittsburgh within a couple of hours. As you may know, Pittsburgh is now the centre of governance for the North American region of the Alliance of Nations after the partial inundation of Washington due to rising sea levels."

"You're pulling your contact out tomorrow, too?" Daniel asked.

"Yes. We have to, for her own safety."

"Is she in danger?" Daniel asked, with concern evident in his voice.

"We think she is. We have reason to believe that as well as causing the unlawful deaths of the first eight test subjects, Blakely has also been responsible for the disappearance of at least one staff member who started to object and was threatening to go public. Our contact is deliberately placing herself in great danger by contacting us as she has done. She is the one who alerted us to your predicament. You have her to thank for your rescue."

Daniel was humbled. "I ... I don't know what to say. I don't think I deserve it."

George didn't disagree. He remained silent and took another hearty gulp of beer.

"There's something I don't understand," said Daniel.

"What's that?"

"Why the heart transplant? Why did they put an artificial heart in me? They told me because it was because my heart was injured in the attack."

"The quantum molecule requires constant blood pressure to operate at optimal efficiency. The surge and slump of normal blood pressure caused by a beating heart interferes with the quantum processes. You didn't receive an artificial heart because of any injuries; it was to support their quantum computer."

Daniel shook his head in outrage. "The bastards!"

"I'll drink to that," said George, taking another sip.

"What do I do until tomorrow night?" asked Daniel.

"Just try to act normally. Play along with them. And make sure you tell them that the headaches are still bad. The headaches indicate that the quantum tendrils haven't finished infiltrating your brain. They won't dare to initialise the new system until the headaches stop."

George pointed to the palm-sized device he had given to Daniel. "Keep that, but don't use it inside the apartment building or the Senticorp complex. Whatever devices they may have given you are definitely being monitored. This device has a secure uplink that can't be traced or hacked, but if you use it inside their buildings they can still see and hear you via cameras and microphones. If you need to use it, step outside the building. My com number is pre-entered. Alternatively, just say, 'call George'."

George drained his beer and stood up. "Thanks for the beer. You should stick around and order another one. I'll see you tomorrow. Stay safe, Daniel."

Daniel watched him walk out the door and disappear into the night. It was precisely what he felt like doing too, but somehow, he had to make it through tomorrow first.

21

Daniel didn't sleep well. In fact, he hardly slept at all. The image of the scarred face of Daniel Mendez – his own face, the face of a hardened criminal – kept flashing across his consciousness. More than the threat that was now hanging over his life or the possibility of having to return to prison to be executed, it was the knowledge of his horrible past crimes that haunted him. After George departed, he had sat in the bar, dredging through every reference to Daniel Mendez that he could find, drinking more beers than he should have as he spiralled down into depression. He had been a truly evil person. There was no other way to describe himself. He had been convicted of three counts of murder, two counts of drug dealing and one count of running an illegal prostitution business, but Daniel suspected that these incidents were just the tip of the iceberg. How many others had he shot or stabbed or quietly choked the life out of? How many women had he abused and forced to demean themselves for his financial gain? How many lives had he ruined by supplying them with life-sapping, brain-rotting drugs?

He detested the person he had once been. His past actions revolted him. Although he could acknowledge that he was a very different person now, the guilt of his past crimes kept him awake through the long hours of the night, calling to him like ghosts who would not rest until justice had been served. Perhaps he deserved to die even now? Perhaps he should just walk out into the night and keep walking until the bomb went off in his head and he sank into grateful oblivion. It was very tempting. Because the truth was that Daniel wasn't sure he could live with himself anymore, knowing the things he had done in the past.

He tossed and turned until nearly 3:00 am, when he finally gave up and got out of bed. He changed into some workout clothes and took the lift down to the basement where there was a fully equipped gym. He punished himself for over an hour until, drenched in sweat and nearing exhaustion, he returned to his apartment and showered. At some point, he must have fallen asleep on the lounge, because he awoke to the sounds of a gentle alarm, telling him it was 7:00 am.

At 7:25, feeling hung over and bleary-eyed, he emerged from the apartment building and joined the small crowd waiting on the sidewalk for the shuttle bus. He spotted the woman from B2 again and casually sidled up to her. He looked at her Senticorp ID tag, this time taking more careful note of her name: Dr Kelly Rearson.

"Good morning," he said.

"Good morning," she replied, her tone light but her face giving him a different message. She gave a subtle shake of her head and looked away, closing off further conversation. Her meaning was clear. *Keep your distance. Don't talk to me. Don't give the game away. Not today.*

It was clear to Daniel that she knew that he was now aware of her identity as the informant. George must have conveyed that information to her last night. He could feel the tension coming off her in waves. She was definitely on edge, and he felt sorry for her. Her whole life was about to be ripped away and, illogically, he felt that he was to blame. He wondered what final arrangements she had made overnight. Did she have family that she would have to leave behind? Friends? A lover? Even a treasured pet? He didn't have any experience with this kind of thing, but he suspected that when she was whisked away tonight, she would be travelling light, simply running into the night and leaving everything behind.

As he stood quietly beside her, he felt ashamed. She was doing this of her own free will. No one was forcing her. She hadn't been backed into a corner like he had. She had a choice. She was willing to sacrifice her comfortable, successful life to save a complete stranger and to stand up for a moral principle that she believed in. She was a hero, and he, by comparison, was a complete coward. He was running for his life: a murderer who was now willing to let innocent, good people, sacrifice themselves for him. As he stood beside her in the early morning light, he vowed that if he got out of here alive, he would make his life count. He would dedicate himself to helping others. He would honour Kelly, and everyone else who was about to help him, and do everything he could to repay their sacrifice.

The shuttle bus pulled up at the curb and they all piled on. Kelly deliberately sat next to someone else and kept her eyes diverted from Daniel. As he sat nearby, he thought he could see her hands trembling slightly. After disembarking less than ten minutes later, Daniel was approaching the main entrance to the Senticorp building when Kelly briefly walked beside him and whispered, "You look like crap. Get a coffee or something, and don't do anything dumb today." Then she moved on and left him in her wake.

He certainly felt like crap, a feeling that was not helped by having forgotten to take his pain meds this morning. But worryingly, his headache was barely there at all. In fact, the slight dull ache he was experiencing was probably more from the beers he had drunk last night than from what was going on inside his head. He figured that must mean that the infiltration of the quantum molecule filaments throughout his brain was almost complete. And that, in turn, meant that he was nearing the point when Senticorp would initialise the quantum computer in his brain – and no one could predict what devastating effect that might have on him. When he met with Nordstrom this afternoon, he would need to pretend that his headaches were still bad. The last thing he wanted was for them to initialise the system on the very day he was about to be liberated.

His shift passed agonisingly slowly. Lee Chen was once again very companionable and helpful, but Daniel's heart wasn't in his work, and he certainly didn't feel like engaging in idle banter. He just wanted the day to end so that he could bring this whole nightmare to an end. Lee soon recognised his grim mood and basically left him alone for the remainder of their shift.

Finally, after a long and tedious day, Daniel's shift ended, and he made his way down to B2. The verbally constipated Dr Marsha Nordstrom fitted the cap to his head, barely acknowledging him, responding to his attempts at conversation with monosyllabic answers. Daniel gave up and submitted himself to the now-routine scans. Thirty minutes later, Nordstrom seemed satisfied.

"How are your headaches?" she finally asked.

"They're still pretty bad," Daniel lied.

"Really?" she said, squinting at the screen in front of her. "That's surprising. Your scan is looking clear of all the pain indicators we've been seeing up to this point. I think it may be psychosomatic. Everything else seems to have stabilised. I think we're ready to ... err ..." she paused, seeming to choose her words carefully, "... to begin the final phase of your treatment."

"I'd prefer to wait until tomorrow, if you don't mind," he replied. "I'm pretty tired."

"Nonsense! You're here now, and we're ready to go. I'll call Dr Blakely."

She activated a comm channel and placed it on speaker. A moment later, Nigel Blakely's voice answered, "Yes?"

"Dr Blakely, it's Marsha. I've just finished Daniel's latest scan. Everything looks clear. I think we're ready to proceed."

"Really? That's very exciting!"

A feeling of panic swept over Daniel, and he broke out in sweat. He began looking at the exit door, planning his escape. There was no way he was going to let them initialise this monstrous thing they'd been growing inside his brain!

"I'm coming straight down! Wait for me!" responded Blakely, ending the call.

"Dr Nordstrom, if we're going to do this, can I use the bathroom while we're waiting for Dr Blakely? I had too much coffee during my shift and I'm busting."

She frowned and considered for a moment, then nodded. "Alright. I'll show you where the facilities are."

"No need. I saw them in the corridor outside the lab entrance."

"All the same, I'll accompany you, if you don't mind. We can't have you wandering off and getting lost just when we're about to ... finish your treatment."

She took his cap off and led him through the main lab area toward the entrance doors into the corridor. He saw Kelly look up from her work in the far corner and stare at him with concern. He felt helpless, unable to communicate with her and warn her that he was about to make a run for it. They walked into the corridor and Nordstrom stopped outside the door to the male bathroom.

"I'll wait here for you. Don't be too long."

Daniel hesitated, glancing down the hall toward the lifts. If he ran now, she wouldn't be able to stop him, but he would still have to wait for the lift. Security would be on him before the lift doors even opened. Somehow, he had to get rid of Nordstrom.

"Is something wrong?" she asked, a note of suspicion in her voice.

"No. I'm fine thanks," he said. He opened the bathroom door and stepped inside. He looked around furiously, searching for some kind of magic escape route, but there were no other exits. The bathroom consisted of two sinks and two small cubicles with inward-opening doors. A mop and bucket were leaning against the wall, ready for the next scheduled cleaning. A desperate plan formed in his mind. He walked to the door again and opened it.

"Dr Nordstrom! You'd better get in here! Someone's collapsed in one of the cubicles!"

Shock registered on her face. "What? Who?"

"I don't know. He looks terrible. Please, he needs help."

She pushed past him and rushed into the bathroom.

"He's in the second cubicle."

Nordstrom reached the open door to the empty cubicle and stopped. She started to turn toward Daniel, with a puzzled expression. "There's no ..." She gasped as he pushed her into the cubicle and quickly pulled the door closed. He grabbed the mop and slid the handle through the vertical bar of the door handle so that she couldn't pull the door open from inside.

"Mr Newman! Daniel! What are you doing? Let me out of here!"

Daniel spun around and raced to the bathroom door as Nordstrom continued to call out. "Help! Help, someone!" As he opened the door into the corridor, Daniel faked a loud coughing fit in the hope of covering the muffled sounds of Nordstrom's calls for help. Fortunately, there was no one in sight and Daniel sprinted down the corridor to the central circular foyer and the solitary lift. He reached the lift and pressed the button repeatedly, willing it to arrive. "Come on! Come on!" he muttered, looking over his shoulder to check that no one was coming.

He guessed that Blakely could be stepping out of the lift at any moment. His brow creased in sudden concern. What if Blakely was on the lift that he had just summoned? He looked around the circular foyer for somewhere to conceal himself and saw the entrance to the nearest corridor just a few metres away. The lift chimed softly, announcing its arrival and the doors began to slide smoothly open. Daniel sprinted to the nearest corridor entrance and dived around it. Had he made it? He peaked around the corner and saw Blakely striding across the foyer toward the far corridor that led to the lab. He was talking on an ear pod comm, saying, "I want you here to witness this with me, my love. You've been a key part of this from the very beginning. How soon can you be here?"

Daniel didn't wait for Blakely to disappear from sight. As Blakely walked away from the lifts and across the foyer, Daniel snuck out of his corridor entrance and quickly covered the few metres back to the lift. The door had already closed. Daniel pressed the button again and the door opened, issuing another soft chime as it did so. Hopefully, Blakely would be too focused on his comm call to Nurse Sylvia to notice the chime.

Daniel jumped into the lift. He scanned his chip and said, "Ground floor." The doors began to close, and he heard someone call out, "Wait!". He glanced out and saw a man in a white lab coat hurrying toward the lift from another corridor. "Wait for me!"

The doors finished closing with the lab worker still several metres away. The lift ascended quickly, and Daniel wondered how much time he would have before the alarm was raised. By now, Blakely would be walking past the bathroom and would almost certainly be able to hear Nordstrom's cries for help – unless he was still focussing on his comm call. Daniel might only have moments left before security were notified and he was trapped in the building. He had to get out.

The door opened and Daniel emerged into a corridor leading to the main entrance foyer for the building. He had barely exited the lift, however, when an alarm began sounding and a recorded message came over the sound system. "All staff report to your designated assembly areas. No one is to leave the building." The message began playing on an endless loop, with the alarm sounding in the background.

"Crap!" Daniel emerged into the foyer and saw people running in different directions with looks of fear and even terror. It was understandable, given the deadly attacks that had taken place recently. The two security guards who were on duty and whom he only vaguely recognised had drawn their weapons and were looking around them in confusion. Any moment now, they were going to get a comm call giving them his details, and then it would all be over.

Daniel hurried toward them. "Guys! Down this way!" he said, pointing back down the corridor. "Some people have been shot in the cafeteria! We need reinforcements!"

They watched him approaching and seemed to hesitate.

"I don't have any weapons," he explained. "I'll stay here and make sure no one leaves. You guys go!"

They hesitated for a moment longer, then nodded and ran

across the foyer toward the corridor. Daniel didn't wait. He turned and ran to the main entrance doors. They didn't open. They had already been sealed.

"Crap!" he said again. Then he wondered if his security tag would over-ride the lockdown. He swiped his tag and the door slid open.

"Hey! Stop or we'll fire!"

Daniel looked back over his shoulder and saw the same two guards. They hadn't even made it as far as the corridor before they had received a comm call. One of them had a hand on his ear, still obviously receiving instructions, while the other was standing with his feet spread wide and his weapon pointed directly at Daniel.

"Don't do it, man," the guard said. "There's nowhere to go. I'm warning you; I will shoot."

They stood like that for a heartbeat, or whatever substituted for a heartbeat with Daniel's artificial heart.

"Lie down on the floor with your hands stretched out in front! Do it now!"

Daniel didn't do it now. Instead, he dived through the door and to his immediate left. A shot whistled through the open doorway, narrowly missing him. He was immediately back on his feet and running, deliberately keeping the transparent wall between him and the guards. The walls were made of bullet-proof material and the guards did not have a clear line of sight to him through the doors which were diagonally to their right. Daniel heard the guards swear, followed by the echoes of their footsteps as they ran across the foyer toward the doors. Meanwhile, Daniel sprinted away from the building, in the general direction of the carpark and the drop-off point where he caught the shuttle bus every afternoon.

The bus hadn't arrived yet, but a small crowd of off-duty workers had already started to gather at the shuttle-stop, obviously before the alarms had sounded. Two shots in quick succession rang out behind him, and Daniel felt the whistle of a bullet tear past his right ear. He began weaving from side to side as the small crowd at the shuttle-stop started screaming and running into the carpark. Surely the guards would not risk hitting innocent people? He was wrong. Two more shots rang out as Daniel continued to weave from side to side, and more screams emanated from the terrified workers who were now frantically running in all directions.

Daniel had no plan; no idea how he was going to get out of this alive. He was kilometres from the CBD and he was on foot. He felt the noose tightening around him. He had nowhere to go and he was hopelessly outnumbered. He reached the empty curb side where, a few moments earlier, tired workers had been waiting patiently, scanning their devices, talking to loved ones and planning dinner. He came to a stop, his breath coming in ragged gasps. He knew it was hopeless. He turned around and raised his hands in the air. There were six guards sprinting toward him now, all with weapons drawn. This was the end. And it was probably what he deserved anyway. He wouldn't fight it anymore.

He heard a vehicle pull up behind him. "Cab for Daniel Newman. Please scan your ID chip."

Incredulously, he turned around and saw a robocab at the curb, its door open and his name in illuminated text above the door. He didn't stop to think. He dived into the cab, swiping his chip as he did so. Several dull thuds sounded against the cab's exterior as more bullets were fired, but the cab was already moving as the door slid smoothly shut. The cab accelerated down the access road and joined the public road, leaving six breathless security guards swearing in frustration.

22

D aniel lay on the floor of the cab, regaining his breath after diving through the door. The driverless cab greeted him cheerily, completely oblivious to the hail of bullets that had dented its exterior.

"Welcome, Daniel Newman. Destination, Quito International Airport, is confirmed. Enjoy your journey."

The airport? George must have decided to pick him up straight from work. But why the change of plans? They'd arranged to meet at Cascades at 7:30, tonight. George couldn't know that Daniel had blown his cover, as it had only just happened, and the cab had already been waiting for him in the carpark when all hell broke loose. And why the airport? Surely, they needed to get the failsafe device out of the back of his head before they took him anywhere. Daniel was relieved but confused.

He unbuttoned the thigh pocket of his trousers and took out the palm device that he had been given last night. He had kept it with him in case of an emergency. He guessed his current predicament qualified as an emergency. He switched the device on, and it established an instantaneous uplink to Solnet. Daniel initiated a call to the only number in the memory.

"Yes?"

"George, it's Daniel."

"Yes, I can see that. Why are you calling?"

"I'm in the cab."

There was a pause. "What cab?"

"There was a cab waiting for me after work."

"That's not good."

Daniel felt a stab of fear. "You mean you didn't send it?"

"No. It must be Blackstar."

"Blackstar?"

"Senticorp's rivals, Blackstar Industries. I told you about them last night. We think they're the ones responsible for the recent attack." He thought for a moment. "Damn it! They obviously know about you, now. Where is the cab taking you?"

"The airport."

"Daniel, you can't let yourself be taken aboard a plane! A minute after you take off, you'll be out of range of Senticorp's tracking signal and the failsafe will automatically detonate."

Now it was Daniel's turn to swear. "What do I do?"

"Try to stop the cab and get out. If that's not successful and you end up in their hands, you must convince them not to put you on a plane."

"There's another complication, George."

"What?"

"I had to leave Senticorp in a hurry."

"How much of a hurry?"

"The kind of hurry where they were shooting at me. I didn't have a choice. Blakely was going to initialise the quantum thingy in my head. I had to run."

There was a long pause.

"George, are you still there?"

"Yeah, I'm thinking. Senticorp will be tracking you, and they are probably chasing the cab as we speak. Things could get a bit ugly at the airport. I can't get there in time to help because I'm still in the CBD. Try to stay alive Daniel! I've got another agent I might be able to get there."

There was a click as George ended the call, leaving Daniel with a rising sense of panic. He started to yell. "Stop the cab! Stop the cab! Pull over! I want to get out."

A calm voice answered. "I am sorry. We are currently travelling on a no-stop freeway. We will reach our destination in four minutes."

"I don't care! This is an emergency! Pull over!"

The voice merely repeated its frustrating message: "I am sorry. We are currently travelling on a no-stop freeway. We will reach our destination in four minutes."

"Damn it!" Daniel tried forcing the door open, but it wouldn't budge. In desperation, he lay with his back along the bench seat and started kicking at the window and door panel with both feet.

"Please desist from destructive behaviour. Deliberately damaging public property is an offense."

Daniel continued to attack the door with his feet, and the inner door panel began to buckle a little.

"You have violated public property code 217E. Airport police have been notified and you will be detained upon arrival."

"Excellent! Call more police. Bring the whole garrison!" Daniel continued to bash at the door panel, but it soon became clear that he was not going to budge it. He stopped and sat up. A few minutes later, the cab pulled into the airport drop off zone and was met by two police officers, waiting at the curb. The door opened with a sick grinding sound and Daniel stepped out.

"Mr Newman, we are taking you into custody for violation of ..."

"Yes, yes. Fantastic! Let's go! I'm keen to get locked up."

The officers looked at each other as if to say, 'looks like we've got ourselves a weirdo'. They grabbed one of his arms each and began walking him along the sidewalk toward their vehicle which was parked about 50 metres away. As they walked, the officer holding his left arm began to advise him of his rights. "As a citizen of the Alliance of Nations, you are entitled to legal representation of your choosing and may ..." But that was as far as he got. He collapsed face down in front of Daniel with a smoking hole in the back of his head. The other officer reacted quickly and spun around as he drew his weapon but was pierced with a laser blast to his left shoulder. He staggered to the side, taking cover behind a large rubbish receptacle, making a call for backup as he did so.

Daniel dived to the ground in the melee and looked back to see two men in dark suits walking grimly toward them with laser pistols drawn. As he looked from his position, cowering on the ground next to the dead officer, the two men fired several more shots at the surviving officer, drilling holes through the bin and piercing the policeman through the chest. A moment later, they stood over Daniel.

"Stand up or we will shoot you dead right here."

Daniel stood, and they hustled him through the door into the terminal, amidst the pandemonium of people running and screaming in every direction.

One of them grabbed his arm and propelled him forward, saying, "Run!" The three of them ran through the open terminal area along with everyone else. They reached a sign for the men's restroom and Daniel was forced through the door. They didn't stop moving as they made their way through the restroom facilities. The two men ditched their dark jackets and ripped off their shirts as they walked, revealing casual, brightly coloured T-shirts underneath. A man was waiting with a small carry bag and as they hurried past him, they were handed a baseball cap each and a brown wig for Daniel. They emerged back into the public area through a different door at the far end of the restroom, looking very different. The sounds of multiple sirens and tyres screeching to a halt could now be heard as police reinforcements arrived.

"Where are you taking me?" pleaded Daniel, as they hustled him toward a smaller corridor that was sign-posted "Private Jet Terminal".

"We're going for a nice plane ride."

"I can't do that! I can't go more than 30 kilometres from Senticorp!"

"Why not? Will you turn into a pumpkin?" It was the slightly taller guy to his left who had spoken. He had a pock-marked face and a couple of large pimples. The guy on Daniel's right was more heavy-set; Daniel would have described him as 'squidgy'.

"There's a failsafe device in my head. A small explosive device. If it loses connection with the tracking frequency, it will detonate!"

"Sure, there is," said Pimples.

"It's true! I'll die if I leave Quito!"

"That's not my problem. Dead or alive, that's what we were told. It makes no difference to us."

Daniel stopped dead. "I'm not going with you."

They both pushed him forward and he stumbled and turned to face them. "I'm not leaving here." People were still running past them in all directions, not sure what was happening.

"I'll give you five seconds to start moving," said Pimples.

"Or what?" said Daniel. "What are you going to do? Shoot me?"

"Yes," said Pimples. He stepped right up to Daniel and stood nose to nose with him. "Last chance, tough guy."

Daniel didn't move.

"OK. We'll do it your way."

He took a gun out of his trouser pocket and shot Daniel in the chest.

23

The shot hit Daniel squarely in the chest. Before he could fall to the ground, his two kidnappers quickly supported him from each side and dragged him to the side where there were seats along the wall. They slumped him into one and Pimples told Squidgy, "Grab one of those wheelchairs." There was a whole 'help yourself' collection of "mobility assistance devices" about 20 metres further along the corridor. The shorter, more solid guy grabbed one and they put Daniel into it and started wheeling him quickly toward the private jet terminal. The whole incident had taken less than a minute and no one had taken any notice of them, such was the panicked mood of the crowd.

Daniel started moaning as he was whisked down the corridor. "Cheer up," said Squidgy, who was propelling his chair. "It could have been worse. He could have used a real gun. You'll start to get some feeling and movement back within a few minutes."

"What the hell was that?" mumbled Daniel, a narrow trail of drool oozing from the corner of his mouth.

"A neural disruptor gun. Hurts like hell, doesn't it" explained Squidgy, cheerfully. He was obviously the chatty one. "Small enough to fit in your palm. Handy little buggers at times like these."

After another 200 metres they took an off ramp to the right, following a sign that said, Private Jet Terminal 4. The ramp descended quickly to the level of the tarmac, and they came to a set of transparent doors with a boarding desk that was now completely empty. Daniel caught a glimpse into a small office through a doorway to the left and saw two prostrate forms in airport uniforms that had been dragged out of sight. A man in a dark suit and sunglasses was holding one of the doors to the tarmac open, and said to them, "You took your bloody time."

"Had a couple of problems to deal with," answered Pimples.

"Get him on board and let's get out of here," said Glasses.

They wheeled him across the tarmac toward a sleek private jet. Despite his dire predicament, Daniel could not help admiring it. It was obviously a skipjet: a rocket boosted craft that would pierce the outer edges of the Earth's atmosphere, temporarily achieving space flight and skipping across the edge of the atmosphere, before hurtling back down to land. It was the quickest and most economical way to fly long distance.

"Please!" begged Daniel. "You can't take me on that! It'll kill me!"

"Shut up!" said Glasses.

They were half-way to the jet when a shot rang out – an ordinary projectile weapon. The bullet ricocheted off the tarmac a metre in front of Pimples. The three Blackstar men crouched down with weapons drawn, looking for the origin of the shot. A voice called out from behind a baggage handling vehicle, near the exit doors for Terminal 3, about 50 metres to their right.

"You have something that belongs to us! We want him back!" While the attention of Daniel's three kidnappers was focused in that direction, he noticed the exit doors for Terminal 5 open, 50 metres to their left, and two men ran onto the tarmac and took cover behind a stack of metal crates. Although they were no longer wearing Senticorp uniforms, Daniel recognised one of them as a member of the security team. A voice from that side then called out, causing the three kidnappers to spin in that direction.

"We have you covered from both sides! Get on your jet and leave him behind, and you won't get hurt!"

No one moved and no one spoke for a few moments. The three men were crouched near Daniel. Pimple and Glasses were in front and Squidgy was cowering behind the wheelchair. Glasses spoke softly to his comrades. "At the count of three we stand up and make a dash for the jet. Les, you push that bloody chair as fast as you can. Pauly and me will cover you."

"Don't do it, Les," pleaded Daniel. "You won't make it."

"Shut up!" said Glasses, glaring at Daniel. He looked at Squidgy. "Les, you do what you're bloody told!" He paused. "OK. Let's do this. One, two, three!"

The three men stood and started running, with Les pushing the chair and the other two firing blindly to both sides. Les didn't make it. Daniel was actually splattered by gruesome brain matter as Les's head exploded. The other two men fell to the ground, both wounded now but still returning fire. Feeling had been gradually returning to Daniels body over the last few minutes, so he quickly reached out to the control panel on the right arm of the chair. He activated the motor, spun the chair around and raced back toward the open doors while bullets and laser fire filled the air behind him.

He kept expecting a bullet in the back as he neared the doors, but nothing happened. He supposed that the two surviving Black-star men were too busy fighting for their lives to worry about him, and the Senticorp guys were not interested in shooting him as they clearly wanted him back alive. One of the doors had been left ajar and Daniel shot through it without slowing down. As he began ascending the ramp to the terminal corridor above, he looked down through the glass wall below and saw four police cars screech to a halt on the tarmac. Officers took cover behind their vehicles and opened fire. It was bedlam.

He reached the level of the corridor and joined the panicked people now running back toward the central concourse. Several uniformed police ran past him in the opposite direction, with weapons drawn and yelling, "Police! Out of the way!" The crowd stood to the side as the police ran through the middle of them and disappeared down the ramp from which Daniel had just emerged. The crowd started surging toward the main entrance again and Daniel slipped into the stream of stampeding humanity with his motorised wheelchair, weaving in and out as he easily outpaced the slower people in the crowd. As he neared the intersection of his corridor with the much wider corridor leading to the passenger plane terminal, he parked the wheelchair against the wall and began walking, looking over his shoulder for signs of pursuit. At least he tried to walk, but he hadn't recovered as well as he had anticipated. His legs were jerking in a strange fashion as he stumbled forward.

He joined the larger corridor which was packed with passengers who had just disembarked from an international flight, and he began stumbling along, trying to keep pace with the general flow. Suddenly a large-framed man grabbed his arm and steered him toward the side wall.

"Not so fast, my man,"

Daniel looked up in shock and then amazement as he recognised the physiotherapist from the hospital. "Carlos? What are you doing here?"

"I'm here to save your skinny white ass, that's what I'm doing."

"But how did you ...?"

"Quick, in here." He guided Daniel into a nursing mothers' restroom and locked the door. As they walked in, Carlos double tapped his ear pod comms. "George? I've got him." He paused and listened. "Yes. Will do. I'll get him to do a quick change and then we'll get out of here." Another pause. "OK. We'll meet you there." He tapped off.

He took some women's clothing from a disposable bag that he had been carrying and gave them to Daniel.

"Put these on. Quickly!"

"Women's clothes?"

"The airport is crawling with Senticorp personnel, some of whom can recognise you. They won't be looking for a frumpy woman. Did you think you were going to just stroll out the front doors looking like that? What was your plan, dude?"

Daniel spoke as he got changed. "I didn't exactly have a plan. I was going to wing it."

"Ducks that wing it often end up as dinner."

"Where did you get this stuff?" asked Daniel.

"I've had it in my car for a week or so. It was one of our ideas for getting you away safely if the need arose." He reached into the bag again and pulled out a long dark wig and sunglasses. "Put these on as well."

"So, you're working with ...?"

"With George, yes. I'm an undercover JUDAN agent. And I'm here to save your skinny white ass. But there's no time to explain. Our problem is that some of the Senticorp people have hand-held trackers. They can home in on the device in your head. The trackers can pinpoint you to within a 10-metre radius."

"So, how will we ..."

"Last night while you were talking with George, he was carrying a frequency analyser. It recorded the frequency of the tracking device in your head. While you were at work today, we bought a whole bunch of these little guys." He pulled a tiny device out of his pocket, about the size of the end of his thumb. "Micro-transmitters. Cheap as chips. We set them to the same frequency. While I've been waiting for you, I've been slipping them into people's pockets and bags as they walk past. By now the hand-held trackers being used by the Senticorp guys will be going crazy."

Carlos pulled a tube of lipstick out of his pocket. "Stick some of this on, too, dude."

Daniel began to shake his head, but Carlos was adamant. "Do you want to live or not?" As Daniel complied, Carlos noted, "Good. You must have shaved this morning. I brought a shaver along, just in case, but we don't need it."

Carlos gave Daniel a scrutinising look. He was now wearing an ankle length skirt over his trousers, and a long sleeve, flowery top. With the long dark hair, sunglasses and lipstick, no one had a hope of recognising him. "You'll do. Now let's get out of here."

24

D aniel and Carlos emerged from the nursing mothers'
restroom and merged with the last of the new arrivals from
the recently landed passenger plane. Daniel felt completely
ridiculous in his long dress, blouse, wig and glasses.

"We're going to stick with the crowd and head downstairs to
the tube," said Carlos. "It's the quickest way into the CBD and the
trains should be jam packed at this time of day."

As they emerged into the large entrance foyer of the airport,
Daniel saw several men scattered through the crowd, staring at
devices in their hands and turning in circles with confused looks
on their faces.

"Head to the travellator in the far corner and keep your head
down," said Carlos. "I'll meet you on the platform downstairs."

Before Daniel could say anything in response, Carlos was
gone, leaving Daniel to blend with the people moving toward the
tube station. He arrived on the underground platform soon after
and stood in the crowd who were waiting for the next train into
the city. Carlos arrived at his side just as the superfast maglev train
arrived and came to a stop.

"Where did you go?" asked Daniel as they finally sat together
at the back of a carriage.

"I stuck some micro-transmitters on the back of two shuttle buses and a couple of cabs. The transmitters are magnetic. I also slipped some into the bags of people on the other platform who are waiting for the train to the tether lift."

As the train accelerated silently out of the airport station, Daniel asked, "How did you know where to find me?"

"I didn't. It was a guess. I just figured that the junction of those corridors was the most likely place to find you if you were ever going to try to come back through the front doors. I knew I had no chance of finding you among all the different terminals."

Daniel nodded. "I see. So, you're working with George's mob?"

"Yes. I work for JUDAN, the Justice Department of the Alliance of Nations."

"So, you haven't been working at the hospital for long?"

"No, dude. We arranged for the usual guy to get sick, and I was the convenient replacement. Carlos the physio! Ha!" The big man chuckled.

"You were pretty good, actually," complemented Daniel.

"Thanks, my man! Maybe I should consider a career change." He chuckled again.

"Why were you there? What was the plan?"

"I only got placed there a few days after your surgery – while you were still unconscious. We were planning to lift you straight from the hospital, but we were still trying to arrange a surgeon when they released you."

"A surgeon?"

"Yes. To take that transmitter out of your head. Which is where we're going right now."

Daniel wasn't looking forward to more surgery. "Is the surgery dangerous?"

"Not as dangerous as leaving it in. Especially now that Senticorp knows you've gone rogue. They could decide to activate the failsafe at any moment." He looked at Daniel in sympathy. "Sorry, dude. But that's the brutal truth. That's why it's really urgent that we get this thing out of your head."

Daniel nodded. "Where are we going?"

"George has got the surgeon set up in a hotel directly above Civic Station."

"You're going to do brain surgery on me in a hotel room?"

"It's the best we can do, considering the circumstances. We were planning to take you to a private hospital and commandeer the operating theatre, but we think Senticorp are now keeping tabs on all the hospitals, looking for that very scenario. They really want you back alive, but if they get wind that someone is trying to remove the failsafe and tracking device, they'll cut their losses and detonate it."

Daniel looked stricken. "They could do it right now, couldn't they?"

"Yes. If they think they've lost you for good."

25

"I think we've lost him for good," said Sylvia.

They were gathered in the executive office at Senticorp: Dr Marsha Nordstrom, Dr Nigel Blakely and Nurse Sylvia Stratham, Blakely's lover.

"But how did he get away? Who is helping him?" asked Blakely.

"It's got to be Blackstar," responded Sylvia. "They must have found out about him after the last break-in."

"And if Blackstar has got him," added Nordstrom, "all they need to do is insert a needle into his brain and extract a sample of the quantum molecule and the enzyme, and they can reverse engineer the whole thing."

Sylvia was pacing up and down and said, "Let's face it, Nigel, he's gone. We're not getting him back."

They were all staring at the large wall screen which showed a map of the city with nearly two dozen blinking red dots, all of them moving in different directions.

"She's right," said Nordstrom. "There are too many decoys out there and we have no way of knowing which one is our subject."

"He has a name, you know," commented Blakely.

"Not to me, he doesn't," answered Nordstrom. "He's filth. So were the others. They don't deserve to live. I say we activate the failsafe."

"I'm reluctant to do so while there's still a chance of reacquiring him," said Blakely. "I've got people scouring the city as we speak, chasing down all of these transmitters. We might still find him and get him back. We've invested too much in this to literally blow it all away."

"But you won't be blowing it all away," said Sylvia. "You'll just be removing a piece of trash. Mendez isn't important; in fact, he's the scum of the Earth. You'll be doing mankind a favour by getting rid of him. We don't need him now. We've perfected the protocol. We know it works. We can start again with someone else – and this time we'll keep him locked up."

Blakely nodded. "Perhaps you're right."

Sylvia walked around the desk and massaged the back of his neck as he sat in his chair. "I know I'm right, my darling. Make the call."

Blakely reached for the comm button.

Daniel and Carlos emerged from the underground tube and stood on the sidewalk, getting their bearings. Carlos spotted the impressive set of transparent sliding doors 30 metres to their left, with sophisticated signage announcing it as 'Civic Towers Apartments'.

"There it is," he told Daniel. "We're nearly there. Keep your head down and try to walk like a girl. You look like a lumbering bear."

"I'm doing my best. My legs still aren't working properly."

Even as he spoke, he stumbled and nearly fell, with Carlos saving him at the last moment. As he fell, his wig slipped down over his face, his dress flew up at the back and his long trousers underneath were momentarily visible. Carlos helped to steady him again and adjusted his wig. He kept a hand on his arm as they walked the remaining few metres toward the apartment complex.

Twenty metres behind them, a man in black trousers and a grey T-shirt was staring at them as he activated a comm.

∾

Blakely's hand was hovering over the comm panel when a blinking light indicated an incoming call from one of the field agents.

"Yes?" he answered.

"Sir, I think I've found him. He's outside Civic Station. He's wearing a wig and is dressed in women's clothing. That's how they missed him at the airport. I'm getting a really strong signal and it's the only one in the vicinity. It's got to be him! There's someone helping him – a big dark-skinned guy. They're entering Civic Towers Apartments as we speak."

"Good. I'll call for backup. Don't lose him! Apprehend him if you can."

Blakely disconnected and initiated an all-channel comm call. "This is Dr Blakely. All available field agents converge on Civic Towers Apartments. Our target has just entered the building. Repeat. Civic Towers Apartments. Get there with all haste!"

He disconnected and smiled. "You see? All is not lost, ladies. A little patience is all that was needed. The day may yet end well for us."

∾

Carlos activated his comm as they walked through the cavernous ground floor entrance foyer of the apartment building. "George. We're here. Where are you?"

"Right here," answered George as he stepped from behind a large indoor plant and started walking beside Carlos. "We're in 714. The surgeon's there and we're all set to go."

They walked to the bank of lifts and George scanned his wrist. About 30 seconds later a lift door opened and they filed inside, along with three other people – an elderly couple and a middle-aged man dressed in dark trousers and a grey T-shirt. George and the elderly couple scanned their wrists. Floors five and seven lit up on the panel. The other man didn't scan himself but merely stood quietly at the rear of the lift. The doors closed and the lift quickly ascended to the fifth floor. The elderly couple got off. The doors closed again. The lift ascended and opened again on the seventh floor. All four passengers got off.

George turned right and led them down the corridor, with Daniel following immediately behind and Carlos in the rear. The man in the T-shirt turned right as well and ambled slowly down the hallway behind them. George reached the door to room 714 and swiped his wrist against the door scanner. The panel light turned green and the door gave a satisfying click.

"Nice and easy, now," said a deep voice behind them.

They turned slowly to find a laser pistol pointed directly at them.

"No sudden moves. Open the door and let's all go inside where we can have a nice little chat."

They remained frozen in place.

"Move now or I'll shoot – starting with the big guy here. I'm deadly serious."

George opened the door and they filed inside. The gunman kept his laser trained on them as they filed into the open plan lounge room. A voice came from the bedroom.

"I'm all set up in here. Bring the patient in and we can ..." A bald man in surgical scrubs emerged from the bedroom and stopped in mid-sentence.

"Please come and join us," said the gunman, waving his pistol at the surgeon. The terrified surgeon put his hands in the air.

"Please. I'm just a doctor. I'm not really part of this. I'm just here to do a job."

"So am I, doc. You can sit in the chair by the window. The rest of you can sit together on the lounge. Nice and easy now."

As they moved toward the lounge, Daniel's right leg gave way and he fell, exclaiming, "Ahh! My leg. Sorry."

The gunman had his pistol trained on Daniel who now lay sprawled on the floor, his skirt around his waist, revealing his trousers underneath. "Get up!" he said. "Nice and slow!" Daniel rolled onto his side and stood up slowly, adjusting his skirt as he did so.

"Now, sit on the lounge, all of you!"

The three of them sat slowly on the lounge, staring at the gunman. He kept his pistol trained on them as he tapped his ear pod comm. "This is Stevenson. I've got them in custody. They're in room …"

BANG!

A gunshot rang out and the gunman fell to the floor.

26

The gunshot was loud in the confined space, causing their ears to ring. Carlos and George watched incredulously as the gunman dropped to the floor, then turned to look at the small pistol in Daniel's hand, still pointing in the direction of the fallen man. Carlos leapt to his feet and crossed the floor to the gunman, grabbing his laser and tapping his ear pod to disconnect the comm call. Then he turned and looked at Daniel.

"What the hell, dude?"

"I recognised him as soon as he walked into the lift. He's a security guard at Senticorp."

"But where did you get the gun? It's small enough to be a toy."

"It's a neural disruptor. It fires some kind of neural dart. I took it from a dead policeman at the airport during the initial attack by the Blackstar guys. I fell to the ground next to the body of a cop with a hole in his head. The pistol had fallen out of his belt when he fell. I slipped it into my trouser pocket, and it's been there ever since."

"And that's why you faked a fall just now?"

"Yeh. I had to get it out of my pocket."

Carlos nodded his head. "Nice work, my man!"

"I didn't know it was a neural disruptor gun until they used one on me at the airport and I recognised that it was the same kind of gun that I took from the cop," said Daniel. He was shaking all over now, a delayed reaction to everything he had just been through. Carlos relieved the gunman of his weapon and comms and went searching through cupboards for something to tie up the now-groaning man. Meanwhile, George walked across to the surgeon who was clearly shaken.

"Dr Carmody, we need to operate, urgently. Do you think you can manage that?"

The surgeon's hands were shaking and he was looking very pale. He sat staring at the fallen gunman, not answering.

"Dr Carmody! This is a matter of life and death! We may only have minutes before they realise that Daniel is compromised and they decide to activate the failsafe."

"Yes. Yes, of course," said Carmody, standing unsteadily to his feet. He walked toward the bedroom. "Quickly, in here."

Daniel and George followed him into the bedroom while Carlos remained in the loungeroom and bound the gunman's wrists behind his back with a cord from a kitchen appliance. The bed was covered with a blue surgical sheet and the nightstand bore a tray with an array of surgical equipment.

"Lie face-down on the bed with your head turned toward me, please, Mr Newman," said Carmody, as he quickly snapped some surgical gloves on.

Daniel lay down as instructed and asked, "You are going to put me to sleep first, aren't you?"

"No. There's no time, and I'm not set up to support an unconscious patient. You will be conscious but drowsy throughout the procedure. I assure you; you will feel no pain at all." He picked up an atomiser and moved toward Daniel. "This is a marvellous concoction. A complete pain blocker, plus a muscle relaxant. It will be very pleasant, although you will later not be able to remember anything that happens in the next couple of hours." So saying, he inserted the atomiser into one of Daniel's nostrils and activated it. Daniel experienced an instant rush of something, followed by an overwhelming sense of euphoria as he seemed to float above his body on a cloud of joy.

Carmody turned Daniel's head to face away from him now, so that he had access to the back of his neck. He quickly shaved the stubble from the top of Daniel's neck and the base of his skull, then grabbed a syringe and injected the area several times.

"This is local anaesthetic," he explained to George who was standing nearby, watching with fascination. Carmody donned a head lamp and surgical magnifying glasses, then picked up a scalpel and said, "You'll need to help me now. Grab a swab and stand beside me. Mop up the blood as I cut."

Carmody sliced along the base of Daniel's skull, while Daniel started snoring peacefully. The surgeon felt the wound with his fingers and cut some more. He paused while George mopped at the blood, then he took a small scanner from the tray and held it over the open wound.

"The device is deeper than I thought. I'm going to have to be very careful here, as it's very close to the base of the brain stem." He put the scanner down and leant closer, focusing his head light and magnifying glasses on the open wound. He began to cut again.

"Damn!" exclaimed Blakely. "Stevenson's still not answering."

"That's because he's been shot!" said Sylvia, as if explaining the obvious to a child. "You heard the shot. They've killed Stevenson and now they've got Mendez. We've lost him."

"Maybe not," said Blakely. "We know he's in that building somewhere. We might still be able to find him. I've got people arriving on the scene as we speak."

"There are hundreds of rooms in that building," replied Sylvia. "What are you going to do, break down every door and search every room? The police will be swarming all over the place before you've searched the first corridor!" She softened her voice. "It's over, Nigel. Blackstar's got Mendez, and you need to end this now."

Blakely sighed. "Yes. I think you're right."

"I know I'm right."

Blakely took and deep breath and reached out toward the comm button that he had hoped he would never have to press.

"There it is!" exclaimed Carmody. The wound was clamped open now, and the shiny black device was clearly visible, nestled up against the white column of the brain stem. "Towel, please," he said. "there's sweat running into my eyes." George picked up one of the white surgical towels and mopped Carmody's brow. "Thank you, that's better. Now swab the wound. I need a clear line of vision. This is the delicate part."

George used a fresh swab to mop up the blood and then backed away. Carmody leant closer. "It doesn't look as though it's physically attached. It's just sitting there." He reached in with some small forceps and gipped the device. He gave a gentle pull. "There is some scar tissue on the side that has partially attached itself to the device. I have to cut it away." He transferred the forceps to his left hand and held out his right without taking his eyes from the wound. "Scalpel!" George slapped the scalpel in his hand and Carmody began to gently slice along the edge of the device, slowly freeing it from the clinging scar tissue.

"Just a few more moments," Carmody said, breathing fast.

"Go as fast as you can, Doc. I think we're running out of time."

"What's the matter?" asked Sylvia.

Blakely's finger was still poised over the comm button. "I'm not sure I can do it. I don't think I can deliberately end someone's life."

"What are you worried about? He's a piece of scum: a murderer, a drug dealer and a pimp, and God-knows what else! He was about to be executed anyway. Trust me, you're doing the world a big favour."

"Do you concur, Marsha?"

"Of course I do! Frankly, I don't see what your problem is. We've killed eight of these bastards already. What's one more? If you're worried about the morality of it, we are simply carrying out a court-ordered, state-sanctioned execution."

Still, Blakely hesitated.

"For God's sake, Nigel! Grow some balls!" Marsha exclaimed.

There was silence for a moment. Then Blakely pressed the comm button.

"Yes sir?" answered a voice.

"Do it."

"Just confirming, sir. You want me to activate the failsafe?"

"Yes. Do it now."

"I think I've got it!" Carmody grunted and twisted his wrist a little. "Nearly there!" He pulled a little harder and the device slid out with a wet sucking sound. He held it up to the light and examined it. "It's such a clever little ...," Carmody began.

"Get rid of it!" yelled George. "Throw it in the bin, now!"

Carmody swung around and dropped the device in the metal bin beside the bed.

The small explosion blew the bin onto its side and filled the air with the pungent aroma of melted plastic and singed metal. The two men looked at the remains of the device in stunned silence, their ears still ringing from the bang.

"My word," said George, "that was cutting it rather close."

27

"It's done," said Blakely, sitting back in his chair and staring at the comm panel, as if the ghost of the man he believed he had just murdered was about to ooze out of it.

"Good!" said Marsha Nordstrom. "Now we can move on with our research. We're done here." She stood up and started moving toward the door.

"We're not done yet," said Sylvia, causing Nordstrom to pause and turn back.

"Why? What's the problem?"

"Two problems, actually," responded Sylvia. "Firstly, there's the mess at the airport. From what I can gather, shots were fired and at least one Blackstar employee was killed. A public gun battle isn't going to go away quietly."

"That situation is under control," said Doug Reed as he walked boldly into Blakely's office. The gruffly spoken Head of Security walked to the bar and poured a double measure of whisky into a tumbler. He took a gulp and sat down in one of the comfortable lounge chairs.

"By all means, help yourself," said Blakely, facetiously.

"I already did."

"In what sense is it under control?" asked Sylvia.

Reed took another gulp before responding. "Our guys were all out of sight when the police arrived. All the cops saw was one dead guy lying on the tarmac and two of his mates firing into some airport property. The Blackstar guys turned their weapons on the cops as soon as they arrived and kept them pinned down while our guys snuck back into the terminal. They all managed to get away."

"How? The cops would have been swarming all around the airport entrance by then."

"Our four guys in the shootout didn't go out the airport entrance. They arrived by flitter on the opposite side of the private jet terminal. They got back through to that side via maintenance corridors which go underneath the terminal corridor above. The flitter was airborne before the cops had stopped hiding behind their patrol cars."

"So, nothing can be linked back to us?" said Blakely.

"Not that I can see. The newscasts are saying that the two remaining Blackstar guys were shot dead by the cops, so those guys certainly aren't talking. There's nothing that can link us to the shootout."

"What about our other personnel who were searching for Mendez in the public concourse and corridors?" asked Sylvia. "Did any of them get detained?"

"They stayed as long as they could. They slipped out with the crowds before the cops shut the whole place down. Trust me, we came out of it squeaky clean."

"Good," said Blakely, clearly looking shaken and out of his depth.

"You were saying that there are two problems," said Doug Reed to Sylvia. "What's the second?"

"The second is more serious," said Sylvia. "It's possible that Mendez isn't dead."

"What do you mean?" asked Blakely, fresh concern written across his features. "The failsafe device is ... well, it's failsafe! We've tested it multiple times. There's no way he could have survived the explosion."

"Unless the device wasn't in him any longer," contributed Nordstrom, catching on to Sylvia's line of reasoning.

"Exactly," said Sylvia. "We have to deal with the possibility, however remote, that Blackstar knew about the failsafe device and initiated an emergency surgical procedure to remove it."

"That seems a bit far-fetched," said Blakely. "We tracked them to an apartment block, not a hospital."

"It would be a simple thing to set up a temporary surgery in an apartment," responded Sylvia. "The surgery, itself, would be relatively simple."

"But how would they even know about the failsafe device?" asked Blakely.

"The break-in," contributed Nordstrom, picking up the argument. "Details of the fail-safe device were encrypted in the files that we believe were copied from our system."

Blakely looked concerned. "So, there's a possibility that Mendez is still alive and in the hands of our competitors?"

"Yes," said Sylvia. "Maybe if you'd acted sooner, my love, we could be surer of his death. But, given the delay before you activated the device, there is a slight chance he could still be alive."

"Damn!" said Blakely. "The technology inside his head is worth billions! We can't let him fall into anyone else's hands. We need to be sure he's dead."

"Exactly," replied Sylvia.

"So, what do we do?" asked Blakely. "How do we make sure the job is done?"

"Simple," said Reed. He took a long gulp of whisky, emptying the tumbler and setting it on the antique wooden side table, deliberately avoiding the drink coaster. "We'll place a 24-hour watch on all exits of the building. We know they're in there somewhere. Eventually, they've got to come out. And when they do ..." Reed formed his hand into the shape of a pistol, pointed it at Blakely and pretended to press the trigger.

"Bang!"

28

G eorge and Carlos sat in the lounge room talking about their
current situation, while Dr Carmody was finishing up with
Daniel.

"Senticorp knows we are in this building," said George, "and
by now they've probably stationed people at all the exits."

"On the positive side," said Carlos, "They don't know what you
or I look like, or Dr Carmody for that matter, so we can come and
go with safety."

"Yes," agreed George, "but Daniel is another matter. They'll be
watching for him. All the surveillance teams will have been shown
his photo by now."

"So, how do we get him out?"

"I'm still working on that. For the moment, we'll just let him
sleep because we've got a more urgent issue to deal with."

"Kelly Rearson?" asked Carlos.

"Yes. Our contact at the Senticorp lab. She's due to be extracted
tonight and I can't risk leaving her in place any longer."

"So, what's the plan?"

"I'm meeting her at a café near her apartment block, at 6:30. I
was planning on bringing her back here to start with, but I can't
risk that now. My goal is to get us all to the airport and safely on

board the skipjet that the Department has made available. I'll have to set Kelly up at a hotel near the airport while we sort out how to get Daniel out of here. That might take a while."

"Yeh, the dude's certainly not in a fit condition to be moved at the moment," agreed Carlos. "And what do we do about this guy?" he asked, pointing to the trussed gunman lying on the floor. The tightly bound man was lying on his side, sleeping peacefully, after Dr Carmody had administered a strong sedative.

"We're just going to have to leave him here when we depart. The sedative should knock him out for at least 12 hours. By the time he wakes, I'm hoping we'll all be safely out of here."

Dr Carmody walked out into the lounge area holding his medical bag. "I'm finished now," he said. "There shouldn't be any complications. I've glued the wound together with plastaskin and injected the site with stem-cell enriched bioplas. You can remove the bandage tomorrow and all signs of the incision should be gone within three days." He placed a small bottle of tablets on the table. "He might need some pain killers later tonight and possibly again tomorrow morning, but after that he should be pain free."

George stood up and shook the doctor's hand. "I can't thank you enough Dr Carmody. Our department will, of course, compensate you."

"How long will he be asleep?" asked Carlos.

"You can wake him now if you like. He's only sleeping lightly. But watch him carefully for the next hour or so. The painkiller I gave him, encephadeine, is also psychoactive and mildly psychotropic."

"Meaning?" asked Carlos.

"Mr Newman will experience a slightly altered state of consciousness and may speak or act a little strangely. Commonly, patients exhibit mild euphoria and a loss of inhibition, a little like being drunk. Just keep an eye on him and make sure he doesn't do anything stupid or dangerous."

We will," assured George.

Carmody continued. "The unique characteristic of this particular drug is that there is no tapering of its effect as it wears off.

One minute he will be experiencing an altered state of consciousness, and the next, he will be back to normal as the last of the drug leaves his system. It's a very sudden transition which could leave him momentarily discombobulated."

"Okay. Thanks. We'll watch him carefully. Would you like me to arrange a cab?" asked George.

"No. I'll walk. My consulting rooms are only two blocks from here."

"Are we sure Dr Carmody is safe to leave by himself?" asked Carlos.

"Yes," answered George. "The Senticorp surveillance teams don't know him. There's no reason to suspect that he is in any danger."

"In that case, I'll take my leave," said Carmody. "Goodbye, gentlemen. And good luck."

Carmody left, and George looked at the time on the wall screen. "It's nearly 6:00. I'll get going. I want to make sure Kelly is not being followed when she arrives at the café." He moved closer to Carlos. "Give me your wrist and I'll transfer the access code for the room, just in case you have to leave and come back." He took out a small device, scanned the chip in his own wrist and then transferred the code to Carlos's wrist. "Reception wouldn't like me doing this, but I won't tell them if you don't."

"Your secret's safe with me, boss."

George walked toward the door. "I'll call you when I get Kelly to safety. Then we'll figure out a way of getting Daniel out of here as well."

"Cool," said Carlos. "I'll look after sleeping beauty." As he spoke, the sound of gentle snoring emanated from the bedroom, and they both smiled.

29

A comm channel started blinking on the desk of Doug Reed, Head of Security at Senticorp. He reached out and opened the line.

"Yes?"

"Boss, it's Sanchez. You told us to call you if there was anything we weren't sure about."

"Yeah, what is it?"

"It could be nothing, but we've just seen a man walk out the front entrance carrying a bag. My guy in the foyer called me to say he's sure it's a doctor's medical bag. The guy sure looks like he could be a doctor."

Reed thought for a moment. It wouldn't be completely unusual for a doctor to make a call to someone in an apartment block. After all, people still got sick from time to time, even in the 24th century. And, of course, there was a good chance the guy wasn't a doctor at all. But what if he had been called to operate on their missing test subject? What if their suspicions were correct and Mendez's failsafe device had been removed? The timing of the appearance of this guy with the medical-looking bag had to be more than a coincidence.

"You were right to call me," said Reed. "Now, listen carefully. Here's what I want you to do..."

～

Dr Charles Carmody was approaching the office block where he had his consulting rooms. He had cancelled all his afternoon appointments and, by now, his secretary would have left for the day. He would spend an hour or so answering messages and catching up with documentation, then head home. Frankly, he was exhausted. The surgery had stressed him more than he had anticipated.

He was mentally listing the most urgent things he now had to attend to, when a dark van pulled up at the curb. It had tinted windows, so he couldn't see in. The nearest window rolled down a few centimetres so that he could just see the top or the driver's head.

"Hey doc! Daniel has started to deteriorate. Something's happened. They told me to come and bring you back."

"Really? What's gone wrong?" He took a step closer. "When I left him, he was fine."

In response, the side door of the van slid open and two men in masks leapt out, grabbed him, and literally threw him into the van. He landed roughly on the floor between two inward-facing bench seats, bruising his shoulder and banging his head against the floor. By the time he started to sit up, the van was already moving, slipping easily into the late peak hour traffic.

Fear now coursed through his veins, his heart pounding and sweat already breaking out across his face. "Please! Please! Don't hurt me! I ... I'm just a doctor. I don't know anything."

There were two men in the back with him, both wearing full face masks.

"That's not quite true, doc," said one of them. "You've just proved that you've treated Daniel Newman."

Carmody glanced at both men, his anxiety level going through the roof. "What do you want?" he asked, his voice quivering.

"It's very simple, doc. You tell us where he is, and we'll let you go. It's a good deal."

"On the other hand," said the second man, "if you refuse to tell us ..." He left the unfinished sentence hanging in the air and lifted his shirt to reveal a pistol tucked into the belt of his trousers.

"You're going to kill me anyway, aren't you?" said the doctor, tears brimming in his eyes.

"Of course not, doc," said the first man. "You can't see our faces, so you can't identify us. That's why we'll be very happy to let you go if you cooperate. The last thing we want is having to dispose of a dead body."

"Yeah," added the second man. "The last time we had to do that, it took us hours to clean up the mess."

"You see, doc?" said the first man. "We're very reasonable people. You help us out, and you get to live the rest of your life. I'd call that a brilliant deal."

The doctor gulped, his heart pounding like a sledgehammer and his breath coming in ragged gasps, as if he had just run five kilometres. "He's in Civic Towers Apartments."

"Come on doc, you can do better than that. We already know that. We need to know *where* in the building he is."

"He's on the seventh floor."

"Close, but no cigar yet. Come on, doc. You're nearly there. Tell us the room number and you get to bounce the grandkids on your knees and watch them get married."

He breathed a long sigh and closed his eyes. "He's in room 714."

"Bingo! Congratulations! Good decision. Now, just sit back and relax. We're just gonna keep you here with us for a little longer, until we have confirmation that you're telling us the truth. Make yourself comfortable doc, it shouldn't be too much longer."

He activated his lapel comm and made a call.

30

Daniel walked out of the bedroom into the lounge area, blinking and looking around him.

"Ah! Sleeping Beauty awakes!" said Carlos. "How are you feeling, my man?"

"Hi Carlos!" said Daniel with a goofy smile. "What are you doing here?"

"We arrived together. Don't you remember?"

"No. What's for dinner? I'm starving!"

"Perfect timing, dude. I've already ordered room service. I got burgers and fries coming for both of us. The food should be here any minute."

"OK. I need to pee."

"Sure, dude. Pee away. The bathroom's that door on the right, next to the front door."

As Daniel walked into the bathroom, there was a knock on the front door, and a male voice announced, "Room Service."

Carlos walked up the short hall and opened the door. "Come in," he said to the waiter holding the tray. He held the door open, and the waiter walked through to the combined lounge / dining room.

"Just dump it anywhere on the table," said Carlos, following him in. The waiter took his time, arranging the two plates with their covers on opposite sides of the table, then arranging the cutlery on each side. When he had finished, he straightened up and said, "Just put everything in the disposal chute when you're finished, sir."

"Sure. Thanks."

The waiter left and Carlos sat at one side of the table. He lifted the lid on his plate and the aroma of the food immediately made his mouth water.

"Hey Daniel! The food's here, dude. Come and get it! I'm starting mine."

He picked up the burger and took a huge bite and then stuffed a few golden fries into his mouth as well. As he chewed, he grabbed a sachet of salt and sprinkled some over the fries. He took a second bite and stuffed another couple of fries in. Delicious!

"Hey Daniel! Come and get it, dude!"

He took a third bite and, as he chewed, decided to check whether Daniel was alright. He walked to the bathroom door and knocked, then noticed that the door was ajar. "Are you OK, dude?" he asked, poking his head through. The bathroom was empty. "Daniel?" he called, walking through to the bedroom. It was empty too.

"Bugger!"

There was nowhere else in the apartment for him to be. Carlos figured he must have slipped out while the waiter was arranging the food. He opened the door and looked up and down the hallway. Nothing. He ran to the lifts and pushed the button. Where would Daniel have gone? Carlos figured that the drugs were obviously still affecting him and he wasn't thinking straight, otherwise he wouldn't have even considered leaving the room. If Daniel walked out the front doors now, he was a dead man!

Carlos looked at the indicators above the three lifts. The first lift was heading down and came to rest at Level 1. The second lift had just started ascending from the ground floor. The lift immediately in front of him now started to descend from Level 8, the floor above him, and a few moments later a pleasant chime sounded as the lift door opened.

Carlos jumped in, scanned his wrist and pressed the button for the ground floor. Agonisingly slowly, the doors closed, and he started to descend. The lift stopped at Level 2 to let a mother with two teenage daughters in. They were chatting excitedly about a show they were going to see. The lift eventually reached the ground floor and, as the doors opened, Carlos pushed past the women, hearing the mother mutter, "How rude!"

Daniel was nowhere to be seen in the lobby. Carlos ran out through the front doors and stood looking up and down the sidewalk. Nothing! He raced back inside. Where the hell was he? He remembered seeing one of the lifts stopped on Level 1, so he raced back to the lift and pushed the button.

Three men wearing nondescript trousers, plain T-shirts and dark casual jackets exited the fire stairs on Level 7 and quickly oriented themselves.

"This way," said one of them.

They strode quickly down the hallway and came to a stop outside room 714. Looking around to ensure that no one was visible, they each drew a small laser pistol from their jacket pockets. Lasers were always preferable when silence was required. One of them aimed at the door latch and fired continuously for several seconds. The mechanism was quickly destroyed, and they pushed the door open and rushed inside, with weapons ready for action. It took only a few seconds to search the apartment and realise that their prey had gotten away.

"It's Stevenson!" one of them said, kneeling over the tightly bound man who was still sleeping on the loungeroom floor. "They must have given him some kind of sedative."

"This food is still warm," said another, standing over the plates. "One burger has only had a couple of bites out of it, and the other hasn't even been touched. They must have only just left!"

The third guy called out from the bedroom, "There's a whole lot of bloodied swabs and other discarded surgical crap in the bin in here. It looks like they operated on our pal."

As he spoke, their lapel comms all chimed and one of them answered.

"This is Matthews."

"This is Sanchez, outside the main entrance. A big, dark-skinned guy just ran out the doors onto the sidewalk. He looked up and down for a few seconds and then ran back inside."

"A hotel staff member?"

"No. A civilian. It has to be one of them. Our guy in the foyer says he pressed for a lift then didn't wait. He bolted through the door to the fire stairs."

"Any sign of the target?"

"Nope."

"Roger that." He disconnected. "Chen, you stay here and take care of anyone who comes back. Gonzalez, you and I will take the stairs and grab the big guy."

The two men ran back down the hallway to the foyer and quietly opened the door to the fire stairs. With weapons drawn they slowly started to descend, listening for sounds from below.

Carlos swiped his wrist against the scanner and opened the fire stairs door on the first floor. He looked up and down the hallway. There was a sign on the far wall directing guests toward the heated pool to the left and the gymnasium to the right. He heard wordless singing or humming coming from the right and turned in that direction. As he rounded a curve in the hallway, he saw Daniel peering through the locked doors of the gym, singing a happy tune to himself. Thank God!

Daniel heard his footsteps and turned toward him. "Hi Carlos! Check this out! There's some cool equipment in there. Can we go in?"

Carlos reached him and grabbed his arm, starting to guide him back toward the lifts. "Not right now, dude. We're kind of busy at the moment. Besides, you haven't had your dinner. You told me you were hungry. Remember?"

"No, I don't remember. What's for dinner?"

"Burgers and fries, my man. Come on, let's go."

They arrived at the lifts and Carlos punched the button.

"Hey, Carlos?"

"Yes?"

"I feel a bit weird."

Carlos put his arm around his shoulders. "Don't worry, my friend. I got your back. Ain't nothing bad gonna happen to you while old Carlos is here."

Matthews and Gonzalez, the two Senticorp men, reached the ground floor fire stairs door without having encountered anyone on their descent down the stairs. They opened the door and caught sight of their man in the foyer. The man saw them and shrugged, shaking his head. The two men retreated into the stairwell again and Matthews said, "He must be somewhere between here and Level 7. We'll go back up and check every level on the way."

They started back up the fire stairs, this time running and not bothering to mask their steps. Matthews held his MFD in one hand and his pistol in the other. When they reached the door to Level 1, he swiped the multi-frequency decoder against the scanner and heard the latch click. They opened the door to Level 1 just in time to see the door to one of the lifts close.

"That might be him," suggested Gonzalez.

They stood and watched which way the lift went. The indicator panel showed it ascending.

"He's probably going back to his room," said Gonzalez.

"Wait and see," answered Matthews. "There's no point in us rushing back up there again if he gets out at Level 3." They waited and watched. The lift stopped at Level 7. The other two lifts were much higher in the building.

"That's it!" said Matthews, turning and opening the door again. "The stairs will be quicker! Let's go!" He activated his comm as he ran. "Chen! Can you hear me?"

"Yeah."

"I think the big guy's coming back to you. Let him get completely inside the apartment, then subdue him."

"You mean, shoot him?"

"No, you idiot! Just cover him with your gun. Don't let him out. We're on our way back up."

The lift opened and Carlos and Daniel turned right toward their room. Daniel was chatting happily, describing the impressive equipment he had seen in the gym. Their room was the fourth door along on the left, but as they drew closer, Carlos saw the singed and melted area around the latch and the door slightly ajar. He held his arm out in front of Daniel and brought him to a stop, then turned and held his finger to his lips. He reached into his pocket and took out the gun that he'd taken from the guard they had captured earlier. He whispered in Daniel's ear, "Don't say anything. Come with me." He grabbed Daniel's arm and hurried him back down the hall to the lifts. He pressed the button, but the lift had already departed for another floor. "Damn!" he whispered.

The sound of multiple sets of pounding feet came from the stair well opposite the lifts. Carlos sensed that they weren't friendly feet and he looked around for somewhere to hide. There was nowhere. The best option was a large potted palm against the foyer wall opposite the lifts, not far from the stair well door and against the same wall. He grabbed Daniel and hurried him across to the palm, flattening themselves against the wall behind it just as the door burst open. Fortunately, the door opened toward them, helping to shield them from their pursuers. Two men burst through the doorway and with barely a glance in their direction they ran up the hall in the opposite direction and straight into their room.

"Quickly!" whispered Carlos, dragging Daniel along with him. He opened the fire stairs door and they went in. Up or down? Somehow, down didn't seem a very safe option. He whispered, "Up we go, Daniel. And stay very quiet!"

"Is this a game?" asked Daniel as they went up the stairs.

"Kind of. But you must be very, very quiet. OK?"

"Sure."

Matthews and Gonzalez ran back into room 714 to find Chen standing alone in the lounge room, pointing his laser pistol at them. Chen lowered his pistol and Matthews asked, "He didn't come in?"

"No. No one."

"Damn it! This is ridiculous!"

"Maybe it wasn't him getting into the lift on Level 1," said Gonzalez. "It must have just been someone else from this floor."

"Maybe. Maybe not," answered Matthews. He thought furiously for a moment. "But this is definitely their room. And they definitely haven't left the building, or we would have seen them. So, they must be in the building somewhere. They haven't got many places to hide, because their access code will only give them access to public areas and public hallways."

He activated his lapel comm. "Boss, do you copy?"

"Reed here."

"They're not in their room, but we must have only just missed them. Stevenson is here, unconscious, and there's blood-stained bandages and other crap. It looks like they operated on the target. There are barely eaten meals on the table that are still warm. They must be in the building somewhere."

"Well find them, damn it!"

"Boss, we need more men. It's a big building."

There was a silent pause for several heartbeats. "Alright. I've got a few more guys I can reassign. But start searching straight away!" The call was disconnected.

Matthews turned to the other two. "I'll coordinate the search from this room. Gonzalez, you go down, one floor at a time. Chen, you go up. I'll send more personnel to higher floors when they get here. Go!"

The two men ran to the fire stairs again and split up. Gonzalez went down and Chen raced up the stairs. When he reached the next level, he swiped his multi frequency decoder, opened the door and ran along both ends of the corridor, but found no open doors or communal areas. He re-entered the stairwell and thundered up the stairs toward Level 9.

Carlos had tried to enter Level 8, but the door wouldn't open.

"Damn! I can't access this level with our room card. We have to keep going." They went up another level and this time when he swiped his wrist the door unlocked. There was a sign on the door that said, Level 9 Immersive Simulation Gaming Area. They opened the door and went through. They emerged from the stairwell into a small foyer. The three lifts were on the opposite wall. To their right was a blank wall and to their left, two large double doors, currently closed, had a sign saying, "Gaming Area Currently Closed for Renovations." Just to be sure, he swiped his wrist on the scanner beside the doors. Locked.

There was nowhere to hide on this floor at all. Carlos pressed the lift button, not knowing what else to do. But almost immediately, he heard footsteps thundering up the stairwell again.

"Is the game over yet?" asked Daniel.

Staring at the stairwell door Carlos withdrew the gun from his pocket again and said, "It's possible it's just about to be, my friend."

31

The lift opened and Carlos dragged Daniel in, swiping his wrist as he did. The doors closed just as he heard the fire stairs door being flung open. He tried pressing a random higher floor, but his room code didn't allow him access. He tried another one: same result. They were sitting ducks in the lift, still stationary on Level 9. If that was their pursuers who had just come through the fire door, all they had to do was walk across the foyer and press the lift door, and he and Daniel would be dead!

Clearly, their room code only gave them access to general access areas, not to other residential floors. Carlos quickly scanned the menu of levels. Level 78 was an observation deck and restaurant. That will do! He pressed the button and breathed an audible sigh of relief as the lift began to ascend, quickly gathering speed. A few moments later, they stepped out onto the top floor of the building.

"Are we still playing the game?" asked Daniel.

"No. We've stopped for a while," answered Carlos.

"Good, because I'm starving."

A small, recessed foyer lined with potted palms on the left and right sides led out into a beautifully appointed public area. This entire top floor was one big open area with floor to ceiling transparent walls all the way around, showcasing the magnificent vista of the city of Quito and its surrounding hills. The lifts formed part of a central hub that also housed two bars, a buffet-style servery for those wanting a quick meal, and a kitchen for ala carte dining. Tables and chairs that were currently half-filled with early evening diners dominated most of the floor space, except for a wide walkway around the transparent walls, currently dotted with gawking tourists.

Carlos led Daniel to the buffet area and offered his left wrist to a waiter who deducted the price of two meals. He grabbed a table that was hard up against the wall of potted palms, directly on the opposite side of the lift foyer. While he watched Daniel walk to the buffet and start filling his plate, he double tapped his ear pod comm.

"George?"

"Go ahead."

"We've got a big problem. The bad guys somehow discovered our room number and broke in. Fortunately, we weren't there at the time."

"What do you mean, 'you weren't there'? Where were you?"

"It doesn't matter. The point is, we're now on the run inside the building and the bad guys are searching for us."

"Where are you now?"

"Top floor. Viewing deck." There was silence while they both pondered their predicament. Carlos continued, "What about if we made a dash straight out the doors on the ground floor? If we run, we could make it down to the subway."

"Too risky. They don't need to capture you. They just need to pop Daniel from a distance. One shot and it's game over. I suspect they may have some long guns in place, prepared for just such a scenario."

"What about calling the cops? JUDAN must carry some serious clout with the local constabulary. We could get a bunch of squad cars to cordon off the front entrance and escort us out."

"Not a good idea, for the same reason we didn't use the cops in the first place. This is the wild west down here and the 'c' in cops stands for corruption. We happen to know that Senticorp has some high-level police officers on their unofficial payroll. The chances are the cops would tip off the bad guys. A long gun would probably be used and the shooter would be allowed to disappear. We can't risk it."

"Damn!" said Carlos, as Daniel sat down and started eating.

"I don't suppose you've got the wig and women's clothing still with you?" asked George.

"No."

There was a longer pause while both men considered other options. They couldn't think of any.

"Sit tight," said George, finally. "I'll contact our local field office down here and see what we can do. Stay in that public area if you can. I don't think Senticorp will risk a confrontation in a public space like that. I'll get back to you soon."

The call ended and Carlos gave Daniel an appraising look. "How are you feeling, dude?"

"A bit strange, to be honest," answered Daniel, swallowing a mouthful of food. He looked around. "Where are we? How did we get here?"

Carlos figured the drugs must have worn off and the real Daniel was emerging again. "We're on the top floor of Civic Towers Apartments."

Daniel put his hand to the back of his head and felt a square bandage there. "Have I had the operation already?"

"Yeah. The device is out, my friend."

"So, I'm safe?"

"Not exactly. The bad guys found our room and we barely escaped. They've got all the exits to the building covered. There's a bunch of them searching the building right now and we're trapped up here with no way out."

Daniel looked at his friend with concern written across his features. He swallowed and said, facetiously; "Is that all? That's a relief. For a moment there, I thought we might be in trouble."

32

D r Carmody was sitting on one of the bench seats in the back of the van, feeling the lump on the side of his head. He was feeling sick in the stomach and slightly giddy, and he couldn't tell whether it was a result of concussion or simply shock. His hands were trembling as well, and his face was dotted with beads of perspiration.

"You're not gonna puke on us, are you doc? I can cope with blood, but they're not paying me enough to deal with vomit."

The two men with face masks were sitting on the bench seat opposite Carmody and the van was now parked in an underground garage a couple of blocks west of where they had grabbed the doctor. By the time they had pulled into the carpark, they had emptied Carmody's pockets and searched through his medical bag, identifying him and noting the location of his consulting rooms and his home address.

"When can I go?" asked Carmody, shakily.

"Just as soon as I get confirmation that ..." He stopped because an incoming comm call was registering on his ear pod. He tapped it.

"Yes?" he answered.

"This is Reed. The doctor's intel was good, up to a point. It was the right room, but the birds had already flown the coop. Looks like we just missed them. We're pretty sure they're still in the building somewhere. We're searching for them now, but no joy so far. So, here's what I want you to do ..."

The masked man listened carefully while the Senticorp Head of Security outlined his instructions. Finally, Reed said, "Is that clear?"

"Yes, boss. Got it."

"Make sure you scare the crap out of him."

"That's my specialty. You can count on me." He disconnected and looked at Carmody, who was still waiting for an answer to his question.

"When can you go?" repeated the dark-clad gunman. "That really depends, doc."

"On what?" asked Carmody, his anxiety rising again.

"On whether you're still withholding something from us."

"I'm not! I swear! You asked me for the room number, and I told you."

"Yes, you did. And it was the right room, so I've gotta give you some points for that. Trouble is, your pals weren't there."

"I don't understand. They ...they were there when I left!"

The masked man took a laser pistol out of his pocket and placed it on his lap, pointing in Carmody's general direction. "The thing is, doc, we're starting to wonder if they have another apartment in the building. You wouldn't happen to know anything about that, would you?"

Carmody's eyes were fixed on the pistol, and fresh beads of sweat broke out across his forehead. "I don't know! I honestly don't know! I only know about that room!"

The man reached into a pocket with his other hand and pulled out a small laserblade, about the size of an old-fashioned pocketknife. He started flicking it on and off, a blue line of sizzling laser appearing and disappearing between the two poles of the blade.

"I'd like to believe you; I really would. I'm a very trusting guy. But my boss would hang me by the balls if I let you go and it turned out you were lying." He kept flicking the laserblade on and off as he spoke. "So, here's what I'm going to do. You can choose whether I shoot you through the kneecap or cut off one of your fingers. I think that's a pretty even choice, don't you?"

Carmody's eyes were flicking back and forth between the two weapons now, and he was visibly shaking. "Please! No! I'm telling you the truth! I don't know anything else! Please, don't!"

"Come on, doc, man up. It's not like I'm threatening to kill you or anything. And I'm being very reasonable by giving you a choice. Which is it gonna be? Knife or gun?"

Carmody shook his head vigorously from side to side, saying "No! No!", and held his hands out in front of him, as if to ward off an attack.

"Finger it is!" said the masked man. "Good choice, doc. I think I would have chosen that, too. Knees can be very tricky to repair." He nodded to his companion who, with lightning speed, grabbed Carmody's left hand and pinned it to his medical bag which was on the seat beside him. The first man activated the laserblade and knelt in front of Carmody who was writhing ineffectually and crying out for mercy. He hovered the blade over Carmody's trapped hand.

"You'll notice that I'm being very kind and doing this to your left hand and not your right. I notice you're right-handed and I don't want to be unreasonable about this." He brought the blade down over Carmody's hand and hovered the sizzling laser line a couple of centimetres above his fingers. "I'll try to only take one, but I haven't done this for a while, so I'm a bit out of practice."

The doctor was sobbing and pleading ineffectually for mercy, and the two masked men noticed a growing wet patch that spread between his legs.

"Last chance, doc. Just tell me where the other room is, and you get to keep all your fingers."

"I don't know! I don't know! I'm telling the truth!"

"I'll count to three, and then I cut. ONE!"

"I don't know!"

"TWO!"

"Please! Please! I'm telling the truth!"

"THREE!"

The man brought the knife swiftly down onto the middle finger of the doctor's hand, and Carmody screamed. The two men let him go and sat back while Carmody held his hand up and looked in terror at his fingers. They were all there! He looked incredulously to the masked men and back to his hand again.

"I love that trick," said the first man. "That's the beauty of a laserblade, you can flick it off at the last second. It fools them every time." Both men chuckled and Carmody sobbed in relief.

"I really do think you're telling the truth, doc. So, we're gonna let you go now."

"Thank you! Thank you! I promise I won't tell anyone."

"I know you won't," said the man with the knife, "because here's the thing." He leaned across until his face was centimetres away from Carmody's, "We know where you live, doc. And we know where your children live." That part wasn't true yet, but it would be easy for them to find out. "And if it turns out you've lied to us, or if you go running to the cops, we'll kill you. And we'll kill your wife. And your kids. And your grandkids if you've got any. We'll do the lot of them. Do you believe me, doc?"

Carmody was sobbing so much, he couldn't speak.

"Nod your head if you believe me."

Carmody nodded.

"Good boy." He gave Carmody two friendly pats on the side of his face. "Now go and have a nice life."

They opened the door of the van and Carmody stumbled out, his legs shaking so badly, he could barely stand. The van backed out of the parking spot and drove back up the ramp to the street. As it disappeared from view, Carmody sank to the ground and sat with his back against a pillar, sobbing and shaking uncontrollably.

33

Doug Reed, Head of Security at Senticorp, placed a call through to Matthews, who was coordinating the search of the apartment block. Matthews was sitting at the dining table in Room 714, eating a hamburger and fries that had been left behind after the hasty departure of Carlos and Daniel.

"Yes, boss?" Matthews said, his mouth full of hamburger.

"What the hell are you eating?" asked Reed.

"They left some food behind. Can't let it go to waste, boss."

"Bloody hell!" said Reed. "I put you there to do a job, not feed your face! Have you made any progress?"

"We're working our way up, floor by floor. If they're here, we'll find them. Unless they hired another apartment, they've got nowhere to go. They'll be cowering in one of the hallways somewhere."

"I suggest you concentrate on the public areas like pools, spas, gyms and restaurants first. They're more likely to be there. I just checked the promo for the apartments. There are bars and restaurants on the top floor. That's where I'd be hiding. Send two men up there, right way. There are two more men on their way up to you now. Get this done!"

"Will do."

The call ended and Matthews opened a comm channel. "Chen and Gonzalez, where are you?"

Gonzalez answered. "I finished the bottom six floors and then joined up with Chen like you told me. We're up to Level 22."

"I'll send two guys to take over from you there. I want you to go up to the top floor and do a thorough search. If they're not there, start working your way back down."

"Roger. We're on our way."

"Carlos, I owe you my life." Daniel was drinking a coffee and Carlos was keeping a watchful eye on their surroundings.

"We're not out of the woods yet, dude," said the big man.

"I know, and I'm sorry I got you into this mess."

"You didn't get me into it. I chose this assignment. I chose this life because I believe that bad guys should be brought to justice."

"Including me?" said Daniel. "Because I've looked into my past, and I'm about as bad as they get."

"'Was', dude. Past tense."

"I'm still the same person, Carlos. I probably killed a lot of people – not just the ones they convicted me for. And I don't want any more people to die because of me." He looked at Carlos. "I definitely don't want you to die because of me. I've taken enough life already. I want you to know that if it looks like there's no way out for us, I'm giving myself up. I'm going to walk out in plain sight and let them take the shot. It won't make up for all the bad I've done, but at least I'll die knowing I've saved one life."

"That's not gonna happen, my friend. We're gonna get you out of here."

Carlos's comm chimed and he took the call. "Go ahead George."

"Are you guys still in the clear?"

"Yes. And Daniel's back with us as well."

"What do you mean?"

"Let's just say he wasn't quite himself for a while. Have you come up with anything yet?"

"Yes. The local field office has moved fast. There's a landing pad on the roof of your building. We've commandeered a flitter and we're about to leave now. Can you get access to the roof?"

"I'll find a way."

"Get there now. We'll be there in about five."

"OK. See you there."

Carlos disconnected and said to Daniel, "Looks like we're getting out of here, dude. Our lift is on its way. We need to get to the roof." As they stood, he took the small neural disruptor pistol out of his pocket and slipped it to Daniel. "Seeing you're compos mentis again, you may as well have this back, bro. I checked it: there are four neural darts left in the chamber. I'll keep the laser."

Daniel took the pistol and slipped it into a pocket. "Let's hope I don't need it." He looked around. "How do we get up to the roof?"

"We ask someone," answered Carlos, scanning their surroundings. He spotted the maître de and said to Daniel, "Come on." They approached a slim, waist-coated man who had just directed a newly arrived couple to a table and was returning to his island service desk.

The maître de smiled and said, "Can I help you gentlemen?" He had a vague European accent.

Carlos held out his wrist and said, "I work for JUDAN, the Justice Department of the Alliance of Nations."

The maître de used a hand-held device to scan his wrist. He scrutinised the screen on the device closely and then nodded. "How can I be of assistance?"

"There's a flitter about to land on this roof, and I need to get up there, fast."

"Certainly, sir. There is an access lift in the far corner of this floor. The floor manager, Mr Khatri, has the code. I am sure he will be happy to assist you. Let me call him for you." He tapped a lapel comm and spoke briefly, then ended the call and said, "Mr Khatri will be right with you." Please wait here.

The maître de moved off to assist someone else, and the two men looked around the dining room impatiently.

～

The lift came to a stop on the 78th floor. The door opened, and Chen and Gonzalez walked out.

"Sweet!" said Gonzalez, looking around at the plush decor and gazing at the view through the transparent wall 30 metres away. Night had fallen and the city skyline was spectacular. Buildings were ablaze with coloured laser lighting, and spectacular holographic images were suspended in mid-air.

"Stay focused, Gonzalez," said Chen. "We're not here to look at the view."

"What are you, my mother? Lighten up, you friggin' sphincter!"

"Lovely," commented Chen, shaking his head. He walked to the end of the small foyer and looked right and left. "There they are!" he said, backing up a couple of steps and positioning himself behind the last potted plant on the left.

"Where?" asked Gonzalez, coming up behind him.

They peered cautiously through the fronds and saw Daniel and Carlos standing in plain view near the maître de's island desk. They were looking around as if waiting for someone. Chen activated his comm. "Matthews, it's Chen."

"Go ahead."

"Bingo! We've found Newman. He's with a big, dark-skinned guy – probably the one who ran out of the building earlier. They're in the restaurant area on the top floor. The only trouble is, there are people everywhere."

"Nice work! Hold tight. I'm sending the other two guys up to you now."

"How are we supposed to apprehend Newman in such a public place?" asked Chen.

Matthews considered his next words carefully, because Chen wasn't aware that Sanchez and the others had been instructed to kill Newman if possible. "You'll have to wait until they leave. Get into the same lift with them and bring them back to room 714."

"Roger."

As Chen disconnected, they saw a thin man wearing a black turban walk up to the two fugitives. After a brief exchange the turban guy led them away, further to the left and out of sight around the central hub. Chen was trying to work out what to do, when one of the lifts behind him opened and two more Senticorp guards arrived. He spoke to the new arrivals.

"They've just walked around the corner, out of sight. You two stay here and guard the lifts. Gonzalez and I will follow them."

"OK." Said one of them, a beefy guy who looked like he lifted some serious weights.

Chen and Gonzalez made their way to the outer perimeter walkway, keeping their weapons in their pockets and trying to look casual. They turned left and walked toward the corner of the building, scanning through the dining area to their left as the view opened up around the central hub. Their quarry came into view again. The man with the turban was leading them toward the far corner of the building, where there appeared to be a single lift. Chen and Gonzalez reached the corner of the walkway and turned left again, walking beside the transparent walls to their right. The lift was dead ahead at the far end of this side and, as they watched, the three men they were following reached the lift. The turban-headed man scanned his wrist and a moment later the lift opened. Daniel and his companion entered, and the door closed again. They were gone!

"Damn!" said Chen, increasing his pace. "We've lost them again!"

"Maybe not," said Gonzalez. "The sign above the lift says, 'Rooftop'. I'm guessing it only goes there."

"So, what do we do?" asked Chen, uncertain.

"I've got an idea," said Gonzalez.

34

D aniel and Carlos emerged from the lift onto the roof top. The warm evening air was heavy laden with tropical scents and a half moon hung low over the distant hills. Theirs was not the tallest building in the city. They were surrounded by slender towers adorned with coloured laser light shows. Holographic images hung in the air above and between buildings, some of them company logos and others simply works of art. Flitters could be seen darting through the air, over and around buildings, their headlights casting beams through the humid air and their red taillights flashing in different rhythms.

A waist-height transparent wall surrounded the perimeter of their building. Large square stacks of air filtration units, each of them about three metres tall, were spaced around the perimeter, just inside the outer wall. The majority of the rooftop was dominated by a large square landing pad, raised three metres higher than the perimeter. It was accessed by a set of metal stairs directly ahead of them. Carlos activated his comm.

"George, we're on the rooftop. Where are you?"

"We're running a little late. We've encountered some red tape getting clearance. We'll be there as soon as we can."

"Copy." He disconnected and turned to Daniel. "We'll wait for them on the pad. Let's get up there, dude."

The two men hurried toward the metal stairs and had just reached them when a laser blast sizzled past Daniel's shoulder and slammed into Carlos's back. The big man collapsed mid-stride and Daniel dived to the ground beside him. A second blast scoured the ground to Daniel's right, narrowly missing his head. As they both lay there, Daniel heard the familiar voice of his shift buddy, Lee Chen.

"Gonzalez! What the hell are you doing?"

"What I was ordered to do, moron."

"No! We can still bring them in. There's no need for this!"

As they argued, Daniel quickly dragged Carlos behind the stairs. His friend was moaning and there was the smell of singed clothes and burnt flesh in the air. Another blast hit the stairs but couldn't penetrate. Daniel figured they must be made of maranium. He snuck a peek around the side and saw Chen and a larger man standing in the open, in front of the lift. The larger man, presumably Gonzalez, had his arm around the neck of the terrified floor manager and was using him as a shield, his laser pistol pointed at the stairs. Chen was standing slightly behind and to the side, his own pistol held loosely in his hand and pointed at the ground, a look of shock on his face.

Gonzales fired again, and Daniel tucked his head in just in time. Carlos groaned and Daniel asked, "Where are you hit? How bad is it?"

Carlos gasped in pain. "Right shoulder. Can't move my arm."

Gonzalez called out, "Newman! Come out or towelhead here gets it! I'm not bluffing!"

"Don't do it, dude," said Carlos. "Stay here. Our guys will be here any minute."

"Newman!" Gonzalez called again. "Come out with your hands in the air. I'll let this guy go and we'll take you back to Senticorp."

"He's lying," gasped Carlos. "If you walk out there, you're a dead man."

"But if I don't walk out there, they'll kill the floor manager."

"They're gonna kill him anyway, bro. You know that. He's seen their faces."

"Newman! Last chance. I'm gonna count to three, and then this guy gets a hole in the head!"

"Don't shoot him!" yelled Daniel. "If I come out, I want you to promise that you'll let him go. My partner is dead, but that man is innocent!"

"Sure thing," answered Gonzalez. "We only want you. We're not animals."

"Don't believe him, bro," said Carlos. "They're not going to leave any loose ends up here. You know that."

"I can't sit by and watch another innocent person die because of me. I couldn't live with myself."

"Are you coming out or do I have to drill this guy?" called Gonzalez.

"I'm coming out! Give me a second!" He looked at Carlos. "Dude, can you still shoot?"

"Yeah. I'm pretty good with my left hand."

"Good. I've got the neural disruptor. If I get close enough, I'm gonna take down the floor manager. Once he's out of the picture, shoot the big guy."

"But he'll shoot you before I get a chance to get off a shot."

"Yes. He will. And once I'm out of the way, you'll have a clear shot."

"No way, dude! No way! I'm not letting you do this!"

"It's my choice. It's my time. I should be dead, anyway. It's what I deserve. You work for the Justice Department, don't you? Well, this is justice."

"Time's up, Newman! I'm counting to three, and then this guy gets it in the head."

Daniel started to get to his feet.

"ONE!"

"No, Daniel!" cried Carlos.

"TWO!"

"Okay! Okay!" said Daniel, emerging from behind the stairs. "I'm coming! Don't shoot him."

He adopted a fake limp and started shuffling toward Gonzalez. He was holding his right thigh with his right hand, the tiny neural disruptor pistol nestled in the palm of his hand.

"Hands in the air, where I can see them!" called Gonzalez.

Daniel raised his left hand in the air but kept his right hand against his thigh as he continued limping forward.

"The other hand, too!"

"I can't. I'm bleeding badly! I'm trying to staunch the blood." Daniel noticed Chen still standing with his pistol pointing to the ground, completely fazed by the situation.

Carlos had shuffled to the right and was peeking around the side of the stairs, his head hidden in the shadows. Daniel was directly in line between Gonzalez and the stairs. "Move to the side!" Carlos whispered to himself. "Damn it, Daniel! Move to the left!"

"I don't care about your bleeding leg! Put that hand in the air, now!"

Daniel gauged the distance. Ten metres to go. He just needed a few more steps to be sure of his shot. He knew he was about to die, but if he could save the others, his life might not have been totally wasted.

"I'm not armed!" said Daniel, still holding his thigh as he shuffled forward. "Have a heart, dude. I don't want to bleed to death."

Carlos still had no clear line of fire and he whispered to himself in frustration, "Move to the side, damn it! Move!"

Daniel took two more steps, then cried out in pain and pretended to stumble, falling to his knees. He raised his right arm and shot the floor manager in the chest, then immediately dropped his pistol and continued kneeling with his eyes closed, his hands both now held out wide in the shape of a crucifix. As the floor manager fell to the ground, Gonzales shifted his weapon and aimed it directly at Daniel's head. He smiled and started walking forward, slowly.

Carlos aimed his pistol at Gonzalez and sighted along the barrel, then swore softly. He didn't have a clear shot. At this distance he was just as likely to hit Daniel. Daniel was about to die, and there was nothing he could do about it.

Gonzalez covered the last few steps and stood in front of Daniel, his laser pointed in the centre of Daniel's forehead and a sick smile now smeared across his face. He kicked the tiny pistol that Daniel had dropped further out of his reach. "Well, well, well. Haven't you caused us a whole lot of trouble today?"

Daniel stayed on his knees with his eyes closed and his arms out wide.

"You know I'm going to kill you, don't you?"

"Just do it," said Daniel, calmly.

"Gonzalez, what are you doing?" called Chen, pocketing his weapon as he spoke. "We've got him, now. We can bring him in. It's over!" He was rooted to the same spot, about five metres away, near the lift door.

"Why don't you just shut up, little man, and leave this to the grown-ups!" said Gonzalez, viciously. He addressed Daniel again. "You sure you don't want to open your eyes and watch it happen?"

"Then I'd have to look at your filthy face. No thanks."

Gonzalez's eyes blazed with fury, and he gripped the pistol with both hands as he took final aim.

The blast of sizzling blue laser fire covered the distance from gun to forehead in a microsecond. The blast tore through his skull causing superheated liquified brain matter and bone to erupt out of the larger hole in the back of his head. The laser momentarily burned a hole in the tarmac directly behind, before it was switched off, then the body fell in slow motion and landed with a thud.

The scene remained a frozen tableau for a moment and then exploded into action. Three men in full black battle dress and armed with laser rifles ran down the stairs from the landing pad, screaming, "Nobody move! Nobody move!"

Chen was frozen to the spot, his arms by his side, his face in shock. Carlos lay back down on the ground behind the stairs, groaning in pain.

Daniel opened his eyes and blinked in confusion. Gonzales lay face down on the tarmac in front of him, a gaping hole in the back of his head. Daniel slowly lowered his arms and looked around. Chen was being cuffed and marched toward the landing pad by one of the agents. Another agent had come to stand beside Daniel.

"Let me help you to your feet, Mr Newman. Are you injured?"

"No. But Carlos is. He's behind the stairs." The third agent heard his comment and ran to attend to Carlos. Daniel shook his head in disbelief. "I didn't hear you land."

"We landed with silent mode activated," said the agent as he helped Daniel to his feet. "Latest technology. Whisper-quiet fusion/ion drive hybrid engines."

They walked toward the landing pad and saw Carlos being helped up the stairs. George was standing at the top waiting for them. Carlos was stumbling slowly, and Daniel and his escort caught up to him as they all reached the landing pad.

"Thought you weren't gonna get here in time, boss," said Carlos.

"Nearly didn't," responded George. "Sorry about that. Let's get you guys out of here."

The walked toward the flitter in the centre of the pad. It was a sleek, all black craft without any visible means of propulsion: no rotor blades and no obvious jet vanes. They climbed through the side door and seated themselves on two inward-facing bench seats. Carlos lay on the floor while one of the agents broke open a field medipack and started first aid treatment. As the flitter silently lifted into the night sky, Daniel's eyes adjusted to the gloom, and he noticed a female figure in the opposite corner to him.

"Kelly?" he asked.

"We didn't have time to rescue Dr Rearson separately," explained George. "It was risky, but given the time pressure we were under, we had to bring her with us."

Kelly looked to be in shock, not quite being able to process the momentous events of the night. Daniel looked at her in sympathy. Her whole world had just been taken from her, and her future was an empty void. He wanted to say something to her, but words failed him. Once again, he felt the terrible guilt that came from knowing that his life was continuing to cause others to suffer.

He glanced down at Carlos. The agent had administered pain relief and was packing the wound and dressing it. "Is he going to be okay?"

"Hope so," said the agent. "The good thing about laser wounds is that bleeding is instantly cauterised. The bad thing is that it burns through everything, including tissue, organs and bones. The doctors will tell us more when we get to the hospital."

"Don't worry about me, bro," mumbled Carlos. "It'll take more than a puny laser to stop old Carlos."

"Nice shot, by the way, dude," said Daniel.

"Not me, bro. Your fat, ugly head was in the way the whole time! I never got a clear line of sight. You should have heard me swearing at you."

"Then who ...?"

"It was agent Garcia," said George, pointing to one of the black uniformed agents on the opposite bench.

"Thank you," said Daniel, realising how incredibly inadequate any words could be.

"You're welcome," said the man, with a slight nod of his head.

"That was a very brave thing you did, Daniel," said George.

"Stupid, more like it!" muttered Carlos. "What were you thinking, dude!"

Daniel hung his head, not wanting to meet anyone's eyes. "I ... I ... just wanted it all to end."

There was silence as the full import of his words sank in. Kelly glanced at him with a look somewhere between concern and sympathy.

"Well, we're not at the end, yet," said George, deliberately misconstruing his meaning. "We still have to get you and Dr Rearson safely out of Quito. And that might present us with a few challenges."

35

The executive office suite at Blackstar Laboratories was in almost total darkness, as it always was. The blinding light of Singapore's midday sun had no chance of sneaking its way past the darkly tinted windows and thick blackout curtains. Eli Tang, CEO and sole owner of the research organisation, sipped his usual glass of cognac. He prided himself that he never took his first sip before noon.

Tang had the rare condition commonly referred to as photophobia – extreme sensitivity to light. His eyes could only tolerate the dullest of red lights, and anything brighter resulted in severe migraines, dizziness and nausea. He was also an albino, completely lacking pigment in his skin, hair and eyes, making him extremely susceptible to sunburn and cancers. He had lived with these conditions since birth, and he knew no different. He lived in perpetual darkness and had grown to love it – to embrace it. He was a creature of the dark, and he found that it placed his business acquaintances and competitors at a distinct disadvantage on those rare occasions when he met with them in person.

It was ironic, then, that he lived in one of the brightest places on Earth; an equatorial city that received more sunlight, in terms of brightness and number of days per year, than almost anywhere else. No doubt, he would have been much better suited to a darker, colder climate, such as somewhere in Northern China. But Tang was an opportunist, and Singapore was a place of great opportunity. Singapore was the location of the largest heavy-lift spaceport on Earth, operated under the auspices of RISSE; the Republic of Independent States Space Expansion. Their aggressive desire to dominate off-world expansion into the solar system and beyond had created a space program that rivalled that of the Alliance of Nations. A 20 kilometre mag-rail launch system was located on the island of Sumatra, to the west of Singapore, which launched reusable payload rockets and re-entry passenger shuttles on an almost daily basis. For Blackstar, that meant access to the rich resources of the off-world mining sites scattered throughout the solar system.

Blackstar Industries, so named because of Tang's favourite colour and also his fascination with black holes – the gravity bending giants of the cosmos – had its finger in many pies. It mined metals on Mars and was the world's largest importer of maranium, an extremely strong and light metal found only on that planet. It had the second largest water harvesting plant on the Moon, melting the huge deposits of frozen water deep below the surface of the Moon's North Pole and supplying water and oxygen to the various Moon bases as well as hydrogen rocket fuel for the staging bases.

While these ventures brought vast amounts of money into the Blackstar coffers, it was the scientific research arm of the company that brought Eli Tang the greatest joy. He was a frustrated scientist, never having even attended school, let alone achieved a degree, but he read widely and had an insatiable appetite to be at the forefront of the latest developments. QBES in particular, the quest to develop Quantum Enhanced Biological Sentience, had been his passion for many years. The Republic of Independent States wanted that technology desperately, to give them an advantage over the Alliance of Nations, and Tang, as a Colonel of RISC (the Republic of Independent States Commissariat) would be a hero of the Republic if he could deliver it to them. But it was the financial reward that interested him the most. His personal empire, Blackstar Industries, stood to make billions from the development of the technology for the Republic.

And he would do anything to make that happen.

A comm channel on his desk started flashing dull red. He looked at the time on his screen. 12:01. Time for his first sip of the day. The crystal glass had already been in his hand, waiting for this moment. The first sip of the day was always the best, not to be rushed. Holding the glass in his right hand he tapped the comm button with his left and simply said:

"Wait!"

He held the tumbler of cognac toward the tiny red glow of his desk lamp, enjoying the way the light sparkled through the silky liquid, throwing off shades of gold and pink. He brought the tumbler to his nose, swirling the golden liquid and sniffing it appreciatively. Finally, when his senses were peaked, he brought the glass to his lips and took a long, slow sip, holding it in his mouth for several moments before giving in to the exquisitely sensual pleasure of swallowing. The vintage cognac slid down his gullet, warming him all the way down, until it exploded in a warm soft glow in his stomach. He savoured the spreading glow for a few more moments before addressing his caller.

"Speak!"

"Sir, I'm reporting back regarding our efforts to acquire the ninth protocol."

"Continue."

"Unfortunately, we were unsuccessful."

Tang remained silent. After several moments, the voice continued.

"Our team had him in their possession at the airport and were about to transport him here when they were ambushed by the original owners. A firefight ensued, quickly joined by local police. Three of our team were killed and the target escaped during the melee."

Tang took another sip of cognac to try to contain his fury. "Do the original owners have him back again?"

"No sir. As you requested, we've been monitoring some of their signals. They were unable to reacquire him as well. It appears that another party has intervened and now has him in their possession. The original owners think it was us."

"Who is it?" Tang asked, leaning forward in his chair.

"Our best guess is JUDAN."

"Damn it! I don't pay you to guess! I pay you to KNOW!"

There was a pause while the voice on the other end allowed Tang to cool down.

"The reason we believe it is JUDAN, is that the target was lifted off the top of an apartment building in a flitter. One of our men on the ground swears it was one of the new XTR flitters with a hybrid fusion/ion drive. Our man used night glasses and thinks he saw JUDAN insignia on the side."

"Tell me you have a plan."

"Yes, sir, we do. While the target was briefly in our possession, he was momentarily disabled with a neuron disruptor weapon. While he was unconscious, our men tagged him – just behind the ear. The micro tag contains a slow-release local anaesthetic, so he won't be aware of it."

"So, you know his location?"

"Yes, sir. That's also how we knew which building to watch prior to him being lifted by flitter."

"Where is he?"

"They've got him at a private property in the Eastern foothills, a few kilometres from the airport. It looks to be a JUDAN safe house. We suspect they're preparing to move him to Pittsburgh for the purposes of giving testimony against our competitors."

"That wouldn't be such a bad thing for us."

"No, sir."

Tang took another sip as he considered his options.

"On the other hand, we're in a race here. The opposition has the formulae for the ninth protocol, and we don't. They don't need to reacquire their test subject. They can simply acquire a new one and start again. We can't afford to wait. We need this living specimen if we have any hope of winning this race."

"Yes, sir."

"What is the level of security surrounding the subject at the moment?"

"Extremely tight. There are several agents staying there full-time, and others are coming and going. It's a 50-acre property with wide open paddocks surrounding the house. There's no chance of approaching unseen. I have two men watching from a distance, but so far we haven't found a weakness."

"Keep watching. If you think there's a chance to grab him, I want you to do so. Failing that, we will have to wait until they move him to Pittsburgh. Hopefully, they will think he is safer there and they will relax their security."

"Yes, sir. I'll keep you informed of any developments."

"And one more thing."

"Yes, sir?"

"This was your last failure. Ever. Do you understand?"

There was a long pause. "Yes, sir."

36

D aniel was sitting on the front verandah of the ranch-style safe house, gazing west across the paddocks. It was early morning and although the sun just had risen, the house was still in shadow because of the hills to the east. The grass in the paddocks was glistening with dew and, overhead, thin wisps of cloud were painted with an underbelly of pink and apricot. Nearby, two foals frolicked with early morning energy, chasing each other around a group of older horses who were busy savouring sweet new shoots of rye grass. A yellow-breasted motmot landed on a fence post at the edge of the paddock and issued its distinctive early morning wakeup call. It fixed its gaze on Daniel and cocked its head to the side, as if wondering what kind of lifeform he was, then lost interest and flew away.

"Yeah, I wouldn't hang around me either, if I was you," Daniel muttered.

"That's a bit harsh, bro," said Carlos, emerging onto the verandah holding two steaming cups of coffee. He had been assigned to stay with Daniel and Kelly until they were safely out of Quito. He plonked himself down into the chair next to Daniel and handed him the mug he was carrying in his left hand. "Strong black, no sugar, just how you like it."

"You shouldn't be using that arm yet, dude," said Daniel, with concern.

Carlos transferred the remaining mug from his right hand to his left, then placed the mug on the arm of his chair. He reinserted his right arm into the sling that was suspended from his neck, wincing as he did.

"One more day in this sling and the doc says I can ditch it."

"So, leave it in the sling all day, you damned fool! I can get my own coffee; I'm not completely useless."

"That's debatable," said Carlos, taking a satisfying sip and sighing with contentment. He glanced at Daniel. "Trouble sleeping again?"

"Yeah."

"It's understandable. You've been through a lot."

Daniel merely nodded. They sat in companionable silence for a while, sipping their coffees and watching the horses grazing in the paddock.

"When do we leave for Pittsburgh?" asked Daniel.

"Looks like tomorrow. George is just finalising the arrangements for the safe house. Once we get you there, our lawyers will be keen to take recorded video testimonies from both of you."

"Just in case Kelly and I get whacked between now and the trial?"

"We've got to cover every contingency, bro."

"Well, I promise I'll do my best to stay alive; I'd hate to let you down."

"Appreciate it. Besides, funerals are a real drag, dude."

Daniel smiled. In the three days he had been here, he and Carlos had strengthened the friendship that had developed during his stay in hospital, spending many hours watching football, walking around the house or just sitting on the verandah. Their recent narrow escape had served to deepen their mutual respect, with each claiming that the other had saved their life.

"How's Kelly bearing up?" asked Daniel.

"Not sure. She hardly comes out of her room, and when she does, she doesn't say much."

"I've noticed," said Daniel. "I've made two or three attempts to strike up a conversation with her, but she just closes down. She's like a frightened rabbit, too afraid to come out of her burrow."

"You can't blame her," said Carlos. "She's putting her whole life on the line for this."

"Yeah. It makes me feel guilty as hell. I did enough damage in the past, and now I'm ruining someone else's life."

"It's not your fault, bro. She contacted us a long time before you came on the scene, as soon as she realised they were starting to experiment on humans. It's just taken us this long to gather enough evidence to act against them."

"What's the state of play in that regard?" asked Daniel.

"Lee Chen, the Senticorp security guard we arrested on top of the apartment block, was flown to Pittsburgh overnight and is currently sitting in a cell, singing like a bird. His evidence will be helpful. As soon as we have your testimony and Kelly's on the record, warrants will be issued for the arrest of Senticorp's key players. So, things are looking pretty sweet."

"I assume Kelly will be granted immunity from prosecution," said Daniel.

"Of course. Although she had no part in the illegal experimentation on humans. She was one of the microbiologists who developed the quantum molecule and the bridging enzyme, but she thought human experimentation was still years away, subject to approval through all the appropriate channels. It was when she suspected that Senticorp had bypassed those approval processes and were effectively murdering people that she contacted us."

"So, she's got nothing to worry about?" asked Daniel.

"Not at all, bro. But she still feels guilty. She blames herself for not suspecting their intentions from the start. It's eating her up."

"She needs to cut herself some slack," said Daniel.

"So does someone else I know."

Daniel took another sip of coffee and watched an eagle hovering over the paddock. Its wingtips fluttered in the breeze, making tiny adjustments to keep it perfectly stationary, its eyes fastened on its prey below. In a flash it folded its wings and plummeted in a steep dive, reaching out with its massive talons as it levelled out at the last possible moment. There was a puff of dust from its contact with the ground and then it rose into the air, beating its huge wings. Some kind of rodent, perhaps a mouse, was gripped firmly in its talons, still struggling feebly, its tail trailing behind as the eagle flew back to its nest in the hills.

"Death is everywhere," said Daniel. "The strong killing the weak and the defenceless. It's a sad but necessary part of nature. But when it happens with humans, it's pure evil."

"That's why we're gonna make sure we nail these guys and lock them away for a very long time. We'll make sure they end up where they belong."

"The thing is," said Daniel, "I belong in there with them, too."

"You've got to stop doing this, dude! You're not Daniel Mendez; you're Daniel Newman. Daniel Mendez, the murderer, died when they wiped his brain."

"Is that a legal argument that's going to stand up in court?" asked Daniel.

"We're working on it, bro. We've got lawyers putting together an argument as we speak. It's new territory, of course. It will have to set a legal precedent, and it will depend on getting the right judge sitting on the case, but we're hopeful."

"Hmmm. We'll see. Whatever happens, I'm ready to face the music. In some ways, it would be a relief."

Carlos was called away a few moments later to oversee the morning shift change, as two new JUDAN agents arrived to relieve the night shift. Daniel was left sitting on the verandah, still thinking about the eagle and the mouse and wondering which one of those he was.

37

The agents watching over them didn't consider it safe for Daniel to go jogging, even around the paddocks. They said it would be too easy for someone to pick him off with a long gun. Instead, the back room of the sprawling ranch house had been converted into a simple gym, with two treadmills and some basic weight machines. Carlos and Daniel worked out together in the afternoons, although Carlos was not yet able to use his right arm. After a shower, they then sat on the verandah enjoying a beer before dinner.

Daniel must have dozed off, because when he opened his eyes, the sun was setting and Carlos was nowhere to be seen. He stretched and yawned. There was the sound of a vehicle approaching up the long driveway, and Daniel peered around the left corner of the verandah to see who it was. One of the two JUDAN agents on day shift came out the front door and walked down the steps, taking up station on the path leading to the driveway, his rifle held confidently at the ready.

"Are we expecting anyone?" asked Daniel, slightly concerned.

"Yes. It's a catering van. The boss is putting on a special dinner, seeing it's your last night here."

Daniel eased back into his chair, relieved, as the van came to a stop, parking parallel with the verandah. The signage on the van said, Costa's Catering Service. A man and woman emerged from the front cabin, dressed in typical all-black catering clothing. They walked to the back of the van and opened the swinging double doors. They reached in and pulled out a carry bag each and started walking up the path toward the JUDAN agent.

"Anyone here hungry?" asked the girl with a smile.

"You bet! Starving!" answered the agent.

"Sorry to disappoint," said her partner. He reached into his carry bag, pulled out a laser pistol, and shot the agent through the head.

Daniel started to stand but the girl was too quick. She leapt onto the verandah and shot Daniel through the chest with a projectile pistol. He crumpled to the floor, landing on his right side facing the door. Blood was pumping out of his chest, spreading in a pool all around him, and he was completely unable to move. All he could do was lie there, watching helplessly as the two assassins strode confidently through the front doors. He tried to scream out to warn the people inside, but all he could muster was a weak moan.

He heard the sounds of running footsteps and caught a glimpse of two more assassins emerging from the back of the van and running around the back of the house. As he lay on the verandah with a surprising amount of blood still pouring out of him, he heard shots being fired from inside; the sizzle of lasers and the explosive sound of bullets. There were yells and the sound of a scuffle, with furniture being overturned and heavy grunting. The scuffle came to an abrupt end with the sound of a single pistol shot.

"Where's the woman?" asked a voice.

"Check all the bedrooms," said another.

As footsteps could be heard walking down the hall, the window at the end of the verandah slid open and Kelly climbed out, her face a mask of terror. She came and knelt beside Daniel, horrified at the pool of blood surrounding him. Daniel shook his head at her.

"Run! Run, Kelly! Run!"

She ran. Down the steps, along the path and across the driveway. She had just climbed over the post and rail fence into the paddock as the original man and woman came out the front door.

"There she is!"

They raised their weapons and fired as Kelly ran into the paddock.

"Run, Kelly! Run!" screamed Daniel.

Kelly kept running and the first shots missed. The girl in black ran to the paddock fence as Kelly raced across the uneven paddock, stumbling at times, her brown hair streaming behind her. The male assassin joined his female assassin at the fence and raised his weapon to shoot, but the woman pushed him aside, saying,

"No! This one's mine."

She took a double grip on her handgun, placed her legs wide apart, and pulled the trigger. The gunshot echoed off the surrounding hills and Kelly was knocked to the ground. A moment later she staggered to her feet and took a few more stumbling steps, holding her side as a dark wet stain began to appear there.

"That was crap!" said the man.

"I was just getting my eye in," replied the woman. "Watch this." She raised her weapon again, took careful aim, and fired.

Kelly's head exploded. One moment it was there, and the next it was a pulpy mess.

"No! No! Kelly! No!" wailed Daniel, sobbing now with frustration and anger. He lay his head back down in the pool of blood. There was so much of it now that it was flowing in a waterfall over the edge of the verandah and flooding the garden below. He watched in fascination. *How could I have so much blood in me?*

He heard a strange fluttering sound above him and looked up to see an eagle descending. It landed on him, wrapped its talons around his left arm and then took off, lifting him higher and higher into the sky. As he dangled helplessly from the eagle, he watched the ranch house shrink to a tiny dot below him. The eagle then started shaking his arm vigorously and calling his name.

"Daniel! Daniel! Wake up!"

He opened his eyes to find a circle of concerned eyes looking at him. Carlos was shaking his arm, while Kelly and one of the agents were standing in front of him with worried expressions. He was sitting in his usual chair on the verandah, an empty beer bottle on the deck beside him and the afternoon sun lowering toward the western hills.

"You were screaming, dude!" said Carlos. "We thought someone was being murdered."

"So did I."

38

George Mallard, Senior Prosecutor with JUDAN, arrived shortly before 5:30. He had visited twice during the last three days, informing them of progress regarding the arrangements for their impending departure and their safe instalment in Pittsburgh. Now, he sat with Daniel, Kelly and Carlos in the loungeroom of the ranch house to bring them up to date on developments.

"Daniel, it is clear to us now, that there were two hostile agencies attempting to capture you at the airport. The gun battle that took place on the tarmac prior to the arrival of the police proves that. One group was obviously Senticorp, who were able to track you there via their implant technology. We are now certain that the second group was Blackstar Industries, Senticorp's main rival in the race to develop QEBS, quantum enhanced biological sentience. They are the ones who arranged for the taxi to the airport and were almost successful in getting you on board a private jet."

"What happened to the jet?" asked Carlos.

"It managed to take off during the subsequent shoot-out with police and it used radar blocking technology to avoid detection in the air, so we don't know where it went." He paused. "We believe that Blackstar were responsible for the recent attacks and break-ins at Senticorp, and that's how they found out about you, Daniel. There is also a third agency involved."

"What agency?"

"As well as being the CEO of Blackstar Industries, Eli Tang is also a colonel in RISC, the Republic of Independent States Commissariat. How familiar are you with world politics?"

"A complete dunce."

"Well, let me fill you in. During the latter part of the 21st century, Mingze Zheng became President of China, and he was completely unbalanced."

"A total nutter," added Carlos, helpfully.

"Yes," agreed George. "He also had an insatiable lust for nationalistic expansion and world domination. Over a period of 25 years, China conducted an aggressive expansion campaign to create a centralised government throughout the whole of Eastern Asia. They called the campaign, in English, RAGE; Republic of Asia Global Expansion. They invaded Malaysia, Indonesia, Philippines, Vietnam, Thailand, Japan, Korea, Laos and Myanmar. Effectively those nations ceased to exist and the whole region became the Republic of Asia. Jump ahead another 25 years, and the Arab Independent States formed an unlikely alliance with the Republic of Asia. This was after several minor skirmishes where they both flexed their military muscles and decided that going to war against each other would be unwise. So, they joined forces and, surprisingly, their amalgamation has lasted to the current day. The result is what has become known as the Republic of Independent States. Over the decades that followed, several other nations aligned themselves with the Republic – all of them opposed to the principles of democracy. The Republic is now a conglomeration of nations, not united by race or religion, but by their political ideology, or at least their opposition to one ideology: Western democracy.

The Republic and the Alliance of Nations have been in a cold war ever since. With the advent of mankind's expansion into space, that cold war has taken on an even bigger dimension. The Republic's new expansion campaign has adopted the acronym, RISSE – Republic of Independent States Space Expansion. Their latest president, Haito Batmati, is determined to dominate the Solar System and beyond, and claim sole rights to its resources for the Republic."

"What's all that got to do with me?" asked Daniel.

"A huge part of the cold war has been the race to acquire new technology to gain leverage over the opposition. And the technology inside your head, Daniel, is a complete game changer. QEBS, Quantum Enhanced Biological Sentience, is an exponential advancement in computing power and portability. The Republic is desperate to get their hands on it and Eli Tang has been commissioned with the task of either developing or acquiring the technology. As I explained a moment ago, he is not only the CEO of Blackstar Industries, but also a Colonel in RISC, the Republic of Independent States Commissariat. The lines appear to be somewhat blurred between Blackstar and RISC. As a high-ranking Colonel, Tang is allowed to run a private corporation as a lucrative sideline, and he appears to employ some RISC agents in his Blackstar security department. We think his recent attempt to grab you was a joint effort between Blackstar and RISC."

"Great! That's just what I need; three groups trying to kill me."

"We think Blackstar and the Republic would be happier to capture you alive but, yes, they can still extract what they need if you are dead."

Daniel looked at Kelly. "Is that right?"

"Unfortunately, yes," she answered. "All they need is a sample of the newly developed long chain molecule that we designed to contain the quantum qubits, and a sample of the bridging enzyme that acts as a conduit between neurons and the molecule. They could obtain those from a ... um ... a dead body, even several days after death." She bit her lip as she looked at Daniel. "Sorry."

"It's nice to know I'll be valuable to someone even after I'm dead," Daniel commented, facetiously.

"Getting back to what happened," said George, "the people pursuing you through the apartment block were entirely Senticorp personnel. There is no evidence that Blackstar were involved at that point. That's because Senticorp had a tracking device and Blackstar didn't. Now that the device has been successfully removed, we are confident that neither organisation can trace you to this location."

"How much longer will we be here?" asked Kelly.

"Tomorrow morning you will be taken from here by flitter to the airport. A skipjet will be waiting for you inside a hanger on the far side of the airport, away from the public terminals. I will meet you there. We will board inside the terminal out of sight from prying eyes, and we have priority clearance for take-off as soon as you are on board. About an hour later, we will be landing at a private airfield near Pittsburgh. From there you will be taken by ground vehicle directly to your secure accommodation, a very comfortable house in an outer suburb of Pittsburgh.

"Over the following two days your testimonies will be recorded and you will be briefed by our lawyers in preparation for a future court appearance. If all goes well during those recorded testimonies, we should be able to secure indictments and arrest warrants for several key people at Senticorp, including, of course, Dr Nigel Blakely. We hope to have them locked up and awaiting trial within a few days."

"How long until the case goes to court?" asked Daniel.

"It could take months, as I'm sure Blakely will hire some fancy lawyers to slow things down. But we will be pressing for a trial as soon as possible."

"So, what happens to us in the meantime?" asked Kelly.

"You won't be needed at the main trial. The judicial system has changed a lot in recent years. You will be part of a pretrial hearing, within a couple of weeks. You will give your testimonies and be cross examined, and all of that will be recorded for the full trial when it finally occurs."

"So, we'll be free to go after the pretrial hearing?" asked Kelly.

George looked a bit uncomfortable. "You will be free to go,

Dr Rearson. In fact, we will be arranging a new location and a full witness protection program for you." He glanced at Daniel. "It's a little more complicated for you, Daniel. You are still regarded by the courts as Daniel Mendez, a prisoner who was scheduled for execution and who was illegally released from prison. Until we can have your status changed, you will be remanded in custody."

"Sent back to jail, you mean?" said Daniel.

"We are arguing for continued house arrest at the safe house. In fact, you are technically under house arrest here."

"I see."

"Boss, that's just not fair," complained Carlos.

"I agree," said George. "But we have our best lawyers working on having Daniel Newman legally recognised as a distinct and separate person to Daniel Mendez. It is just going to take some time."

There was silence as they all digested this. Then George clapped his hands and said, "In the meantime. I thought we all deserved a treat! I've arranged for caterers to come and prepare us a special dinner tonight."

"No!" Daniel cried out, before he had even realised that he had spoken.

"What's the matter?" asked George.

Daniel's face had gone pale. "They're not called Costa's Catering by any chance, are they?"

"No," answered George, slightly confused.

"What's the matter, bro?" asked Carlos. "You don't like Greek food?"

"It's not that. It's just ... it doesn't matter. I just had a flashback to a dream ..."

"Yeah, that was one wild dream you had this afternoon, dude."

"Yeah. It certainly was. It was so ... vivid."

They all looked at him with concern.

"Don't worry, bro. Ol' Carlos has got your back. Ain't no bad dudes gettin' in here tonight!"

George stood. "How about we turn our thoughts to more

pleasant things? I've brought along a selection of very nice wines if anyone is interested."

Three hands shot up, immediately.

The food was delicious; international cuisine, served by a catering crew who didn't brandish a single lethal weapon all night. The caterers had been carefully vetted and their van thoroughly searched at the front gate prior to entry. The party was small, just Daniel, Kelly, Carlos and George, with the agents on shift swinging by from time to time to avail themselves of some food.

Kelly seemed to spark up after the afternoon session with George, as if she finally started to believe that everything was going to be alright. She made a special effort and came to dinner with make up on and wearing a short, very tight dress. Daniel was taken aback, never having seen her in that light before, and Kelly seemed to enjoy the effect she was having on all three men.

The wine flowed, and so did the conversation. Kelly joined in, talking more in one evening than she had in the entire three days previously. After dinner was over and their dessert bowls had been removed, they sat in the lounge room, sipping a superb port. Shortly after 9:30 pm, George made an exit, wishing them good-night and promising to meet them at the aircraft the next morning. As he left, he asked Carlos to join him briefly on the verandah to discuss final arrangements for tomorrow.

Finding themselves alone, Daniel asked Kelly, "How are you feeling about ... well, everything? It must be a huge thing, leaving your whole life behind?"

She nodded and looked down at her wine glass. He thought she wasn't going to answer, but eventually she said, "It's pretty devastating, but I had to do it. I couldn't stand by and watch what they were doing. And I certainly didn't want to be part of it. I only stayed on as long as I did, because George told me he needed me there."

"I'm sorry you've had to go through all this, Kelly. Have you got family that you're leaving behind?"

"No. Both parents are dead. My sister lives in Brazil and we don't see much of each other. I only moved here for the job, so there's nothing particularly tying me here anymore." She was sitting in the lounge chair opposite Daniel, and he was having trouble not looking at her legs. They were exceptionally nice legs, as far as legs went, he mused.

"Tell me about your dream this afternoon," she said.

He shrugged. "It was so real. A bunch of assassins turned up and killed us all. It was ... incredibly vivid."

"You were calling out my name."

"Was I?"

"Yes. Several times."

"I guess I didn't want to see you get hurt. I ... I didn't want someone else to die because of me. I've been responsible for too much death already."

"If you're talking about Daniel Mendez, that's not who you are any longer. You can't keep carrying that around."

"No?" he asked. "Then what am I supposed to do with it? How do I live with myself, knowing the things I once did?" Maybe it was the wine, or maybe it was the sympathy in Kelly's eyes, but Daniel found his own eyes welling up with tears.

"Let me ask you something," Kelly said, leaning forward, which unfortunately only added to Daniel's discomfort as it presented him with a view of another part of her gorgeous figure. "Would you do any of those things now?"

He almost recoiled. "Of course not!"

"That's right," she agreed. "Because it's not who you are. It goes against every fibre of your being. And that's why I know that Daniel Mendez is dead. He's completely gone. And you need to let him go."

Daniel merely nodded. "I guess so."

"I know so. You have a new life to live. Don't let Mendez kill that as well." She placed her half-finished glass of port on the coffee table and stood up. "I'm going to bed now." She hesitated a moment and then, on an impulse, walked over to Daniel, leaned down and kissed him briefly on the cheek. She turned and walked toward the hallway, leaving her perfume lingering in the air behind her. As she reached the entrance to the hallway, she turned and smiled. "By the way, I don't want you to get any wrongs ideas. I'm gay." Then she turned and disappeared, leaving Daniel in a swirl of emotions.

39

The skipjet was an impressive looking aircraft: a sleek, slim-lined thing of beauty. As Carlos, Daniel and Kelly entered the hangar, accompanied by four armed agents, Daniel marvelled at its design. He had researched it briefly overnight. The two wing-mounted engines provide the thrust to propel the aircraft to the edge of space in about 12 minutes, at which point they shut down. The massively powerful direct fusion drive jet engine at the rear of the aircraft then kicks in, accelerating the aircraft into space itself and skimming it across the surface of the atmosphere. Because the aircraft doesn't ever reach true orbital velocity, as soon as the DFD is shut off, the aircraft starts to gradually lose altitude until there is sufficient air density to reignite the standard jet engines. Its sub-orbital velocity means that heating upon re-entry is minimal and is easily dealt with by the innovative thermal dissipation skin of the aircraft.

As they walked around the rear of the aircraft, Daniel paused to look up at the huge rear nozzle of the direct fusion drive. The silent, brooding engine seemed to emanate an aura of incredible power.

George Mallard met them at the foot of the stairs and led them inside the aircraft. The economy section at the rear had comfortable seating for 30 people but as there would be no one else on this flight, they were able to sit in the business class area, which accommodated less than half that number. They sprawled in luxurious reclining chairs and quickly strapped themselves in as the hangar doors opened and the plane taxied out. With priority clearance already assigned to them, they taxied directly to the end of the runway and, without any delay, surged forward with impressive acceleration, leaving the ground in an astonishingly short distance and leaping skyward. Daniel felt himself pressed deeply into his chair as the plane climbed at an angle that seemed very close to vertical.

The acceleration was relentless. The minutes ticked by, and the sky gradually changed colour from blue to a dark indigo as they continued to streak upward. Eventually, their ascent path flattened to a gentler angle. The engines roared for another minute or so, still pressing Daniel deeply into his chair, and then, without warning, they shut down. The G forces from acceleration were instantly cancelled and the passengers all felt incredibly light. They were not completely in free fall, as their forward momentum was not sufficient to counteract the pull of Earth's gravity, but it was fast enough to significantly diminish its full effect.

Carlos was sitting next to Daniel and said, "I just lost about 50 kilograms, dude!"

Kelly, who was sitting across the aisle from Daniel, commented, "Instant weight loss! A girl's best friend."

Without pausing to filter or even think about his words, he said, "You don't need to lose anything, you're absolutely perfect just the way you are!" Then he remembered her parting comment the previous evening about her sexuality, and he immediately felt awkward. Not wanting her to be offended, he mumbled, "I'm sorry, I didn't mean ... I wasn't trying to ... you know ... I was just pointing out ... umm ... without inferring any kind of ... you know ... untoward or inappropriate ... thingy ..."

"Beautifully expressed, bro," said Carlos. "I couldn't have put it better myself."

Kelly laughed out loud and said, "That was very sweet. Thank you. With such smooth repartee, it's hard to imagine how any girl could resist you!"

Before Daniel could reply, they were all slammed into the back of their seats as the direct fusion drive kicked in. It went from zero to full thrust instantly and the passengers experienced G forces greater than anything previously. They continued to climb at a moderate angle, the DFD imparting greater lateral velocity as well as altitude. Gradually, the colour of the sky visible through the side windows changed from indigo to black, and the Earth's atmosphere became visible as a thin blue band on the horizon. Their craft had now transformed, however briefly, from an aircraft to a space craft.

After what seemed like barely a minute, the DFD switched off, and they were released from the pressure of acceleration. They were coasting now, skimming across the top of the Earth's thermosphere, beyond the stratosphere, on the very edge of space. Their momentum continued to carry them upwards at a shallow angle until, very gradually, the Earth's massive gravitational pull began to assert itself. While their lateral velocity reduced slowly, their climb rate reduced much more quickly until it ceased altogether.

They began to fall back toward the hungry ground, executing a parabolic arc as their temporary spacecraft curved back toward Earth. Now, for a short period of time, the passengers experienced complete weightlessness. Daniel couldn't help himself. He unclipped his harness and allowed himself to float up from his chair, although he maintained a firm grip on his armrest with one hand. He ended up inverted and looked like he was doing an impossible one-armed handstand on the armrest. He pulled himself toward the chair and then pushed himself away again, up, down, up, down, as if he was doing push ups.

"How's that, dude?" he asked Carlos. "Not bad, hey?"

"A bit boring, bro. I do those all the time."

Kelly just shook her head and said, "Boys, boys."

"Sir, you need to resume your seat," said the sole flight attendant, who was seated at the front, facing them. "Realignment and air braking will commence very shortly."

Daniel reluctantly pulled himself back into his chair and clipped himself back into his harness. He looked out the side window and saw some short bursts of outgassing from various points on the nearby wing as the pilots used attitude controls to align the plane ready for air braking. The nose of their craft gradually pitched down toward their point of entry into the stratosphere. As Daniel continued to watch through the window, he heard a whining and grinding sound, transmitted to him through the hull of the plane and he saw huge spoilers rise from the upper surface of the wing.

Almost immediately, thin wisps of condensation began trailing off the spoilers as the plane began to encounter increasingly dense air molecules inside the stratosphere. As they continued to fall, the trails of condensation became a constant stream of white cloud bursting over the whole wing structure. The sound of the turbulence grew to a steady roar and the supersonic aircraft was buffeted like it was a toy caught in a thunderstorm.

Weightlessness had ceased now and everyone on board was gripping their armrests tightly as they were occasionally bounced from side to side.

"This is fun!" said Daniel in a show of bravado. He glanced across at Kelly and noted that she had her eyes closed as she clung grimly to her armrests. She must have sensed him watching because she briefly opened her eyes and glanced across at him. She quickly closed her eyes again but reached out her hand across the aisle. Daniel responded and reached out to hold her hand and was surprised by the strength of her grip.

The turbulence did not last long. The roaring soon died down and the buffeting ceased. Kelly opened her eyes and released Daniel's hand and looked across to him, mouthing a silent "Thank you."

In the comparative quiet that followed, the whine of turbines starting up could be heard and, shortly after, the passengers experienced the smooth pressure of the jet engines reasserting themselves as they were pushed gently back into their seats.

As normal atmospheric flight resumed, Daniel said, "That was awesome!"

"Pretty cool, hey dude?" agreed Carlos.

"It's something I'll remember for the rest of my life. Even if it's only ..." Daniel couldn't bring himself to say the words.

"Don't go there, bro. Don't go there. You're gonna have a long and happy life. I'll give you a money back guarantee on that, my friend."

"So, just explain to me: how do I get my money back if you're wrong?"

Carlos just shook his head and smiled.

Fifteen minutes later, they landed at a small, private airfield on the outskirts of Pittsburgh. The plane exhibited deceleration that was equally as impressive as its acceleration at take-off, jamming the passengers forward against their harnesses. The plane taxied into a large hanger, beside which a large black van was waiting for them. There were three armed JUDAN agents waiting outside the vehicle, carefully scanning the environment for signs of any threat.

The plane came to a stop inside the hangar and the engines shut down. The hangar doors were closed, and the flight steward opened the cabin door and a set of stairs extended automatically from the fuselage. Daniel was about to stand up when George knelt in the centre aisle beside him with an apologetic look on his face.

"This is the part I haven't been looking forward to, Daniel."

Kelly frowned and looked across at him with concern.

"What do you mean?" asked Daniel.

"Now that we're back in the heartland, so to speak, I am expected to follow appropriate protocols." He paused. "I'm afraid I'm going to have to handcuff you. My superiors insisted. Technically, you are a recaptured, convicted prisoner under house arrest – at least until the court says otherwise."

Daniel said nothing, merely lowering his head and staring at

the floor. Carlos shook his head and said, "This is so wrong, dude."
It wasn't clear whether he was addressing Daniel or George.

"I'm very sorry, Daniel," continued George. "It's only until we
get you to the safe house, then we can take them off. But those
agents outside need to be able to report that due process was
followed."

Daniel continued to say nothing. He simply held out his hands
and looked directly at George, who nodded and quickly clipped
the cuffs on him. Daniel stood and walked down the aisle of the
plane, all signs of his previous enjoyment of the flight now
completely absent. He descended the stairs with a grim look on
his face. As they all started walking across the floor of the hangar
toward the open side door, Kelly caught up with him and slipped
her arm through his.

"Care to keep a girl company?" she asked.

"You don't have to take pity on me."

"I know. I just want those arseholes out there to know that
someone is still willing to treat you decently, as an innocent man."

"But I'm not, am I."

Kelly dragged him to a stop and spun him around to face her.
"Now you listen to me, Daniel Newman! I'm not going to let you
talk like that anymore! Do you hear me? You're a good man. I
haven't known you for long, but I know you well enough to see
that. You have a good heart. And I refuse to let you wallow in the
shadow of someone else's past."

"Is everything okay?" asked George who had stopped alongside them.

"Just give us a moment, will you?" asked Kelly.

George nodded and kept walking to the side door where he
stopped and waited with Carlos.

"Now here's the thing, Daniel. I want to be your friend. Not
because I feel sorry for you, but because I think you're a nice guy.
And I happen to like you. Would you like to be my friend?"

He nodded. "That would be nice. I'm not exactly over-run with
friends at the moment."

"Okay. But friends speak the truth to each other. And now that you've just officially accepted me as your friend, I get to speak the truth to you."

"Maybe I was a bit hasty in agreeing to the whole 'accepting you as a friend' thing," he said.

She thumped him on the arm and continued unabated. "So, today's truth is: Stop focusing on the past and start believing in yourself."

"Is there going to be a different truth every day?"

"I haven't decided. I haven't quite mapped out the whole rehabilitation program yet."

"Are you guys finished yet?" called George impatiently.

"Yes," answered Kelly. They started walking again and she reinserted her arm through his, asking, "Have you ever had a platonic friendship with a gay woman before?"

"I've got no idea. I only woke up two weeks ago."

"Trust me," she said, "you're gonna love it."

40

The safe house was a comfortable two-story home on a secluded three-acre block in the hilly township of O'Hara, on the north-eastern outskirts of Pittsburgh. The property was bordered by trees around its perimeter and the house could not be seen by any neighbours. Given the fact that various official visits would be taking place over the next few days, it was ideal. The bedrooms were all upstairs and the ground floor was devoted to open plan living. There was to be a similar security arrangement to the safe house in Quito. There would be two armed agents on site at all times, rotating in shifts. Carlos would be on site through the day but was no longer staying overnight with them. George, as the agent in charge, would be coordinating the legal side of things.

As they sat around the dining table, discussing the arrangements for the next few days, a strange feeling came over Daniel. The voices of the others started to distort and echo. Their faces blurred and then transformed into hideous-looking creatures. The floor beneath him started to give way and his chair started to sink into what seemed to be a pool of black mud. The others were still sitting on firm ground, but his chair sank until it had disappeared. He was under the table now, up to his armpits in mud, and sinking rapidly. He struggled frantically, calling out, but he continued to sink. The legs of the table turned into writhing snakes and began winding around him, squeezing his chest tighter and tighter until he could barely breath. Gasping, he called out for help, reaching up toward the table above. He felt a hand grasp his and heard Kelly's voice calling to him from a great distance.

"Daniel! Daniel! Focus on my voice. You're alright! You're safe!"

The vision cleared and he found himself sitting on the floor underneath the table. Kelly was crouched beside him, holding his hand and looking very concerned.

"What just happened?" Daniel asked.

"You tell us, dude," said Carlos. He and George were crouching beside him as well. "One moment you were sitting at the table, the next, you were sliding off your chair and yelling out."

"It ... it was so real. There was black mud. I was sinking into it. And there were snakes. I hate snakes."

"You're okay now," said Kelly.

"But am I? That ... that isn't exactly normal."

"No, it's not," agreed Kelly. "How are you feeling now? Any dizziness? Headaches? Residual vision?"

"Nope. Nothing. I feel completely normal again."

They helped him up from the floor and sat him in a comfortable lounge chair. Carlos fetched him a glass of water while Kelly and George stood looking at him with concern.

"Maybe I should call a doctor," suggested George.

"No. I'm alright now. I'm probably just tired and a little dehydrated. Let's just wait and see."

The others all looked dubious but agreed to hold off on calling a doctor after Daniel continued to insist that he was fine. They all resumed their places at the table and continued eating lunch, but Daniel couldn't help noticing occasional glances from each of the others from time to time. They were all probably wondering if he was losing his marbles.

So was he.

41

E li Tang answered his comm.
"Speak."

"Sir, as suspected they've flown the target to Pittsburgh."

"Do we know his exact location?"

"Yes sir. The tag we implanted at the airport is the latest micro-technology. We can pinpoint him anywhere on Earth to within a metre."

"I didn't ask for a description of the technology. I asked for his location!"

"They've got him in a house in O'Hara, just outside Pittsburgh."

"Access?"

"It's very private: a three-acre property completely surrounded by trees, which suits us, as we can get to within 100 metres of the house without being seen. We've had two watchers in place for the last couple of hours. It looks like there are two armed guards on sight – probably in shifts again. There appear to be two senior agents with the target at the moment, but we suspect they won't be staying overnight."

"Do you have a plan?"

"A night operation. Early hours of the morning. If there are only two guards, we should be able to overcome them quickly and easily. The rest should be simple."

"Make it happen."

"Yes, sir. I'll start assembling a team right away."

42

Daniel was having trouble sleeping. After a day of relative inactivity, he wasn't particularly tired when he eventually went to bed. He had tossed and turned for about two hours before finally falling into a light slumber. Now, however, he was awake again and sleep was once again eluding him. He looked at the dim readout on his nightstand. 2:15 am. He lay there for another ten minutes and then decided to get up and make himself a hot milk. He padded quietly down the stairs and walked into the kitchen.

"Lights at 30 per cent," he mumbled. He grabbed a mug, activated the beverage dispenser and selected "Milk; protein enhanced; low fat; temperature 65 degrees."

His mug filled with warm milk which he started to sip as he padded to the transparent sliding doors at the rear of the dining room, commanding the lights to be turned off as he did so. He looked out at the back garden, partially illuminated by a half moon that was now high in the sky, shining through thin wisps of scattered cloud. As he watched, a guard walked around the corner of the house, his rifle held at an angle. He seemed to be talking on his comm. As Daniel continued watching, he saw movement among the trees at the far end of the yard. Two dark-clad figures emerged from the tree line and sprinted toward the guard who had now stopped walking. He was intent on his comm call and had partially turned his back on the tree-lined perimeter.

Daniel tried to open the sliding door to warn him, but it was locked and he couldn't find the latch in the dark. He started banging on the door and yelling, trying to attract the guard's attention, but the guard was too absorbed in his conversation to notice. Daniel continued banging the door and yelling and watched in horror as the running figures drew near. The guard finally seemed to hear Daniel and looked toward him in alarm.

But it was too late. As the guard started to turn to see what was behind him, the first intruder drew near and shot him through the chest with a laser, and he crumpled to the ground, lifeless. Both intruders then moved swiftly toward the sliding doors as Daniel backed away into the darkened room. They didn't seem to be able to see him yet as their attention was fixed solely on opening the door.

"Daniel? What's happening?" Kelly was standing at the bottom of the stairs. Daniel could only vaguely see her in the darkened room.

"Intruders! Get back upstairs now! Call George!"

As she backed away up the stairs, one of the intruders fired a laser into the door mechanism which disintegrated with a sizzling, crackling sound. Daniel dived behind a lounge as the two men entered the house. As he crouched behind the lounge, he heard more sizzling from another laser and, a moment later, he heard the front door being forced open.

"Where is he?" asked a voice.

"Hang on," answered a second. "It's saying he's right here, in this room. Over there."

"Lights on," said a third voice.

"Bingo!" said the first voice.

Daniel looked up into the barrel of a laser pistol. The man who was holding it was also holding some kind of scanning device.

"Stand up! You're coming with us. Either we shoot you and carry you, or you walk. Your choice. You've got ten seconds!"

Daniel knew he had no choice. "I'll walk." He stood and saw

four men, clothed entirely in black, including black face masks. One of the men activated a comm and said, "Bring the van to the front door. We've neutralised both guards."

As they marched him toward the door, one of the men asked, "What about the woman? We saw a female walking in the garden this afternoon. She must be still in the house somewhere."

"Irrelevant," said the man who had found him. "We were told to just get him. We got what we came for. Let's go."

They pushed him roughly out the door as a dark van came to a sliding stop in the circular gravel driveway. They slid the side door open and shoved him in, quickly jumping in after him. The door slid shut and the van took off in a spray of gravel and dirt. There was no window in the rear of the van and Daniel was bounced around as he sat awkwardly on the floor, surrounded by the four heavily armed men who were sitting on inward facing bench seats on either side of him.

"Is this a dream?" he asked.

"Shut up!"

"How did you find me?"

"I said shut up! Last warning."

"You're Blackstar, aren't you? Why are you doing this?"

Before he even saw it coming, one of the men smashed his rifle butt into the side of Daniel's head and he slumped unconscious to the floor. "Moron!" the man said as he leant his rifle back against his seat.

"What did you do that for?" asked one of the others. "Now we'll have to carry him!"

"At least we don't have to put up with his whining anymore."

"Well, just don't expect me to carry him, that's all. You whacked him, so you can carry him."

"Shut up or I'll whack you too."

43

"Where are they now?" asked George, as he drove recklessly toward the JUDAN head office, disregarding traffic signals and road signs.

A tactical specialist in the situation room at head office was looking at an image being transmitted by a drone that was flying 50 metres above the speeding van.

"They're heading north, along Dorseyville Road."

Silent perimeter alarms around the safehouse had been tripped when the intruders first set foot on the property. Drones from the JUDAN headquarters in Pittsburgh had been launched instantly, and the fast response team of six specialised soldiers, rostered on for that evening and who until that moment had been playing cards in the ready room, had been mobilised seconds later. They were now in a stealth flitter, on their way to intercept the van.

"Where are they taking him? What's your best guess?"

"Just a moment. I've sequestered a satellite and I'm scanning ahead as we speak." There was silence for a few moments, and George let the specialist do his work while he pulled into the underground carpark.

As he ran to the lift, the specialist updated him. "There's a new private airfield four more klicks up the road. I'm zooming in now.

Bingo! There's a small jet parked there. The door is open, stairs have been extended and two armed men are in view, at the bottom of the stairs."

"Okay," replied George as the lift arrived and he got in. "How many weaponised drones are in play at the moment?"

"Three, keeping pace with the van."

"Alright. Send two ahead to the airfield. Have them hovering in place and ready to engage when the van arrives. Keep the third on the van. Redirect the flitter to the airfield as well."

"Roger."

George arrived in the situation room, puffing from a short run along the corridor. He took a seat beside the specialist, whose name tag read 'Regan Coffey', and studied the various screens. One was a view of the van as seen from above and slightly behind by the drone. Another two were a blur of motion, as two drones raced ahead to the airfield. A fourth screen was obviously a satellite feed. The specialist had zoomed out to encompass the whole scene in one shot. A red triangle indicated the speeding van and another red triangle indicated the plane, parked at the end of a runway at a small airfield. Three blue circles indicated the weaponised drones. One was overlapping the red triangle of the van and the other two were now taking up station over the plane.

"I'll position them about 30 metres apart, so that we get optimal angles for crossfire."

"Good," agreed George.

"Sir, I need to clarify our end game, here. Is this a terminal action or immobilisation?"

"Terminal. We can't take any chances."

"Roger that. I need your authorisation, sir."

George scanned his wrist on the security scanner and said, "This is George Mallard. Terminal action is authorised."

"Thank you, sir." Coffey tapped a few keys on a screen. "Drones are now initialised for terminal action. Please confirm, sir."

"I confirm."

"I'll need you to identify the friendly before the drones open fire, sir. The quicker the better."

"It should be fairly obvious," replied George. "The call we got from Dr Rearson indicated that he was taken while still wearing pyjamas."

"Roger. Do you want an audio feed from the drones, sir?"

"Yes. Let's listen to what's going on."

The red triangle of the van turned into a short access road and approached the plane. The satellite image zoomed in close as the van came to a stop. The two guards near the plane approached the van. The van doors could be heard opening and two black clad figures quickly emerged.

A voice said, "We got him. It was a piece of cake."

Two more black-clad figures emerged from the van, carrying a person in light clothing between them, one holding his arms and one holding his legs.

"Bugger! How come I get the heavy end?" said one voice, grunting and puffing.

"That's because you aren't as smart as me," said another.

"Shut up, both of you and get him in the plane!" said someone else.

"Zooming in," said Coffey.

Daniel's face appeared on the screen; his eyes closed.

"That's him," said George.

"Roger that," said Coffey. He zoomed out and tapped his screen. Daniel's image had a blue circle superimposed over it and all the other figures at the scene were suddenly marked by red squares, including a driver of the van who had now emerged.

"Seven targets identified. Please confirm, sir."

"Confirmed."

The two men who were carrying Daniel began to move toward the steps leading up to the plane, while the other figures seemed to cover them while scanning their surroundings.

"Awaiting your fire order, sir."

"Fire."

The specialist tapped a command. Instantly all four screens in front of George lit up with blazing light. The speakers in the situation room relayed the sizzle and bang as the drones all fired multiple blue bolts of laser at the same instant. Each of the targets was hit by more than one laser blast. It was all over in less than a second.

"Seven targets down," reported Coffey.

"Watch for any more bad guys attempting to exit the plane," said George.

"Roger." Coffey positioned a drone to hover just in front of the plane's open doorway, then he placed a call to the flitter. "Airborne One, do you read?"

"Go ahead, base."

"The airfield is secure. Seven targets neutralised. One unconscious civilian will need to be stabilised and air-vacced. I advise caution, as there may be more bad guys inside the aircraft."

"Roger. We have the plane in sight now. Out."

Coffey lowered one of the drones to hover over Daniel, sending back an image of his unconscious face, with blood trailing from the left side of his head. Meanwhile, the satellite feed showed the flitter landing and the six JUDAN soldiers fanning out in a disciplined formation. One of them carried a medikit to Daniel and began basic first aid. Three ran into the aircraft while the remaining two took up covering positions at the base of the steps.

A few moments later, a pilot emerged from the plane with his hands in the air, ferried down the steps by the armed JUDAN soldiers and was taken into the flitter. Two of the team then carried a still-unconscious Daniel on board the aircraft on a stretcher. As the team moved among the bodies and finished securing the site, one of the soldiers was heard to say, "Bloody drones. They get all the fun, and we have to clean up the mess."

44

Daniel woke up with a splitting headache. He looked around and didn't recognise the room. Kelly was sitting in a chair beside his bed, and she looked up with relief when she saw Daniel open his eyes.

"You're awake! Thank goodness," she said.

"I had a terrible dream."

"It wasn't a dream, Daniel. Blackstar abducted you. You were knocked unconscious."

He lifted a hand to the left side of his head, where the centre of the pain seemed to be. The skin was numb on the surface, but his head was pounding.

"I seem destined to wake up in strange places with pounding headaches. Please tell me I haven't been turned into a zombie this time."

She smiled. "The doctor says you're going to be fine. They glued the gash in your head together and kept you sedated for six hours. You might have some mild, residual concussion, so you'll need to rest and take it easy."

"Where am I?"

"This is the private medical centre in the secure basement of the JUDAN building. It's where they stitch back together all their wounded heroes," she said, smiling at him.

"Huh! Some hero I am! I couldn't even save myself, let alone anyone else."

She stepped forward and rested her hand on his arm. "You kept me safe. You warned me and told me to go back upstairs. They didn't come looking for me, but if I'd stayed downstairs who knows what they might have done."

The door opened and George and Carlos walked in. Carlos started singing, "*Daniel my brother, you are older than me. Do you still feel the pain of the scars that won't heal?*"

"What's that supposed to be?" asked Daniel.

"Elton John, bro! It's a classic from the 20th century!"

"Well, it's appropriate, because right now that's about how old I feel." Daniel looked at George. "It was Blackstar, was it?"

George sighed. "Yes. Several of the dead operatives have criminal records and have been linked to Blackstar in the past. The jet was hired and the pilot and the company he works for claim to know nothing about the clients who hired their services."

"But how did they find us so quickly?" asked Kelly.

"That's got me perplexed as well," said George. "You were only in the safe house for about 18 hours before they struck. We've searched the house top to bottom for bugs and can't find any. We simply have no idea how they found you so quickly."

"I think I know," said Daniel.

George's eyes opened wide and his eyebrows shot up. "How?"

"They used some kind of tracking device to locate me hiding behind the lounge. They zeroed straight in on me. I saw the device one of them was holding in his hand."

George frowned and activated his comm. "This is George Mallard. I'm down in the med centre. Send Adams down here immediately with his bug scanning gear."

They didn't have to wait long. A man entered who looked like a clown without makeup to Daniel. He was completely bald on top but had fuzzy clumps of red hair on both sides of his head. Daniel had to try hard to keep himself from laughing. He glanced at Kelly and saw her give him a surreptitious goggle-eyed raised eyebrow expression that only made it harder for him not to laugh.

Adams was clearly very excited about the chance to use his fancy gear, and he chatted enthusiastically about its technical specifications as he switched it on and initialised it. It only took a few seconds before it located the source of the problem, giving off a high-pitched whine as it hovered behind Daniel's left ear. Everywhere else on his body was clear.

Adams then used a different device to scan the tracker and he studied the screen carefully before announcing that the device that was embedded in Daniel's skin was truly a thing of exquisite technical beauty. He spoke of its range and frequency modulation and sensitivity, but all Daniel heard was, "blah, blah, blah."

"But how did it get inside me?" asked Daniel. "It's not something they'd be able to do without me knowing, surely!"

"While you were briefly in their custody at Quito airport, was there any time when you were not fully conscious?" asked George.

Daniel thought hard and nodded. "Yes. When they shot me with the neural disruptor gun."

"They must have done it then," said Adams chirpily. "It would only take a second. It's impressively small and would only need a tag injector. If it included a long-lasting local anaesthetic, which is how I would do it, then you wouldn't feel a thing, even after you regained full consciousness."

"I don't care how they got it in him. Let's get it out!" said Carlos. "We could put it in a parcel and send it to the other side of the world."

"Not so fast," said Adams, enjoying his moment of importance. "We can certainly do that, but it will stop transmitting within an hour after its removal. It doesn't have a battery, but uses the glycogen molecules from the cells of the body for its power. So, if you want it to keep transmitting, you'll need to put it into someone or something else."

"Does anyone own a cat they want to get rid of?" asked Daniel.

"That's not such a stupid idea," said George, considering the suggestion seriously.

"I know it's not. That's why I suggested it," said Daniel. "I'm not completely stupid."

"That's debatable," mumbled Carlos, which caused Daniel to crack his first smile since waking up.

"Leave it with me for a few hours," said George. "If we're going to use this as a decoy, I want to set everything up properly. We'll leave the device where it is for the moment."

"In my head," clarified Daniel.

"Err, yes."

"Well, I suppose there's a whole lot of other crap in there that shouldn't be. I guess one more bit won't hurt."

"So, you admit that your head is full of crap, bro?" asked Carlos.

"You're lucky I'm in bed in a weakened state, dude," responded Daniel.

Kelly chose to ignore the flippant exchange. She addressed George, saying, "This means you can't take Daniel to a new safe house, because they'll only find him again if you do."

"Neither of you are going to a new safe house," replied George. "You will stay right here for the next day or so. We have a secure basement facility, including several apartments that are completely impenetrable. The JUDAN headquarters is the most secure building in all of Pittsburgh. Obviously, the basement apartments have no windows or outdoor space, which is why we didn't put you there originally, but at least you will be perfectly safe there. It doesn't matter if Blackstar knows where Daniel is for the moment, because they can't do anything about it."

Daniel looked at Kelly and sighed. "Looks like we're not going to Space World tomorrow, honey. You'd better break it to the kids."

45

D aniel and Kelly were taken to a secure apartment in the basement of the JUDAN building soon after lunch. It was comfortable and functional, but it wasn't going to win any home décor awards.

"It's basically a bomb shelter," explained Carlos who showed them around. There certainly wasn't much to it: three bedrooms, bathroom and an open plan lounge / dining / kitchen. Two guards were stationed directly outside their door and Carlos would also be staying with them as a third member of the security team. His shoulder was now fully healed, thanks to fast-acting cellular nanobot technology.

Late in the afternoon, after they had played several games of cards, George turned up with a cat.

"I thought you were joking, boss," said Carlos.

"Not at all. It was a good idea. I got the kitty from a local animal pound for unwanted pets."

George put the cat down and they all watched as the cat prowled around the loungeroom, exploring its new surroundings. After a short time, it jumped onto one of the lounge chairs, curled up and went to sleep.

A doctor arrived shortly afterward. He opened a bag of medical equipment and sat Daniel down on a kitchen chair.

"This will only take a few moments, as the device is not very deep," he explained. He administered a local anaesthetic, and after waiting a few minutes, made a quick incision. Using a pair of tweezers, he pulled out the device.

"It's tiny!" exclaimed Kelly who, as a scientist, was looking on with professional curiosity. "It's the size of a grain of rice!"

"Carlos, can you grab the cat please," asked George.

"Sure boss." Carlos walked into the loungeroom, calling "Here, kitty, kitty."

The doctor poked around Daniel's wound for a few moments, then sealed it with plastaskin. Carlos returned with the cat and held it while the doctor quickly inserted the transmitter underneath a fold of skin in the cat's neck, using a tag injector that looked like an oversized syringe.

"All done," the doctor said happily, as he straightened up. He packed up his medical bag and left, while the cat jumped to the ground and returned to the lounge chair that it had apparently claimed as its own.

"Don't get too attached to that thing," said George, "because I'm taking it now."

"Where is it going?" asked Daniel.

"It's about to have a very long trip. It will board a flitter on our rooftop and be flown to the airport where it will be transferred to a skipjet departing for Zurich, Switzerland. On arrival it will be taken to the JUDAN world headquarters there, where we will let it stay for a few days. The device will then be removed and destroyed. Anyone tracking it will assume we have discovered the device and destroyed it."

"You're hiring a skipjet just for a cat?" asked Daniel, incredulously.

"No. Fortunately, we have two officials flying back to Zurich today. The cat will just tag along for the ride."

"So, how long do we need to stay here?" asked Kelly.

"A couple of days, just to make sure no one is still watching the building. Tomorrow, our lawyers will be recording your testimonies, so I suggest you get a decent sleep tonight. It could be a long day tomorrow."

George departed with the cat a few minutes later, leaving the three of them wondering how they would fill in the rest of the afternoon and evening. They ate an early dinner of creamy pasta and beans and started to watch a movie, but Daniel and Kelly kept falling asleep, the events of the last 24 hours finally catching up with them. In the end, they all gave in and went to bed, hoping for an unbroken night's sleep.

They didn't get it.

∽

Daniel opened his eyes and blinked. His light was on, and Carlos and Kelly were in his room. Carlos was standing beside him and Kelly was sitting on the side of his bed, holding his hand. Both were looking at him with deep concern.

"Are you awake now?" Kelly asked.

Daniel blinked in the bright light. "Where am I?"

"In a basement apartment in the JUDAN building," answered Carlos.

Daniel looked around. "Where did the wolves go?"

"There aren't any wolves here," explained Kelly, squeezing his hand. "You were dreaming."

"And you were screaming, bro," explained Carlos.

"I was?"

"Yeah, dude. Like you were being eaten alive or something."

Daniel's brow furrowed as he tried to make sense of what was happening. It had been so real. It took several more minutes for the dream to fade and for reality to reassert itself. Kelly made Daniel a mug of warm milk and made him drink it, claiming it would help him sleep. Half an hour later they all retired to bed again and Daniel slept fitfully until morning.

46

E li Tang glanced at the digital time readout on his desk console. It was the second brightest light in his almost completely dark office, the brightest being the dull red glow from his desk lamp. The bright sunlight of a hot Singapore afternoon had no chance of penetrating his darkened windows and the thick blackout curtains. He glanced again at the time. They must almost be there by now. He grunted and placed the call. After a few moments a voice answered.

"Yeah. Who's this?"

"It's your employer."

"Oh! Sorry Mr Tang! I wasn't expecting your call."

"Clearly. I believe you have some disappointing news for me."

"How did you ... Yes, sir. Sorry. I was just about to call you."

"I am told that our target was in our hands but, due to your incompetence, slipped out of our grasp once again."

"I ... we ... hadn't anticipate their use of weaponised drones."

"Why not? Did you think they were going to come after you with sticks and stones? This is the Justice Department we're talking about, you fool, not a bunch of amateurs! Unlike you!"

"I'm sorry, sir. But we still have a strong signal on our target. I promise you ..."

"No more promises! Your incompetence is appalling! Did you know that present in the very house where our target was staying was the scientist largely responsible for developing the bridging enzyme?"

"The woman?"

"Yes! The woman! She has intimate knowledge of the quantum molecule as well. She was there for the taking and you left her! You had within your grasp a living specimen of the ninth protocol AND one of its key designers, and you let both of them slip through your hands!"

"I ... I didn't realise who she was. How did you know?"

"I have other sources." In the background, Tang heard a door chime. "Is that someone at your door?"

"Yes, sir. I'll ignore it. They'll call back again if it's important."

"No. Answer the door. I'll wait."

"No, your call is more important. I can ..."

"I said answer the door!"

"Yes, sir."

Tang heard footsteps and the soft swish of a door being opened, followed almost immediately by the sizzle of a laser blast. A moment later there was a thud as a body hit the floor.

"You're dismissed," said Tang as he disconnected the call. He reached out and took a satisfying gulp of golden cognac, holding it up to the glow of the red desk lamp as he swallowed the smooth nectar. He placed the tumbler on a coaster and activated a comm to his personal secretary.

"Miss Liu, please get our deputy security chief on the line."

"Yes, Mr Tang."

A few moments later, a comm line lit up and Tang took the call.

"You know who this is?"

"Yes, sir," said the voice on the other end.

"Congratulations. You've just been promoted."

"Promoted? Thank you, sir. What happened to ...?"

"He was underperforming and had to accept forced retirement. I'm expecting you to do better."

"Of course, sir. I'll do my very best."

Tang took another sip, then said, "You are aware of our recently failed efforts to procure a certain asset?"

"Yes, I am sir."

"Where is the asset now?"

"Our tracking system indicates that it's on the move again. It's just left JUDAN headquarters and appears to be heading to the airport."

"Keep tracking it and mount a retrieval operation as soon as possible. In the meantime, I also want you to maintain close surveillance on the JUDAN building. The woman who was staying in the same house is now a priority target as well and we don't know whether she is travelling with the asset or still in the building. Her name is Kelly Rearson. She is highly valuable to us and must be taken alive. Watch all the exits, including the rooftop landing pad. Is all of that clear?"

"Yes, sir."

"Don't fail me. I don't want to have to retire you as well."

47

George arrived shortly after 9:00 am the next morning and took Kelly and Daniel to a secure meeting room on the 60th floor. The room was dominated by a large rectangular table, and the entire back wall was a floor to ceiling window, giving expansive views of the city and its suburbs. Two Justice Department lawyers were already seated at the table waiting for them, and introductions were made.

The lead lawyer was Claudia Fallon, a hard-faced woman in her 50s, dressed in a no-nonsense grey business suit. Her short, grey-streaked hair was sticking out at odd angles, looking like it had never been brushed in its life. Her dark-suited companion, Saul Berring, looked to be in his late 40s and his dark hair, by comparison, looked as if it had been styled to within an inch of its life and sprayed with lacquer. Neither smiled as they were introduced.

George Mallard sat next to Claudia Fallon, and Kelly and Daniel sat opposite them. Saul Berring fiddled with his desk-mounted recording gear while Claudia explained what was about to happen.

"These testimonies that you are about to provide will be recorded and used as initial evidence to procure indictments, arrest warrants and search warrants. But they won't be able to be used in a trial. Prior to the trial, you will need to be properly deposed, in the presence of defence lawyers who will have the right to cross examine you under oath. That deposition will be recorded and used in the trial proper. Do you have any questions?"

They both shook their heads.

"Good. We'll start with you first Mr Mendez, and we'll ask Dr Rearson to wait in the adjoining room."

"Newman," said Kelly, her tone expressing a measure of annoyance.

"What?" asked Fallon.

"His name is Daniel Newman."

"Not legally," she answered. "As far as the law is concerned, his name is Daniel Mendez. Whatever name he was given by his liberators is irrelevant."

"Captors, not liberators," said Kelly, getting angrier.

"Dr Rearson, he is a condemned prisoner who should have already been executed. He was illegally set free, taken to safety and given a false identity. The courts will view that as liberation, not capture."

"But he's ..."

Daniel placed a hand on her arm and said, "It's okay, Kelly. I'll handle this. Why don't you go and grab a coffee?"

She glared at Fallon for a few more seconds, then got to her feet and marched out of the room.

"Good. Let's get started," said Fallon. She looked at Berring. "Start recording."

Daniel's session took longer than expected. They took him through his entire experience, day by day, often going back to a previous day to clarify a point that later became pertinent. Finally, the questions ended, and Daniel asked, "Will this be enough to get them arrested?"

"Along with Dr Rearson's testimony, yes," replied Fallon, as she finished tapping on her data pad. "You did very well, Mr Mendez."

Daniel bridled at the mention of that name, but let it pass. "What is being done to secure some kind of pardon for me? After all, I don't have any first-hand knowledge or memory of Mendez's past crimes. That persona has been completely erased from my brain."

Fallon glanced uneasily at George who was sitting beside her, then said, "We will certainly be making an argument for your pardon, but there are no guarantees."

"I thought JUDAN, the Justice Department of the Allied Nations, no less, could guarantee me clemency?"

George answered, "We could certainly grant you immunity from prosecution for any crimes you might have committed over the last couple of weeks, in return for your testimony. But your past convictions are an entirely different matter. You were convicted and sentenced in a court of law, and only an appeal to a higher court can now overturn that conviction."

"But surely there is a strong case, for me being a completely different person?"

"It is certainly an argument that we will be making," said Fallon, "but you need to understand that it is an argument that currently has no legal precedent. There has never been a person who has been legally declared to be a completely new person in the same body. This is much more than a mere change of name. The court will have to be convinced that the persona, once known as Daniel Mendez, no longer exists."

"When will you be presenting my case?"

"We have a hearing before a High Court Judge a tomorrow," said Fallon. "We'll have to see how it goes from there. The testimony that Dr Rearson is about to give, regarding the physiological changes to your brain, will be absolutely vital to our argument."

"Hang in there, Daniel," said George. "We're going to do all we can to help you."

"What happens if you fail to convince the judge?"

There was an awkward silence. "Let's not worry about that until we have to," said George.

They broke for lunch, which consisted of self-serve food arranged on a central table in an adjoining room. After loading their plates, Kelly, Daniel and Carlos sat at a small circular table near the transparent wall, eating their lunch as they gazed out at the city below.

"So, they still can't guarantee you a pardon?" asked Kelly.

"No. They have to be convinced that Mendez no longer exists, and that might prove difficult."

"Not if I can help it. I'll convince them, Daniel."

"Thanks. I appreciate your optimism. But I have to face the possibility that ..."

"Stop!" Kelly exclaimed. She gripped his arm and leant toward him. "Here's today's truth. Are you ready for it?"

"What's this?" asked Carlos.

"I made the mistake of officially accepting her as my friend," said Daniel. "Now she gets to tell me stuff. I didn't realise what I was getting myself into at the time."

"Always read the fine print before you commit, bro."

"Are you boys finished?" asked Kelly, with mock severity. "As I was saying, here's today's truth: Stay positive! Stop living tomorrow's problems today!"

"That's technically two truths, and you only get one per day," said Daniel.

"Yeah, but I missed giving you one yesterday, so this is a catch up."

Daniel looked at Carlos. "Can she do that?"

"I haven't read the fine print, bro, but I think she might have a point."

The missile burst through the window, narrowly missing Daniel's head and exploding against the far wall of the room. A fireball engulfed them, and people were screaming. Daniel was thrown to the floor, a piece of shrapnel jutting out of his shoulder. An armed intruder ran into the room and started firing a laser gun. Daniel got to his feet and rushed the intruder as the weapon swept toward him and Kelly. He tackled the man to the ground and smashed the hand holding the weapon to the ground, forcing him to release it.

Someone grabbed him and pulled him off the intruder.

"Daniel! Daniel! What are you doing? Stop it, Daniel!"

He was pinned to the ground now and couldn't move, staring at the flames engulfing the ceiling.

"Daniel! It's alright! Nothing bad is happening." He saw Kelly's face above him. "Focus on me. You're okay now."

The flames disappeared and the room returned to its former state. Daniel looked around in confusion. "What ... what just happened?"

"I don't know, dude, you tell us," said Carlos, who was kneeling beside him.

"There ... there was a missile. It exploded ... and fire ... and a man with a gun."

"You tackled a waiter, dude. He was holding a jug of juice."

Daniel shook his head and looked at Kelly. "What's happening to me?"

"I don't know."

48

C arlos accompanied Daniel back down to their basement apartment, to rest after his bizarre break with reality. Meanwhile, Kelly met with the lawyers to record her testimony. Once again, Claudia Fallon took the lead role as questioner, with her associate, Saul Berring, sitting beside her monitoring the recording equipment and only making occasional contributions. George Mallard, the Senior Investigator with JUDAN, sat alongside Fallon, keeping watch over the proceedings.

Sitting opposite them, Kelly tried to dispel the notion that she was on trial. The meeting began with them showing her a signed document guaranteeing her immunity from prosecution, in return for her testimony. Not that she had committed any crimes, because as the interview progressed, it became abundantly clear that she had not taken an active part in the unlawful experimentation on humans and had, in fact, immediately raised the alarm when she became aware of those illegal experiments.

The first part of Kelly's testimony related to the technology that she had helped to develop. She explained about the quest for QEBS, Quantum Enhanced Biological Sentience, a truly sentient artificial intelligence. She discussed how it was believed that true sentient artificial intelligence was only going to be possible with quantum computers, but that up until now, the essential sub-atomic elements of a quantum computer, qubits, could only survive and operate at an extreme temperature of minus 273 degrees Celsius.

She explained, "For decades, scientists have been desperately searching for a way to make qubits function effectively at room temperature. The theory is that it might be possible to manufacture a molecule inside which qubits could operate at normal temperatures. Senticorp have developed such a molecule."

"And you helped them develop the molecule?" prompted Fallon.

"Yes. Blakely hired me ..."

"For the record, Dr Nigel Blakely?"

"Yes. He hired me because of my previous work with molecular design. His team had reached a bottleneck in their research, and I was able to help provide the breakthrough. We designed the first room temperature quantum computer. At first it was only a few molecules of processing power, but even that was thousands of times faster than a standard computer. The problem with the molecule, however, is that it needs a biological host to survive for more than a few minutes. So, we inserted the molecules into the brains of rats and used nanobot technology to grow the molecules into micron-thin structures that permeated every part of the brain. The molecules bind to neurons in the brain. In essence, the super-fast quantum computer residing in the molecules is blended with the natural senses and cognition of the brain."

"And then they started doing that to humans?" prompted Fallon.

"Not at first. It was always the end goal, of course, the ideal that one day we might be able to use this technology to assist people with brain injuries. But it was understood by everyone in the laboratory that that sort of thing was still decades away, subject to all the usual legal loopholes and approvals."

"So, when did you become aware that Senticorp had circumvented those due processes?"

"About 18 months ago. I contacted JUDAN straight away."

Kelly went on to disclose how she had become aware of a succession of people being injected with the quantum molecules by Doctors Nigel Blakely and Marsha Nordstrom, as well as her growing suspicions that the test subjects were not surviving.

Claudia Fallon questioned Kelly for a considerable period, extracting evidence that could be used to indict Blakely and others of a number of felony charges. Finally, she was satisfied that she had enough, and they moved on to Daniel's specific case.

"The key issue regarding Mr Mendez's situation..." began Fallon.

"Mr Newman," corrected Kelly.

"Well, that is precisely the dilemma, isn't it Dr Rearson? Is there any way it can be proved that the persona of Daniel Mendez no longer resides in Daniel's brain? In what sense has it been erased?"

"I can answer that question at two levels. Firstly, as a research scientist, I can assure you that the invasion of Daniel's brain by the quantum molecule structures has irreparably altered his persona and erased the episodic memories that defined who Daniel Mendez once was. These significant changes were certainly evident in the experiments we did with animals. As our research progressed, we eventually began to experiment with higher order animals such as dogs and monkeys. In every case, once the new quantum molecule structures were in place in their brains, these animals lost all memory of previous learnt behaviour and no longer recognised their previous owners or previous siblings and parents. Furthermore, we also noted global personality changes. Animals that were once aggressive or uncooperative became gentle and compliant; they had totally different personalities. Brain scans of these animals revealed that the new quantum molecules had significantly altered the signal paths in the hippocampus, neocortex, and amygdala. All three of these form the reservoir of an individual's memories and are at the very heart of who they are."

Kelly concluded, "In short, I can guarantee that Daniel Mendez is gone. Not only does Daniel Newman have none of

Mendez's memories, but he also has a completely new personality."

"I see," said Fallon, who appeared to be less than completely convinced.

George prompted Kelly further, "You said you can answer this question at two levels. The first was as a research scientist. What is the second?"

"At a personal level, I can attest that the personality traits that the new Daniel exhibits are the antithesis of Mendez as I understand him to have been. He was, by all accounts, a callous, vindictive, cruel sociopath. The new Daniel is none of those things. He is warm, empathetic and highly principled, and demonstrates an undeniable abhorrence for the things that Mendez did."

"So, you're basically saying that the courts should let him walk free because you think he's a nice guy now," said Fallon.

"No. That's not what I'm saying, and you know it! I'm saying that as a research scientist I can guarantee that his brain is significantly different to that of Mendez, and I can see that difference clearly demonstrated by Daniel's attitudes and actions."

"The judge is going to need more than just the opinion of a scientist," said Fallon. "No disrespect intended. To make the kind of landmark decision we are going to be asking for, the judge will want to see some kind of hard evidence – perhaps before and after images of Daniel's brain wave activity or something similar."

"I'm sure those kinds of images will be on Senticorp files somewhere," responded Kelly. "I assume you will be taking all their records into custody?"

"Yes, we will," answered George. "And we'll be prioritising the search for images of that nature."

"It would also be wise to arrange for a psychiatric evaluation," suggested Saul Berring, Fallon's assistant.

"Yes," agreed Fallon, looking at him. "Get it done this afternoon."

George asked Fallon, "Have you got everything you need? Are we done here?"

"Yes, we are," answered Fallon. Turning to Kelly, she said,

"Thank you, Dr Rearson. On the basis of the testimonies we've recorded here today, we won't have any trouble obtaining immediate indictments. You're free to go."

As Kelly stood to her feet, she asked, "What about Daniel's case? What's the chance of him being granted a pardon?"

"For that to occur, the judge will have to recognise him as a new, distinct persona."

"I'm aware of that, but that wasn't my question. What are his chances?"

Fallon glanced at George Mallard then back to Kelly. "Thirty percent at best."

49

D aniel was rushed to a quickly arranged psychiatric evaluation and was gone for several hours. He arrived back at the basement apartment after 7:00 pm to find Kelly and Carlos creating chaos in the kitchen. There were pots and cooking paraphernalia everywhere and Kelly had somehow managed to smear what looked like pastry mix through her hair.

"Wow, you guys are busy," Daniel commented as he entered the disaster area.

"I'm cooking my secret culinary weapon – creamy gnocchi fungi – guaranteed to win over a man's heart," said Kelly.

"Or a woman's, I presume," replied Daniel.

Kelly looked momentarily discomforted and then rallied. "Yes, that's true." She smiled at Daniel and pushed a strand of wayward hair out of her eyes, adding another blob of white goo to her forehead and her hair in the process.

"What can I do to help?" he asked.

"Just sit and relax," answered Kelly. "You've had a pretty tiring day. We've got this!"

Carlos grabbed a beer from a cupboard and placed it in the insta-chiller for ten seconds then handed it to Daniel who sat at the small dining table to the side of the kitchen.

"Drink up, bro. We're celebrating. George has just informed us that the arrests have been made."

"Wow! That was quick!"

"Yeah. A bunch of the bad guys are now locked up: Dr Nigel Blakely, Dr Marsha Nordstrom, Nurse Sylvia Stratham, and several security personnel whom you identified."

"And what about the laboratory?" asked Daniel.

"The whole of Senticorp has been sealed off and is under 24-hour guard by JUDAN officers. A digital forensic team is onsite, sifting through their records."

"We got them, Daniel!" said Kelly. She seemed exuberant, as if a great weight had been lifted off her shoulders. As she turned and smiled at him, her hair a mess and her face smeared with goo, Daniel had an overwhelming urge to hold her in his arms and kiss her. He shook his head to try to dislodge the idea – an idea that he knew would never come to fruition given Kelly's previous admission about her sexuality.

"Why are you shaking your head?" asked Kelly, frowning slightly.

"I ... um ... was just wondering what's going to happen to me now."

"That's the problem for another day," said Carlos. "Tonight is for celebrating! Drink up, dude! It's craft beer that I ordered in especially."

"Yes, tonight you have to abide by my truth, remember?" said Kelly.

Daniel had a sip of beer and said, "Which one? There were two as I recall."

"Both! Stay positive and stop living tomorrow's problems today."

"Are you going to be writing all these down? Because if there's going to be a new one each day, I'm going to have trouble remembering them all."

"Yes, that's a great suggestion," said Kelly as she stirred a creamy concoction that was simmering on the micro-pulse cooker.

"I think I'll publish it as a book. I'll call it, 'Kelly's Hints for a Happy Life'."

"You could subtitle it, 'Practical Tips for Gloomy Pessimists'," suggested Carlos. "Perhaps we could even put a picture of Daniel's face looking glum on the cover."

"Ha, ha, you two. Very funny."

Half an hour later, with the kitchen looking like a chaos bomb had gone off, they were sitting at the table eating together and drinking wine.

"Well, what do you think?" Kelly asked Daniel, her eyes shining with enthusiasm.

Daniel looked at her and his heart melted again. "Beautiful. Absolutely beautiful. Although your hair is a mess and there's still some goo on your face."

She slapped him on the arm. "Not me, you goose! The gnocchi!"

"Oh, that!" He smiled. "That's beautiful too. You'll make someone a wonderful wife someday ... or ... um ... whatever it is you call it ..."

She laughed. "Wife is fine." She looked at Carlos. "What about you, Carlos? Is there someone special in your life?"

"No. My job is pretty intense. It doesn't leave much time for intimate relationships. But one day I'd like to settle down and find somewhere peaceful to raise a whole bunch of chubby little cherubs. Some place in the country where I can grow vegetables and go fishing occasionally."

"Sounds wonderful," said Kelly. "I wonder where I'll end up after this. This whole witness protection thing is a big unknown."

Carlos nodded sympathetically. "On the positive side," he said, "I don't think your life is in any real danger now that we've made the arrests. We've got the bad guys locked up and they don't pose a threat any longer."

"What about Blackstar?" asked Daniel.

"That's a different matter, dude," agreed Carlos. "All we have are suspicions about their involvement, but we don't have any hard evidence. No one was captured and there is nothing physically tying them to any of the violence in recent days. But as far as Kelly is concerned, we don't think they pose any threat. They were only after you, Daniel, not her."

"So, they could remain a threat to Daniel?" asked Kelly.

"Yes. If Daniel's case is successful and he is granted his freedom, we will have to enrol him in our witness protection scheme as well."

Daniel dived into the clear sparkling water. It was a beautiful aqua-blue and was lukewarm. Columns of coral rose from the seabed and hundreds of brightly coloured tropical fish were swimming in and out of the structures. Daniel swam down, equalising the pressure in his ears as he did so. He swam around a huge column of pink coral and saw two electric eels entwined in an intricate mating dance, their vivid blue colouring looking iridescent in the crystal-clear water. He pushed back up to the surface and breathed in the warm tropical air, spending a few moments floating on his back with his eyes closed, revelling in the sun's warm rays.

Turning back over, he dived again, quickly reaching the bottom and then swimming between the columns of coral, watching tiny, coloured fish dart in and out of their homes in the living aquatic forest.

"Daniel! Daniel! Open your eyes!"

He felt a tug on his arm and saw Kelly swimming behind him. How was she able to speak underwater?

"Daniel! Can you hear me? Open your eyes!"

But my eyes are open, he thought. He beckoned her to follow him and started to swim again, but she held onto his arm and pulled him back.

"Daniel! You're dreaming again. Open your eyes! Please, Daniel."

He opened his eyes. He was lying face down on the floor. *How did I get here?* He sat up, blinking as he tried to process the sudden shift in reality. Carlos and Kelly were kneeling beside him, concern etched deeply into their faces.

"What were you doing, dude?" asked Carlos.

"I ... I was swimming. There was coral and ... fish. It was beautiful. And it was so real." He looked at his friends. "What's happening to me?"

No one said anything for a moment. No one needed to. Because it was very clear that something was very wrong with Daniel. And it was getting worse.

50

Daniel must have dreamed again overnight, because they found him sleeping on the loungeroom floor the next morning. He couldn't remember how he had gotten there or what he'd dreamed. What was troubling about these episodes was the vivid nature of the dreams and their extremely sudden onset. Even more concerning was the fact that Daniel was now having episodes during the day, while he was awake. These were clearly more than just dreams; they were psychotic episodes.

George was called down for an urgent meeting, shortly after breakfast. After he was briefed on the latest overnight episodes, he asked Kelly, "Do you have any idea what is going on?"

"Unfortunately, I think I do." She looked at Daniel, uneasily.

"Go on. I'm listening," said Daniel.

"We witnessed this kind of increasing episodic psychosis in some of the animals we experimented on. It's one of the reasons why we thought it was much too soon to even think about human trials."

"It didn't seem to worry Blakely and his little gang," said Daniel.

"No. They're monsters for what they've done to you, Daniel."

"Do you know what's causing these psychotic episodes?" asked George.

"It's complicated, but I'll try to explain it as clearly as I can." She paused and considered her words carefully. "The quantum-friendly molecules are introduced to the brain and, via pre-programed nanobots, are replicated and multiplied to form a pervasive structure throughout the brain – tiny filaments only a micron in diameter. These filaments attach to the neurons – specifically to the axon terminals. This is effectively like attaching a powerful booster to an aerial or ramping up the sensitivity of a digital array. Of course, until the quantum programming in these filaments is initialised, the new structure just sits there doing nothing. At least it should do nothing."

"But sometimes it does do something?" asked Carlos.

"Yes. Kind of. You see, there is a structure throughout the brain called the limbic system. It's a linked structure that permeates most areas of the brain and has strong links to the hypothalamus, amygdala and hippocampus. In some of the animals we studied, the new quantum molecule filaments caused the limbic structure to become over-sensitive – over-stimulated if you like – and the animals became increasingly psychotic, experiencing an escalating series of psychotic breaks with reality."

She paused, unwilling to go on.

George asked the question they were all thinking. "What happened to those animals in the end?"

Kelly looked at Daniel, then looked away. "If left untreated, their psychotic episodes became increasingly frequent, and their lucid moments became increasingly rare. In the end, they ... um ... they became completely psychotic, living in their own over-stimulated imaginations, no longer able to sense the real world around them. We had to put them down."

Daniel was staring at the floor, nodding his head. "Uh huh," was all he said.

"You said 'if left untreated'. So, there is a treatment?" asked George.

"We tried all sorts of things including electroshock therapy and administering antipsychotics. The only thing that worked was initialising the quantum system in the molecular filaments. Once the quantum structures were activated, the filaments were no longer sitting there acting as a kind of passive aerial for the limbic system to latch onto. The activation of the qubits – the quantum particles within the molecular structure – rendered the new structure unreadable or unrecognisable to the limbic system, and the psychosis ceased almost immediately."

Kelly continued. "Think of it like tuning a digital aerial. If it is untuned, the aerial just generates massive static, magnifying all kinds of rubbish that is residual across the electromagnetic spectrum. But once it is tuned to the correct, precise frequency, all the static and rubbish is excluded, and you get a clear picture. That's what initialising the quantum system did in most cases."

"What do you mean, 'in most cases'?" asked Carlos.

Once again, Kelly looked uncomfortable. "On two occasions, the quantum molecule filaments must have been poorly formed or faulty in some way. When we initialised the system, they … had some kind of a meltdown. The animals suffered massive brain seizures and died."

"And what about the other cases - the ones who were successful?" asked George.

"Their psychosis ceased abruptly. Unfortunately, the early ones only lived for several more days. The active quantum system seemed to be short-circuiting their neurons. That was the point at which Dr Blakely began experimenting with humans. He thought that the human brain could cope better with the activated quantum system. But, of course, he was wrong. The victims in the human trial died too. It was only toward the end that we developed the new enzyme, to form a perfect bond between the quantum filaments and the neurons."

Daniel looked at Kelly. "Why didn't you tell me about the psychosis before this?"

"Because the psychosis complication only occurred in about 25 percent of cases in our experiments on animals. We still don't know why some test subjects were susceptible to it while most were not. I was just hoping that you were one of the lucky 75 percent. I didn't want to worry you unnecessarily."

Daniel nodded. "I see." He leant forward and rested his head in his hands, then looked at Kelly again. "So, what you're saying is that if we do nothing, I'm eventually going to lose touch with reality and become completely psychotic."

Kelly had tears in her eyes now, and her voice was barely a whisper. "Yes. Your psychotic episodes will become increasingly frequent and longer in duration. Eventually you will become permanently disconnected from the real world."

Daniel nodded. "Uh huh."

Kelly reached out her hand and gripped his arm. "But there is hope, Daniel! We could initialise the quantum system. It would definitely resolve the psychosis!"

"As long as the quantum structures in my brain are properly formed and don't melt down in the process," said Daniel.

"But that was only in the very early cases, Daniel. The nanobot programming, which was responsible for the formation of the structures, was refined over time. None of the later cases experienced a meltdown."

"And then what?" he asked. "The quantum system has never been successfully initialised in a human brain, has it? We have no idea what would happen."

Kelly nodded, a tear sliding down her cheek as she did so. "That's true. We don't know what will happen. You would be the first human to have the system fully initialised. But I don't think we have a choice."

"There's no 'we' involved here," he responded. "Surely, it's my choice and mine alone."

Once again, Kelly nodded. "Yes. I guess it is."

"So, I have to decide whether I want to gradually slide into psychotic oblivion or have a quantum computer switched on inside my head with completely unknown consequences."

There was silence in the room for several moments.

"Yes," Kelly whispered. "That appears to be the choice."

"How would you go about initialising the system?" asked George. "Do we have the facilities here?"

"No. The technology and specific software is at Senticorp, in the B2 lab. We would have to take Daniel back to Quito."

"How much time do I have left?" asked Daniel, looking directly at Kelly.

Kelly's face fell. "Once psychotic episodes start occurring while awake, the progression is quite rapid."

"How long, Kelly? Tell me."

"You probably have less than 48 hours before complete psychosis takes over."

Daniel nodded and looked at the floor.

"I'm so sorry Daniel," Kelly said, reaching out and gripping his arm. But Daniel was no longer listening. His eyes had glazed over, and he began making strange sounds and movements. His psychosis had swallowed him again and he was no longer with them.

51

The comm light blinked in the darkened room. A pale, almost pure white hand festooned with gold rings reached out and accepted the call.

"Speak."

"Mr Tang, it's …"

"Yes, I know who you are! Get on with it."

"The asset was taken to their International Headquarters in Zurich. We have a surveillance team in place and an exfiltration team ready to move at a moment's notice."

"Withdraw your men."

"Sir?"

"Withdraw them all. You're wasting your time. It's a decoy."

"A decoy?"

"It's a damned cat!"

"A cat? How do you know?"

"Don't question me! Ever!" He paused to calm himself and took a sip of cognac. "I have a highly-placed, reliable source. Our two targets, the man and the woman, are still in the Pittsburgh building. I want eyes on that building. Watch every exit, including the landing pad on the roof. Station men on the rooftops of surrounding buildings. They can't stay in that building forever, and when they leave, I want to know where they go."

"Yes, sir."

52

Soon after lunch Daniel was summoned to a meeting with the two solicitors to discuss his case. Once again George was part of the discussion, and Daniel had asked that Kelly be present as well. There was no recording gear this time; just two grim faced lawyers bringing him some news. As in the previous meeting, the stern featured Claudia Fallon did the talking while her offsider, Saul Berring, sat beside her.

"Mr Mendez," began Fallon.

"Newman," interjected Kelly.

"Leave it, Kelly," said Daniel. "I think I can already see where this is heading."

"Mr Mendez," Fallon said again, "We spent over an hour in a formal session with one of our high court judges first thing this morning. We made our argument for the legal recognition of you as a new persona, distinct from Daniel Mendez, and therefore not guilty of Mendez's crimes. We presented the evidence we had gathered yesterday, including Dr Rearson's expert testimony and the psychiatric report. The judge considered the issue carefully and, because we are on a very tight timeframe with this case, she was kind enough to expedite a finding a few moments ago. I have an extract that I would like to read to you."

"Okay," said Daniel. "Let's hear it."

Fallon tapped her data pad screen and then began to read.

"This court acknowledges the many positive changes in character and temperament that have been observed in Daniel Mendez in recent days. The explanation that these changes have resulted from the persona known as Daniel Mendez being wiped from his brain seems highly conjectural at best. Our experience in dealing with convicted felons, particularly those whose crimes warrant the death penalty, is that they often undergo a 'born again' type of transformation when they are faced with their impending execution. While these transformations may well be genuine, often arising from sincere remorse over the felon's past actions, the transformations do not cancel the serious nature of their previous offences nor quash the sentences imposed. Justice must still be served. Furthermore, it is beyond the bounds of this court, as well as beyond the bounds of all sensible reason, to infer from a transformed character that one persona has been extinguished and another has somehow been born in its place. There is no precedent for this court to assert that two separate people can inhabit the same body, albeit one after the other, and this court finds no incontrovertible evidence sufficient to set such a precedent. It is the finding of this court, therefore, that Daniel Mendez be returned to confinement and that the sentence of execution previously imposed upon him be duly carried out."

There was stunned silence in the room. Kelly began quietly sobbing and Daniel hung his head.

Kelly wiped her eyes and glared at the two lawyers. "How hard did you try?"

"We presented the strongest possible argument, Dr Rearson," said Fallon.

"I doubt that. In fact, I doubt it very much! I could tell, yesterday, that neither of you were convinced about Daniel's new persona. So, if you don't believe it, I can't imagine that you were very convincing when you presented the argument to the judge."

"Judges prefer to deal in facts and hard evidence, Dr Rearson," said Fallon. "They are not often swayed by conjecture or opinion, even from someone as respectable as yourself. Unfortunately, in this case, there was not enough tangible evidence to support our argument. It was always going to be a remote chance at best."

"When does he have to go back to prison?" asked George, who looked and sounded crestfallen.

"As soon as possible. This afternoon if that can be arranged."

Kelly shot to her feet. "I withdraw my testimony!"

"What do you mean?" asked Fallon.

"If this is how you are going to treat Daniel, if the court is determined to execute an innocent man, then I refuse to help. I refuse to testify."

Claudia Fallon's mouth opened and closed several times, but no words came out.

"I refuse to testify, too," said Daniel. He looked up at Kelly and tried to put on a brave face.

"And without our testimonies," continued Kelly, "you really don't have a case against Senticorp."

"We have Lee Chen, the security guard," quipped Fallon.

"Sure," agreed Kelly. "He might help you get a few gun-happy security guards convicted of firing their weapons unlawfully, but he knows nothing about the major crimes that went on in that laboratory. Without our testimonies, Nigel Blakely and the other key players will walk free, and you'll be left with egg on your face." She stared at Fallon until the older woman was forced to look away.

Fallon drummed her fingers on the desk, biting her lip. "So, you're asking for some kind of reduced sentence in return for your testimonies?"

"We're asking for a complete pardon," said Kelly.

"You won't get it."

"You haven't asked yet," said Kelly.

Fallon shook her head as she considered the proposal. "A capital case like this can't just be pardoned. Not by a high court judge."

"Then take it to someone who can."

George cleared his throat. "Ms Fallon, why don't you go back to your judge and explain the situation. I'm sure she is very keen to see Senticorp brought to justice. See what kind of deal can be made. In the meantime, I will make representations to the Chief of JUDAN in Zurich, to see what can be done from our end."

Fallon nodded. "Very well. I'll try to get an answer this afternoon."

53

"How long was I gone that time?" asked Daniel. It was late afternoon and Daniel had experienced two more episodes since their meeting with the lawyers.

"Nearly 15 minutes," answered Carlos.

"The episodes are getting longer," said Kelly.

"Yes, but you're not moving around as much anymore," said Carlos. "This time you just sat in the chair, with a blank expression on your face."

"Where were you this time?" asked Kelly.

"I was inside some kind of giant silver sphere that was rotating around me. Then the sphere opened, and I floated out into a dark void that gradually began to fill with swirling-coloured shapes. There was a lot more, but I can't adequately describe it."

"Your episodes are becoming increasingly abstract and unrelated to the real world," said Kelly. "Unfortunately, that is typical of spiralling psychosis. I wish I had good news for you, Daniel, but this is only going to continue getting worse unless we intervene."

"You mean switch on the quantum computer in my brain."

"Yes."

"Without really knowing what it's going to do," Daniel persisted.

"We can't know for sure. But one thing we can be certain of is that if we don't do anything, you are going to become completely catatonic and unresponsive within another day or two."

"It won't make much difference in the long run," said Daniel. "If they're going to execute me anyway, what's the point of trying to fix the psychosis?"

"Don't give up hope, Daniel."

"Is that your truth for today?" he asked.

"Yes, it is. Hope is the ability to see the light, even when you're surrounded by darkness."

"Is that some kind of famous quote?" asked Daniel.

"No. I just made it up. Pretty good, hey?"

Daniel smiled. "You should put it in your book. It's just a shame I won't be around to read it."

"Don't talk like that, Daniel! We have leverage. They are desperate to convict Blakely and his gang. They need our testimonies – especially mine. I'm pretty sure they're going to cut a deal."

The front door to the basement apartment opened and George walked in.

"They're going to cut you a deal," he announced without preamble as he sat in the loungeroom with the others.

"What kind of deal?" asked Daniel.

"The International Chief of JUDAN, our 'el supremo' in Zurich, had a lengthy conversation with the Attorney General for the Alliance of Nations. They are willing to commute your death sentence to a life sentence, with the possibility of parole after a minimum period of ten years. Plus, you will serve your sentence in a minimum-security prison. After two or three years, providing your behaviour is exemplary, you will be granted day release for outside employment."

"That's not good enough!" said Kelly. "Daniel deserves a full pardon!"

"It's the best deal he's going to get," responded George. He looked at Daniel. "It's a good deal, Daniel. I'd take it if I were you."

Daniel nodded. "It's actually better than I'd hoped for. I guess I'll ..." Daniel's eyes glazed over, and he was gone again.

Eighteen minutes later, Daniel blinked and looked around him. Kelly was looking at him with concern. George and Carlos were no longer there.

"How long?" Daniel asked Kelly.

"18 minutes."

He nodded.

She came and sat beside him. "We really need to fix this problem. It's getting worse. Soon your psychotic episodes will be longer than your lucid moments. We need to initialise the quantum system in your brain, Daniel. It's the only way to stop the psychosis."

He nodded. "Yeah. You're right."

She took his hand. "You're going to live a long and happy life, Daniel Newman. You're going to get through this and come out the other side."

"But what's on the other side?"

"I'll be on the other side. I'm your friend, and you're stuck with me."

"You gay girls sure are persistent."

"You bet we are!" She smiled and kissed him on the cheek. "Now, freshen up if you need to, because we're leaving for Quito as soon as possible. George and Carlos are arranging the details as we speak."

As if on cue, George's face appeared on the comm screen on the loungeroom wall. Kelly accepted the call, and George began to explain what was happening.

"I've been in contact with the high court judge overseeing your case here in Pittsburgh. She has been instructed by the Attorney General and is now processing the documentation for your commuted sentence. She has also granted us permission to take you to Quito for medical treatment for your condition."

"How soon do we leave?" asked Kelly.

"Carlos is on his way down to collect you now."

54

Eli Tang made a call to his new Head of Security.

"Sir?" answered the voice.

"I have new information," said Tang. "They're going back to Quito; to the Senticorp laboratory. They are going to initialise the quantum system. I want you to assemble a team at Quito and wait for them there."

"You want me to stop them from doing that?"

"No. Of course not! Let them finish the job. It will make the prize much more valuable. Allow them to complete the initialisation before you make a move."

"Yes, sir."

"Now listen carefully. Here is what I want you to do ..."

55

Daniel had another episode during the skipjet flight to Quito. He slipped into psychosis as the plane was taking off and did not regain normal consciousness until the plane was descending back through the Earth's upper atmosphere.

"You mean I missed our whole time in space?" he asked Kelly, who was sitting beside him this time.

"Afraid so. But you didn't miss much. Just spectacular stars, an amazing view of the moon, and a flying saucer filled with little green men who were waving and taking photos of us."

"Oh well, in that case it was hardly worth staying awake for." He smiled at her and glanced out the porthole window, watching the contrails stream off the wing as the plane descended into the thickening atmosphere. The ground wasn't visible, hidden underneath a thick carpet of fluffy clouds which were still far below them.

"Kelly, I want to thank you for what you did today. By threatening to withdraw your testimony, you literally saved my life. I'd be headed back to jail and certain execution if it wasn't for you."

"I couldn't let the bastards treat you like that, Daniel. You clearly don't deserve to be punished for something that you would never even remotely consider doing now and have absolutely no memory of doing in the past. It's so unfair that you still have to go to prison at all."

"I understand their perspective, though," said Daniel. "They have to be seen to be carrying out justice, and there is no legal precedent for accepting that the same body can contain two distinct people, consecutively."

Kelly shook her head in frustration. "It all comes down to the question of what constitutes a person. One day, maybe soon, the law will have to recognise that the essence of a person's consciousness and persona doesn't reside in the arms and legs and guts of a physical body, but in the mind, and the mind can be wiped and made new. As it stands, the fools don't realise they're punishing the wrong person, because Mendez is gone."

"I can live with my punishment. I'm not happy about it, but I can live with it. There's a sense that it might even help me – help me to feel that appropriate consequences are being enforced for my past crimes."

"For Mendez's past crimes, you mean."

"I guess. Although I will always carry around a measure of guilt for what I – he – did. In fact, when I finally get released, I want to do something to try to make up for my – his – past. Something that will help others and give back to the community."

"Like what?"

"I don't know. I might get a degree and become a social worker or a nurse. Or maybe I could study law and do community law work, helping the victims of crimes and injustice."

"You're a good man, Daniel Newman."

"Not really. I'm a bad man just trying to make a fresh start." He looked out the window. "Of course, this whole conversation could be moot if my brain ends up getting fried." He looked back at her. "What's the chance of success?"

"I really don't know. I'd like to tell you not to worry, but the truth is, this has never been done before with a human. This is brand new territory. There are several different scenarios that could play out." She hesitated, biting her lip.

"Go on. Tell me. I'm a big boy, I can take it. Besides, friends always tell each other the truth. Remember?"

"I hate it when people quote me back to myself."

"I'm waiting."

"Okay. The first possibility is that the initialisation could be a success, your new personality remains intact, and you end up with a whole lot of processing power inside your head."

"That's my favourite one so far," he said.

"The second, is that the initialisation could be a success, but your persona – the memories and personality that comprise the real you – gets wiped and you end up different again."

"So, Daniel Newman dies, just like Mendez did?"

"Yes," she said with reluctance.

"I'm not a huge fan of that one. What's next?"

"The third possibility is that the initialisation doesn't work at all, and you are left just as you are."

"Not so good, either," he said. "Next."

"The fourth is the possibility that the initialisation is partially successful. This would mean that the quantum molecule filaments become activated and no longer function as a booster for the limbic system, but the qubit physics within the molecule fail to do their thing. In this scenario you would be permanently cured of your psychosis but still be ..."

"Permanently dumb," finished Daniel.

"Dumb is a bit harsh," she countered playfully. "I would describe it as only mildly stupid."

"That's very kind of you."

"You're welcome."

"So far, I like numbers one and four," said Daniel. "But there's a fifth, isn't there? That's the scenario where you flick the switch, or whatever, and my brain is completely fried and I die, instantly."

"Yes. That is the final possibility. But I'm pretty sure that's not going to happen."

"But it could," he said.

"Unlikely."

"But possible," he persisted.

"Highly improbable."

"How improbable? Would you like to make a wager?" he asked.

"Sure," she said with a lopsided smile. "I'll bet you dinner at a nice restaurant that you won't die."

Daniel smiled. "So, if I live, I have to buy you dinner, but if I die, you have to buy me dinner?"

"Yep."

"Call me stupid, but there's something not quite right about that bet."

Kelly laughed. "It's a good bet. Come on, shake on it." She held out her hand toward him.

But Daniel's eyes had glazed over again. He was gone.

56

The skipjet landed at Quito airport but they had to wait nearly 30 additional minutes for Daniel to resurface before they could disembark. Once he regained normal consciousness they quickly transferred to a flitter and made the short flight to Senticorp. Both George and Carlos, the two Justice Department agents, were armed, but they weren't really expecting any trouble. The key players at Senticorp had all been arrested and the whole facility was now a crime scene. The only people onsite were JUDAN personnel – armed agents and digital forensics teams.

The sleek flitter landed on the rooftop landing pad and the four occupants disembarked and made their way to a lift. The lift quickly descended one floor to the executive level where Blakely's office and several other offices were located. The lift door opened, and they were greeted by an armed JUDAN agent who checked their IDs before allowing them to proceed down the corridor to the central lift.

A few minutes later, the four emerged into the circular foyer on B2 level where another armed agent was on duty. They walked across the foyer and down the corridor to the laboratory that was signposted, 'QEBS'.

"Quantum Enhanced Biological Sentience," said Daniel as

they drew near to the door. "My whole life has been ruined, because of one man's quest for glory."

"Not ruined, Daniel. Reborn. At least that's what we're all hoping for, today," said Kelly.

The lab was relatively quiet, compared to Daniel's previous visits. There were just two people sitting at workstations in the main laboratory area and two more in separate offices, all of them dressed in Justice Department uniforms. They all looked up and stared at Daniel as the group walked in, and Daniel thought he heard one of them whisper to the other, "He's the ninth protocol!"

The agent sitting at Marsha Nordstrom's desk came out and greeted them. "We've been expecting you, Agent Mallard," she said to George. "Is there anything we can do to help?"

"No. Dr Rearson, here, is in charge of proceedings from this point." He looked at Kelly. "Unless you need assistance?"

"No," Kelly answered. "It's a one-person job." She nodded toward the smaller lab where Daniel had undergone scans. "Is the lab free?"

"It's all yours, Dr Rearson."

They entered the smaller lab and Daniel saw the familiar equipment that he had come to regard with a degree of loathing. Now he was going to submit himself to a final procedure that could end his life or turn him into a vegetable. He felt a wave of panic sweep over him, and he had to supress an urge to turn and run.

"It's going to take about 10 minutes to get things ready," Kelly said. She sat at the main console and began activating the complex system, totally focused on her task while Daniel and the two men stood looking on.

"How are you feeling, bro?" asked Carlos.

"Pretty much what you'd expect when there's a possibility my brain might be about to melt down."

Carlos nodded. "Yeah, man. It doesn't get much heavier than this."

"I'm sure you'll be fine, Daniel," said George. "Kelly knows what she's doing."

"You do know what you're doing, don't you, Kelly?" asked Daniel.

"Yes. I've done this many times before; only on animals. The process is the same, though." She continued staring intently at several screens as various systems came online.

"So, what you're saying is that there's not much difference between Daniel's brain and the brain of a chimp?" asked Carlos.

"Not much," agreed Kelly, still concentrating on her tasks.

Carlos chuckled. "It doesn't surprise me. I always suspected there wasn't much going on up there."

"You're so encouraging, dude," said Daniel.

"Don't mention it."

"I just did."

"Well don't mention it again."

"You're so encouraging, dude," said Daniel with a smile.

"I told you not to mention it again!"

"I forgot. Remember, I've only got a monkey brain."

Both men smiled and nodded to one another, in recognition of their shared light-hearted ritual.

Soon afterward, Kelly announced that she was ready to begin the procedure. She handed Daniel a thin transparent skullcap and told him to put it on.

"This is different from the cap I wore during my scans," he said.

"Yes. The other cap was used just for scanning and mapping your neural pathways. This is a much more sophisticated interface. A NIT – neural interface transceiver."

"It's years since I've had nits," he said, trying to make light of the situation.

Kelly smiled and continued. "This NIT and its associated software is the most technologically advanced neural interface on the planet. No one else has anything like it. It has the ability to stimulate individual neurons of our choosing or, in this case, to target complex molecular structures such as your newly-developed quantum molecule filaments."

Daniel looked at the transparent cap in his hand, turning it over. "It just looks like clear silicone. There are no wires or electrodes or flashing gizmos."

"The NIT uses micro-circuitry. Millions of circuit pathways, only microns thick. Trust me, it's an incredibly complex piece of gear you're holding in your hand." She looked at him. "Are you ready to put it on?"

He nodded. "I guess so." He hesitated a moment longer, then slipped it onto his head.

"Looks like you're about to take a shower, bro," said Carlos.

Daniel looked at Kelly. "Just explain to me again; what will happen if this actually works? Will I suddenly know a whole lot of stuff I didn't know before?"

"No. It doesn't work like that. As with any computer system, facts and information need to be input to a computer before it can retain and recall that information. You won't know anything more than you already do. What should happen, if the system works, is that your brain will operate much more efficiently and quickly. You will be able to absorb, retain and understand new information many times faster than you currently can. For instance, you will probably be able to read a whole page of complex information at a single glance. You will think much faster and more clearly. And you will be able to solve problems rapidly."

"That's why George asked me what the square root of 1,081 was, on the night I first met him."

"Yes. You already know the basic rudiments of maths, and without the aid of a computer you could probably work out the square root of 1,081 in about half an hour, using a series of calculations that got you closer and closer to the answer. But this quantum system would enable you to do the same calculations in a fraction of a second."

"I see. So, I'm either going to come out of this as a math nerd, a vegetable or ... dead."

There was a silent pause. No one knew quite what to say. Daniel looked at the three of them who were all gazing at him in concern.

"I might not recognise any of you after this," he continued. "I might not even be me. This 'me' might be about to die, and a new 'me' emerge. If that's the case, let me just say ... thank you. To all three of you."

He held out his hand to George. "Thank you for all you've tried to do for me, George." They shook hands.

"You're welcome, Daniel. Good luck."

"Thanks, dude," he said to Carlos. "You were my first friend."

Carlos pushed his hand aside and enveloped him in a big bear hug. "I still am your first friend, bro. No past tense needed."

Daniel turned to Kelly and saw that her eyes were brimming with tears. "Kelly ... I don't know what to say ..."

She hugged him tightly. "You just come back to us, okay? You come back to me. Because you owe me a dinner, and I mean to collect!" She disentangled herself from him and wiped her cheeks. "Now, I need you to lie on the bed," she said, indicating the medibed in the corner of the room. "You could experience disorientation or giddiness during the initialisation, so we don't want you falling over."

Daniel lay on the bed and stared up at the ceiling. His anxiety level was skyrocketing, and he had broken out in sweat.

"I'm just calibrating the NIT now," said Kelly. "It takes a few moments to locate and lock on to the quantum filament structures."

Daniel looked across at his three companions one last time, as if trying to store their images in his memory.

"Okay. Are you ready?" asked Kelly.

"Not really," said Daniel, "but let's get it over with."

Suddenly, his eyes glazed over and his body stiffened.

57

Daniel's psychotic episode lasted for almost 90 minutes. It was his longest break from reality so far. Kelly had been just about to initialise the quantum system when the episode seized him.

Finally, Daniel's face cleared and he looked around. "It worked!" he said, enthusiastically. "I'm alive and I still recognise you all! I'm still me!"

"No. I'm sorry, Daniel," said Kelly. "I haven't initialised it yet. I was just about to when you had another psychotic episode."

"Really?" Daniel was crestfallen. "How long was I gone"

"Nearly 90 minutes."

"Where are George and Carlos?"

"Just outside, talking with the other agents. I'll get them."

Kelly was back a few moments later, with George and Carlos in tow.

"How are you feeling, bro?" asked Carlos.

"I'm completely over this," Daniel said. "I just want to get this finished. Please, just do it. Either fix me or kill me – one or the other – but I don't want to go on like this any longer." He looked at Kelly. "I'm ready."

She nodded and sat at the console again.

"Okay, take two."

"Goodbye, guys," said Daniel.

Kelly wiped a tear that had strayed down her cheek.

"Initialising in three, two, one, now."

Daniel's eyes blinked rapidly for about 20 seconds then steadied. Daniel raised an arm and looked curiously at his hand, moving his fingers as he did so.

"Oh my goodness, it's working!" exclaimed Kelly, pointing at the console. One of the screens was showing a video feed that seemed to be coming from Daniel's eyes. The screen was showing everything that Daniel was seeing. "The quantum system is online!" Kelly said excitedly. She pointed at another screen "Look, we're receiving a data uplink!" Complex graphs were scrolling across the screen, indecipherable to George and Carlos but obviously meaningful to Kelly. "I can't believe it! It's actually ..."

Suddenly the video screen went blank, and Daniel's arm flopped to the bed and his eyes closed. He remained immobile and Kelly scanned the data screen.

"Is he ... is he dead?" asked Carlos.

"No. He's alive. His brain readings have all returned to normal, but the quantum system just stopped working. It just shut down."

She looked at Daniel's readouts. "He appears to be sleeping. I'm going to try to initialise it again." She fiddled with a few settings, then said, "Initialising in three, two, one, now."

They all looked at Daniel. Nothing happened. Kelly stared at the screens. Nothing was happening there either.

"What's going on?" asked George.

"Um ... The quantum filaments are no longer responding to my input. It looks like ... they're completely dead. I'm getting nothing from them at all. They must have ... shorted out." She looked at Daniel with concern.

"Does that mean that Daniel is ... gone?" asked Carlos, looking at his friend.

Kelly rushed over to him and took hold of his hand.

"Daniel? Can you hear me?"

Daniel's eyes opened. He looked around in confusion. "Where

am I? What am I doing here?" He sat up and Kelly stepped back a little.

"Daniel, do you know my name?"

He stared at her and frowned. "You look like a doctor."

She stepped back and held her hands to her mouth, her eyes brimming with tears.

Daniel smiled. "So, you'd better wear something less 'doctorish' tonight when I take you to dinner. Where do you want to go?"

"You bugger!" she said, launching herself at him and smothering him in a hug.

"Dude, that was just plain cruel!" said Carlos.

"Sorry. I couldn't resist."

Carlos chuckled and shook his head.

"That wasn't funny, Daniel!" Kelly said, wiping a tear from her cheek. "Don't you ever do anything like that again!" She walked back to the console. "Now, leave the cap on for a second. I'm trying to work out what just happened."

"Did it work?" asked Daniel, coming to stand beside her.

She didn't answer. She scrolled through several screens and tweaked a few settings, then stared at the readouts for several moments.

"Well," asked Daniel. "Is it working?"

"There's good news and there's bad news," announced Kelly, finally.

"Tell me the good news first," said Daniel. "I haven't had a lot of good news lately."

"The good news is that your limbic system is no longer supercharged. By resetting the quantum filaments, they have ceased to function as magnifiers or boosters overstimulating your limbic receptors."

"Plain language, please," said Daniel.

"You won't be having any more psychotic breaks. You're cured."

Carlos slapped Daniel on the back. "Congrats, dude!"

Daniel just stood there with a huge look of relief on his face. "So, what's the bad news?"

"Nothing too major," assured Kelly. "The quantum system is completely unresponsive. It's failed."

"So, I'm not going to be a genius?"

"Afraid not."

Daniel nodded. "I can live with that. Genius is over-rated anyway."

"It's just as well, bro," said Carlos. "One guy shouldn't have killer good looks AND a super-intellect. It wouldn't be fair on all the other guys in the world."

"True, dude, very true," answered Daniel.

"Oh my goodness!" said Kelly with feigned exasperation. "You guys certainly live in your own fantasy world."

"Daniel, what is the square root of 1,081?" asked George.

Daniel frowned, as if trying to dredge the answer up from the depths of his mind. "I'm sorry, George. I have absolutely no idea."

58

They got into the lift on B2 level and selected the top floor of the Senticorp building. As the lift began ascending, Daniel asked, "Now that the whole quantum thing has turned out to be a big flop, what happens to all those filaments in my brain?"

"Nothing," said Kelly. "They're only a micron in diameter, so your brain won't even notice them They will just sit there like a disused circuit."

"Sounds like how most of his brain already operates," said Carlos.

"Ha, ha. Has anyone ever told you you're hilarious?"

"All the time, bro, all the time."

Daniel smiled, then looked at George. "So, what's next for me?"

"We need to take you back to Pittsburgh where you will be transferred to a low security correctional facility. Unfortunately, we can't put it off any longer. I'm sorry, Daniel."

"That's okay. You did your best for me, George, and I appreciate that."

Kelly made an observation. "Daniel will still need full protection, even during his incarceration, because the quantum molecules and linking enzyme in his brain are incredibly valuable. If a competitor could obtain those, they are only one or two tweaks away from a successful breakthrough."

George nodded. "We'll make sure he's adequately protected. And you, as well."

The lift door opened and they emerged onto the executive floor. They walked along the corridor toward the lift that would take them to the landing pad above. The armed JUDAN agent saw them coming and pressed the lift button for them.

They were about five metres from the lift when George suddenly stopped. He reached out and grabbed Daniel and Kelly, stopping them in their tracks while Carlos kept walking. Carlos reached the lift and turned back with a frown on his face, standing beside the guard.

"George? What's wrong?"

George had drawn his laser pistol and was pointing it at the JUDAN agent. "Don't raise that weapon or I'll shoot!"

"George, what are you doing?" asked Carlos.

"That's not the same guard who was here when we arrived!" said George.

"I'm the new shift," the confused agent explained. "We just changed."

"I don't believe you. None of the other agents downstairs were different."

"They're on a different shift timetable."

"I don't think so," said George. "That wouldn't make sense."

"George, put your gun down. Please!" said Carlos.

George continued to keep his weapon trained on the frozen agent. "If you really are a Justice Department agent, who is the local duty officer?"

"I don't know. I'm not from the local field office. A bunch of us have been dragged in from the office in Macapá, Brazil, to help with the shifts."

George shook his head. "I don't believe you." He quickly glanced at Daniel and said, "We're going to leave via another route." When he looked back toward the lift, Carlos had a pistol in his hand, pointed directly at George.

"Drop your gun, George."

"What the hell is going on?" asked Daniel in confusion.

"George is working for Blackstar," said Carlos. "He's obviously organised some alternative transport for you."

"That's not true," said George, his gun still pointed at the guard. The guard made a slight move to raise his rifle, but George yelled, "Move that weapon one more centimetre and I will shoot!" The guard froze again.

Carlos kept his gun aimed in the centre of George's chest. "The game's over, dude. Drop your weapon. I'm not letting you take them out of here."

Daniel and Kelly had stepped slightly to the side, toward the walls of the corridor, leaving George in the centre facing the other two in front of the lift.

Carlos kept looking at George but spoke to Daniel. "He's been working for Blackstar all along, bro. We only began to suspect this morning, when a call was logged from somewhere in the JUDAN building in Pittsburgh to Blackstar Laboratories in Singapore. The chief of station informed me before we left. He suspected it was George and told me to be on my guard. I'm sorry dude, we should have taken more direct action."

"That's complete bullshit!" said George. "He's lying, Daniel! It must be him."

Carlos moved slowly toward the side wall of the corridor, away from the guard, opening their angle of fire.

"Stop moving!" said George. "Daniel, Kelly, your lives are in danger here. We need to go. Please! Trust me!" He took a step backward, but Daniel and Kelly remained where they were, confusion written on both their faces.

"You made another call to Singapore, yesterday, as well George. And about 30 minutes later, the Blackstar surveillance around the Zurich head office where the cat had been taken was removed. They stopped watching that building and started focusing solely on the Pittsburgh building."

"I didn't call anyone!"

"George, last chance! Drop your weapon. I promise you won't

be harmed. We'll get you a good lawyer. You've been a good JUDAN agent. I'm sure there must be extenuating circumstances that have led you to this. We'll help you, dude. Please, George, surrender. It's over."

Carlos took one more step to the side. George swung his gun across to cover him and, as he did so, the guard saw his opportunity and started to raise his weapon. George swung his pistol across and fired, hitting the guard in the chest with a sizzling bolt of laser. Then George's chest seemed to explode as a laser blast scored a direct hit. George was flung backward, his pistol flying through the air, and he lay on his back, immobile, with a smoking hole in the middle of his chest. Daniel turned to see Carlos's pistol still pointed at the spot where George had stood, a wisp of smoke rising from the end of the barrel and the distinctive smell of ozone lingering in the air. He slowly lowered his pistol, as if in shock.

With a shake of his head, Carlos seemed to snap out of his shock. He pocketed his pistol and strode to the lift which had closed. He pressed the button and, as the door opened, he turned to Daniel and Kelly who were still standing in shock.

"Quickly, bro! We probably haven't got much time. There may be other Blackstar agents in the building. I need to get you out of here, to safety."

Daniel started to move toward George, to check on him, but Carlos yelled, "Dude! He's dead! And we're running out of time! We need to go! Now!"

Carlos was in the lift, holding the door open, beckoning them to follow. After a moment's hesitation, Daniel grabbed Kelly's arm and led her to the lift. The door closed behind them, and the lift ascended.

59

C arlos, Daniel and Kelly ran across the tarmac to the waiting flitter on the Senticorp rooftop. They scrambled into the rear passenger compartment and Carlos yelled at the pilot, "Go! Go!" as he slid the door closed.

The flitter took to the air and Carlos breathed a sigh of relief. "Are you guys okay?" he asked.

They both nodded. Daniel and Carlos were sitting next to each other facing forward and Kelly was sitting on the opposite bench seat, with her back to the cockpit and facing the men.

"I'm sorry you had to witness that, Kelly," Carlos said.

She just nodded again, her hands trembling slightly.

"You're shaking," said Daniel. He moved across to her and sat next to her, drawing her closer and reaching both hands over to clasp both of hers.

He glanced out the window, then said to Carlos, "We're not heading back to the airport."

"No. I decided to take you somewhere safe until I can be sure you're out of danger."

"But how did the pilot know where to go? You didn't tell him your change of plan when we got in."

Carlos just stared at Daniel, and a sly expression crept across his face.

"How long have you been working for Blackstar?" asked Daniel.

Carlos took his pistol out of his pocket and lay it loosely across his lap, casually pointing it in Daniel's general direction, his finger hovering over the trigger.

"You're a smart guy, dude. What made you suspicious?"

"The pilot. He's different as well. They wouldn't swap a flitter pilot who was half-way through a mission just because of a shift change."

Carlos nodded. "Like I said, you're a smart guy, bro."

"I think you should stop calling me 'bro', now. Don't you?"

"If that's what you want," said Carlos. "But I really do like you. I want you to know that."

"Gee whiz, that means a whole lot to me right now."

"No need for the sarcasm, dude. I'm just doing my job."

"Why? Why Blackstar? Have they got some kind of hold on you?"

"No hold. Just money. Tang is a very generous guy. I've been a big help to him over the years, giving him sensitive information. And he's been very generous to me in return. Of course, now that my cover is blown, this is my swan song – my retirement gig. The big man has promised me a very nice golden handshake for delivering you two."

"How did you do it?" asked Daniel. "How did you swap the guard and the pilot?"

"Easy, dude. They just walked through the front door at Senticorp soon after we arrived. They had JUDAN uniforms and fake IDs saying they were from the Macapá Field Office, sent to provide additional support. Then it was a simple matter of getting to the top floor and dispatching the guard and the pilot. No great loss. The bodies are probably stashed in an office up there somewhere."

"Why didn't you just abduct me long before this? You've had plenty of chances."

"The Blackstar agents were supposed to do the job so that I

could stay embedded at JUDAN. I kept feeding them as much information as I could. But those morons kept dropping the ball. Tang finally got sick of their incompetence and decided to use me as his trump card."

Daniel looked out the window. "So, where are you taking us?"

"A private airfield, east of here. Then you're both going on a lovely plane ride."

"Why can't you let Kelly go? Tang just wants me; he doesn't need her."

"Oh, but he does! You're the goose who lays the golden egg and she's the chef who knows how to cook the omelette. He wants both of you – you're both equally valuable."

Daniel kissed Kelly on the cheek and said, "Kelly I'm really sorry."

"What for?" she asked.

"For this!"

He shoved her violently to the side and shot Carlos in the chest.

60

C arlos slumped sideways in his seat, dropping his laser pistol. A strangled groan came from his mouth and his eyes rolled up into his head. Daniel picked up the laser and handed it to Kelly who was returning herself to an upright position on the seat after having been pushed sideways.

"Here. Keep this trained on him. He'll be out for a few minutes."

Without waiting for a response, he launched himself through the open hatchway into the cockpit and placed the barrel of the neural disruptor pistol against the neck of the pilot who was sitting in the right-hand seat.

"Don't move ..." was all he managed to get out before there was the sizzle of a laser burst and his left shoulder was instantly engulfed in agony. The pilot had obviously heard the commotion behind him and drawn his weapon, laying it across his lap.

As the blast of the laser hit him, Daniel's trigger finger in his right hand convulsed automatically and the neural disruptor gun discharged directly into the pilot's neck. The pilot slumped sideways into the small space between the two front seats and Daniel cried out in agony as he staggered back against the hatchway bulkhead.

"Kelly! Help me!"

Kelly came up behind him.

"Daniel! You're shot!"

The flitter was starting to angle down and spiral to the left.

"Help me get him out of the seat!"

She pulled the pilot from behind and Daniel shoved his torso sideways with his right hand, his left arm hanging uselessly by his side. The pilot plopped onto the floor in the hatchway. The flitter's descent became steeper and Daniel fell into the pilot's seat. He grabbed the control wheel with his good hand and pulled back. The flitter levelled out.

"Help me!" he called.

"How? What do I do?" There was panic in Kelly's voice.

"Get into the other seat. There are dual controls. Help me figure out how to land this thing."

The control wheel was the standard design that had been used for centuries; a comfortable handgrip for each hand centred around a central control column. Pull back for up and push forward for down. That much was clear. But the flitter had only small, streamlined vanes, rather than wings, and did not fly through the air like a conventional plane which used lift from the wings to keep it aloft. Instead, the flitter had four variable pitch engines built into the undercarriage and one on the tail which provided lift as well as forward propulsion. To land, Kelly and Daniel would have to cancel all forward momentum and angle the engines directly down, while gradually reducing power.

Daniel tried to explain this to Kelly, gasping in agony as he did so.

"Sure," said Kelly, sarcastically. "Just tell me which of these buttons and knobs and levers does what, and it should be easy."

"We'd better strap ourselves in first," he replied, "because if we can't work out how to do it, we'll have to go to Plan B."

"What's Plan B?"

"Crash it," he replied.

"I like the sound of 'Plan A' a hell of a lot better!" said Kelly.

She fastened her harness then took hold of the duplicate

wheel on her side while Daniel clumsily fastened his with his one good hand. For the next few minutes, they flew in circles over farmland to the east of Quito, having quickly worked out how to turn and how to increase and decrease altitude, using the control column. There was also a central throttle lever that increased or decreased the engine thrust of all engines equally – a master throttle control. They played with that for a few minutes, soon working out the minimum thrust setting before they started falling out of the sky.

But they couldn't find the engine's pitch controls, which would have enabled them to pivot the thrusters for a vertical landing.

Daniel heard two sets of moans coming from behind him and realised that the two incapacitated men were starting to come good again.

"Where's my neural disruptor?" he asked. "Can you see it anywhere? I must have dropped it on the floor somewhere here."

Kelly looked around and lifted the legs of the pilot who was starting to move.

"I can't see it."

"Where's the laser pistol I gave you?"

She bit her lip and gave him an apologetic look. "I don't know."

Daniel looked back over his shoulder through the hatchway into the passenger cabin and saw Carlos trying to sit up.

"I'm scrapping Plan A. It's time for Plan B," he announced. "Look for a nice flat field."

"Flat? Are you kidding? This is hill country, Daniel."

"Well, find me the flattest hill you can. And I'm going to need you to help me land this thing."

"You mean crash it."

"Whatever. I'll take us down using this control wheel thingy, and when I say to, you pull that throttle thingy all the way to zero."

"Oh my God, we're going to die," she said.

"Yes, that's true. We're all going to die eventually. But I'm hoping today isn't the day for us."

"I can't believe you. Even when we're about to die, you're being flippant."

"What can I say? – I'm a funny guy." He spotted something about a kilometre ahead. "What about that grassy bit over there?"

Kelly looked and said, "I don't know. It still looks pretty hilly."

They were flying very low by now and they flew over the next ridge, barely skimming it.

"There! Straight ahead! I'm going to try for that!" he said. "I'll drop down lower and try to land on the next slope. Drop the throttle as low as you can for me."

They began losing altitude following the descending slope of the ridge they had just crossed. Daniel was planning to land on the upward slope of the next hill, pulling back on the control wheel as Kelly cancelled the throttle.

The pilot was now partially up on his hands and knees, trying to roll over into a sitting position in the crammed passage from the cabin.

"We're not landing here!" said Carlos.

Daniel glanced back and saw the barrel of a laser pistol pointed directly at his head. Carlos was on his knees, not yet steady enough to stand, and had obviously located one of the lasers that had been dropped – either his or the pilot's.

"Where do you suggest I land?"

"You're not gonna land it. He is!" said Carlos, indicating the still groggy pilot. "Throttle back up and gain altitude. Now!"

"The thing is," said Daniel, "if I do that, I know I'm a dead man. Tang isn't going to let me live, is he? I may as well die here and now, my way, rather than hand myself over to him."

The flitter continued to lose altitude.

Carlos changed his position and pointed the laser at Kelly. "You might not care about your own life, dude, but I know you care about her. I've seen the way you look at her. So, I'm going to make you a really generous offer. You pull up now, and I won't blow her head off. That's a very good deal."

The flitter kept falling out of the air and Kelly and Daniel locked eyes. Kelly gave the tiniest shake of her head.

"I'm starting to count! One! ..."

The flitter was losing altitude fast, almost skimming the grassy slope that they were following.

"Two! ..."

The hill in front was looming up quickly and it was much higher and steeper than Daniel had anticipated.

"Crap!" he said and heaved back on the control wheel, calling out as he did, "Plan B!"

"Three!"

Three things happened simultaneously.

Kelly pulled the throttle lever to zero.

The pilot tried to stand up.

And Carlos pulled the trigger.

The laser blasted a hole in the front windscreen, the pilot's head having connected with the pistol as he tried unsteadily to get to his feet. Not that Daniel had time to notice. He was pulling back on the control wheel with his one good arm, trying to arrest their descent and flare their approach. The flitter bottomed out of its descent and the nose lifted and, for a few seconds, the aircraft gained a few sluggish metres in altitude as Daniel tried to match their angle of inclination with the looming hill's upward slope.

It didn't work.

The tail of the flitter hit first because Daniel had been too aggressive on the control wheel. The tail gouged into the grassy hill then flipped the craft onto its nose. From that point, the occupants lost all sense of up and down. An outside observer would have seen the flitter flip back into the air, tumble end over end, and then hit the ground again with a sickening crash. It continued tumbling up the hillside, making a horrendous grinding and tearing sound as it reconnected with the ground over and over. The tail was the first large piece to be shorn off, hurtling through the air to eventually smash into a small grove of trees to the right, slicing cleanly through the first two saplings and flattening several others. It was followed by dozens of other smaller pieces of wreckage that were flung far and wide as the flitter continued its devastating tumble up the side of the hill, quickly becoming a mangled mess.

Finally, the remains of the flitter came to rest in a deep gouge in the grass, two thirds of the way up the hill. The countryside was silent once again, except for the panicked lowing of a handful of nearby cows and the mournful cries of some black ravens who had been disturbed from their roost among the smashed grove of trees.

Gradually, the cows stopped lowing and resumed their grazing, and the cries of the ravens faded as they flew into the distance. Finally, all that could be heard was the tick-tick-ticking of the engines as they cooled and contracted.

No one moved.

61

Daniel's eyes fluttered open and closed several times, as if trying to decide whether the world was worth joining. Apparently, they decided it was, but the decision must have been a close one because they only half opened, looking as if they were ready to snap shut again at the first hint of anything even remotely unacceptable.

"There he is," said a voice. "I'll go and get the doctor." Footsteps faded down a corridor.

He looked to his right and saw Kelly sitting in a chair, wearing a white gown.

"Are you an angel?"

She smiled. "I've been called worse."

"Am I dead?"

"No. You're in a secure hospital facility in the basement of the JUDAN headquarters in Quito."

"Bloody hell! This is getting ridiculous."

"Yes, you are starting to make a bit of a habit of this," she agreed.

He noticed that her arm was in a sling. "Are you injured?"

"Just a broken collar bone, three cracked ribs and a missing spleen," she answered. "I'm in the room next door."

He felt the bandages on his shoulder. "What's my damage?"

"The laser blast pretty much destroyed your shoulder, so you've got a nice new titanium shoulder now."

"To match my artificial heart," he said. "If I keep going like this, I might be able to collect the whole set."

"Yes, you are slowly accumulating upgraded parts. You've only got two cracked ribs, and you kept your spleen, so I get to have a lot more sympathy than you."

"Duly noted."

"How long have we been here?"

"About 24 hours. They kept you sedated for a while after your surgery. I think it's because boys can't handle pain like us girls can."

"Is that right?"

"It's a fact."

"Fair enough."

"Speaking of facts," she said. "You lied to me."

"I did?"

"Yes. You said we were going to do a crash landing. That was all crash and no landing."

"That's a bit harsh," he replied. "I'd say it was more like ninety eight percent crash and two percent landing."

She shook her head. "No way. I'm willing to concede one percent landing, but that's as far as I'll go."

"You're a harsh marker."

They smiled at each other, and Daniel said, "So, we didn't die, hey?"

"Apparently not," she said.

"What about Carlos and the pilot?"

The doctor walked into the room at that moment, and Kelly got up, wincing and holding her side as she did.

"You really should still be in bed resting, Ms Walker," said the doctor.

"Ms Walker?" said Daniel looking at her.

She leaned over and kissed him on the forehead and whispered, "I'll explain later, Mr Fieldman," then she shuffled out of his room.

"Now Mr Fieldman, how are we feeling?" the doctor began.

Daniel wondered what the hell was going on but played along. "Not bad for a tin man," he replied.

"Tin man! Ha! Yes, very good. Very good. Tin man, indeed. Ha, ha!"

Oh dear, thought Daniel. *This is going to be more painful than my injuries.*

62

K elly came back after the doctor left and told him they had a visitor. She had barely sat down beside his bed when George Mallard walked in.

"You're not dead!" exclaimed Daniel.

George held his arms wide, as if to allow for full inspection. "Not at all. Very much alive and well."

"But ... he shot you."

"Laser-proof vest," explained George. "A light-weight, high tensile composite of boron nanotubes and maranium. The latest thing." He smiled. "Cracked some ribs of course, and I got knocked unconscious when my head hit the floor. Knocked some sense into me, my wife reckons."

"Did you know Carlos was working for Blackstar?" asked Daniel.

"Not really. The chief of station and I became suspicious that there was a mole in our midst because of several leaks over the last few months, but we didn't know who it was."

"I've got so many questions, I don't know where to start," said Daniel.

"In that case, I'll start," said Kelly. "Where did you get the gun? You know, the gun you shot Carlos with, inside the flitter."

"I've been carrying it around in my thigh pocket ever since the incident at Quito airport when I picked it off the ground beside the dead policeman. After the kidnap attempt in Pittsburgh, when I was thrown into a van in my pyjamas ..."

"Which we will henceforth refer to as 'The Great Pyjama Heist'," interjected Kelly.

"... err, yes, fine. After the 'Great Pyjama Heist', my clothes were brought to the Pittsburgh Basement flat by an agent, and no one noticed the tiny pistol in the pocket."

"Wrong," said George. "We found it. I instructed them to leave it there. I figured you couldn't kill yourself or anyone else with it, and it might actually come in handy."

"How right you were," said Daniel. Then to Kelly, he said, "When I moved across to sit next to you on the flitter, I slipped it out of my pocket and into my hand. Then I grabbed both of your hands and held them between us, with my gun hand underneath, wedged between our thighs."

"Is that what it was? I thought you were starting to get a bit fresh with me."

Daniel looked at George. "What happened to Carlos and the pilot?"

George shook his head. "They died at the scene of the crash. They were found more than a hundred metres from the wreckage. We think they were catapulted out of the flitter when it first impacted."

"Why didn't we die?" asked Daniel.

"Three reasons. Air bags, a maranium cage and seat harnesses, which Carlos and the pilot weren't wearing at the time. The outer fuselage of the flitter was a mangled wreck, but the inner cage of the cockpit and passenger compartment is made of the toughest metal known to man, so it was completely intact after the crash. Plus, you were both instantly enveloped in airbags. Technology and clever design saved your lives. Even so, you were both unconscious when we found you."

"And that's another question," said Daniel. "How did you find us?"

"A tracker planted behind your ear."

"What? You took that out."

"Yes and no. Our doctor took out the tracker from Blackstar. But I got him to put one of our own in just before he glued the wound together again. You didn't feel it because it was numb."

"And you did that in case I ever got taken again?"

"Yes."

"Did Carlos know about the new tracker?"

"No. Do you remember that I sent him to go and get the cat from the loungeroom just as the doctor was getting ready to glue up your wound? That's when we slipped the new one in."

"So, you didn't really trust him?"

"I didn't know who to trust at that point. I hoped he wasn't the traitor, but I couldn't be sure."

"What about Blackstar?" asked Daniel. "Can the Justice Department take action against them now?"

"Unfortunately, no. We don't have any hard evidence linking them to any of the recent criminal actions, and the only person who claimed to be working for them is now dead. Blackstar remain out of our reach, even though we are convinced of their involvement. Plus, RISC has been involved in this from the very beginning – the Republic of Independent States Commissariat. No doubt they have already covered their tracks and those of Blackstar. Which brings me to your ongoing predicament; both of you remain in danger."

"You mean, it's not over?" asked Daniel.

"I wish I could assure you that it was, but I can't. Blackstar have made three unsuccessful abduction attempts and I strongly suspect that they aren't going to stop until they get what they want. And remember, your situation remains doubly tenuous because, ultimately, it's the Republic of Independent States that is behind these abduction attempts. As a Colonel of RISC, Eli Tang has the almost unlimited resources of the Republic at his disposal. They will not stop until they have you in their possession."

"Me, too?" said Kelly.

"Yes. Both of you are firmly in their sights, now. Initially, it was just Daniel, but once they discovered that you, Kelly, were one of the creators of the technology, you became a target as well. Ideally, they would like to get their hands on both of you, but either one of you will do."

"So, they are going to keep hunting us, wherever we go," said Daniel, bluntly.

"Yes. Which is why both of you must die."

"Is this where you take a gun out and shoot us with an evil laugh?" said Daniel.

"I don't have to shoot you," George answered. "Because you're already dead. We've already set the scenario in motion. The moment I arrived at the crash site I saw an opportunity. Both of you were unconscious but not mortally wounded, so I brought you back here in body bags. Even though we arrived at the crash site with two flitters and eight agents, the only other person there who knew you weren't dead was the senior medic, whom I would trust with my life. All the other agents at the scene were told you were dead."

"Four occupants, and all four dead," said Daniel.

"Yes. And that is the story that has been reported in the news bulletins. Kelly, I'm sorry, but your sister now believes you are dead. At some distant point in the future, it may be possible to contact her, but not for a very long time."

"And you think this is necessary?" she asked.

"Definitely. Even if we place you in the witness protection program and give you a new identity and a new location, I am fearful that Blackstar's resources will allow them to eventually track you down. But if they are convinced you are dead, they won't be searching for you anymore."

"But I'll still need a new identity?"

"Yes, which is why we've given you the temporary name of Sally Walker while you're here. You can choose a new name for yourself once we've settled on a new location. We will set you up with a job and a home and everything else you will need in order to start a new life."

"What about Daniel? Does he get the same deal?" asked Kelly.

"Not exactly. Like you, both Daniel Newman and Daniel Mendez need to die. If we placed him back into prison under either name, Blackstar would almost certainly reach him there. If they couldn't get him out, they would simply arrange for him to be murdered in prison and then they would obtain a sample of his brain tissue. I'm sure they could do it."

"So, he's not going back to prison?" Kelly asked, a note of hope in her voice.

"It's not that simple. He remains a convicted felon in the eyes of the law, and the Justice Department is committed to upholding the law. We can't just go around arranging fake deaths for convicted criminals and setting them free, even if we disagree with the court's findings."

"So, am I going back to prison?"

"That's one option, yes. We could place you back into the prison system under a fake name and get you to serve out your reduced sentence. The problem with that, though, is that Blackstar will understandably be suspicious about the death stories that we've fabricated, at least initially, and they will be searching for any signs of either of you emerging as new identities. In your case, Kelly, their search for you will be next to impossible, because we have the whole world in which to place you. It would be like looking for a needle in a haystack. But in your case, Daniel, the prison system is a much smaller world. All Blackstar would need to find is a new inmate matching your description and with a similar sentence. Even with a new name, they may still find you."

"Where are you leading with all this?" asked Daniel. "Clearly you have some other plan."

"Yes. We do. We are going to send you into space."

"You're going to send me into space?" asked Daniel. "You're planning to make me an astronaut? Or are you talking about chaining me to an asteroid and getting me to break rocks for the next ten years?"

"More of the former," replied George Mallard. "ANSA – the Alliance of Nations Space Agency – is about to launch a mission to the stars. You've probably heard of the Longshot Mission."

Kelly and Daniel both nodded.

"They're building a massive starship on the Moon," said Kelly. "There's something about it on the news feeds almost every day."

"Yes. The starship has taken nearly 50 years to build and has been in its final stages of pre-flight testing for about six months. As Earth's weather has continued to spiral out of control, our scientists have begun to look to the stars for our future. It is hoped that a new earth-like world could be the answer to our problems, so there is a lot riding on this mission. It is scheduled to launch in about three weeks."

"And you want to put me on board?"

"That's the suggestion. Let me explain. The Justice Department is not ungrateful for what you've just done, Daniel. You brought down a highly placed mole within our organisation and you saved Kelly's life."

"He almost killed me in the process, though," Kelly said.

"Fussy, fussy," said Daniel. "The service might have been a bit rough, but I was cheap. You get what you pay for."

"Remind me to pay for a premium rescuing service next time," she said.

George continued, "In recognition of your recent actions, JUDAN is willing to commute your sentence further. We had already commuted it from execution to life in prison with a possibility of parole after ten years. But that would mean that even when you were released after ten years, you would still effectively be on parole for the rest of your life. And that would have placed severe restrictions on you for your whole life. But the Department is now prepared to offer you a sentence that is reduced even further. They are offering to reduce your life sentence to ten years in total, to be served while you are in cryogenic stasis during the space flight. By the time you wake up, along with the other colonists, 38 years will have passed on Earth and you will be a free man."

"Free, but no longer on Earth," said Daniel.

"That's right."

"And where will that be, exactly?"

"The planet hasn't been named yet. They're leaving that up to the colonists when they arrive. But the star that the planet orbits is called Tama, which is the Maltese word for hope, named by the Maltese scientist who discovered it. The star system is 37 light years from Earth. The starship will reach a maximum velocity of 99 percent of the speed of light and, to an outside observer, will take 38 years to travel there. But due to Einsteinian relativistic effects, the colonists on board will experience only 7 years of space flight. And, for the majority of that time, they will be asleep, effectively frozen in cryogenic stasis. Because of that, their bodies will barely age at all."

"So, I would sleep for 38 Earth-years and, when I wake up, I will have served my time and be a free man?"

"Exactly. Furthermore, no one on board will know of your prisoner status: not even the captain. This will just be an agreement between you and the Justice Department. You can even keep your name, Daniel Newman, because once the starship launches, you will be beyond the clutches of Blackstar and the Republic, even if they managed to find out you were on board."

"What's this new planet like?" asked Daniel.

"There's plenty of video footage of it on Solnet. ANSA launched probes there about 100 years ago, and they've been receiving images and data for the last 12 years. It's very Earth-like. Similar mass, temperature, atmospheric composition, axial tilt and orbital distance. It even has oceans and continents. In short, it looks like a wonderful place for humanity to make a fresh start. There's a lot of hope riding on this mission."

Daniel considered the plan silently.

"I don't see that you have a choice, Daniel," said George. "If you stay on Earth, you will be a criminal for life and, very likely, that life won't last very long, because Blackstar and the Republic will almost certainly get to you."

Daniel nodded. "I appreciate the offer, George. It's very generous. Can I think about it for 24 hours?"

"Certainly. It's a big decision."

"If I agree, when would I depart?"

"In a few days. As soon as you are well enough. The doctors tell me that the nanobot technology and stem-cell therapy will have you almost as good as new in a couple of days. You will be taken to the Moon where you will join the other colonists who are in the final stages of their training. There are 200 of them and they've been up there for a month, after having spent 18 months in intensive training on Earth. You will have a lot to catch up with."

"I see. So, I leave in a couple of days?" Daniel said, looking at Kelly. She gave him a sad smile and then looked away.

"Yes," said George. "In the meantime, you might be interested in watching your funerals. They'll be held tomorrow morning, in the botanical gardens, and we'll be providing a livestream of the services. Your caskets will be cremated, and the ashes buried under a tree in the garden. Do you have a choice of tree or plant?"

"What about something spikey and carnivorous for Daniel?" suggested Kelly.

"Ha, ha. Very funny. And what are you suggesting for yourself? Something pretty and fragrant, I suppose?"

"No, I was thinking of a really tall tree so that the birds could sit in the branches and poop all over the people below. I'd like to make an ongoing contribution to people's immersive experience of being in nature."

"Nice," said Daniel with a smile.

"In terms of your testimonies in the case against Senticorp," continued George, "clearly your 'deaths' mean that you will no longer be able to be deposed by the defence lawyers. It does weaken the case slightly. However, the Attorney General has already granted special dispensation for your recorded testimonies to be heard in court, giving them the legal credibility due to the obvious efforts made by Senticorp to apprehend you."

"Do you think Nigel Blakely and his cronies will be convicted?" asked Daniel.

"Our lawyers are extremely confident. Thanks to your testimonies and some of the additional evidence we have extracted from the data files at Senticorp, they are all going to spend many years behind bars."

"Sometimes, I absolutely love our justice system," said Kelly.

64

"What are you going to decide?" asked Kelly the next day, as they sat drinking coffee in Daniel's room. They had just watched their funerals, which Kelly had described as a 'big letdown'. (*Very disappointing! After all the taxes I paid, I only get a three-minute monologue by a crinkled old celebrant and a horrendous recital of something from the Dark Ages by an out of tune piper!*")

"I don't think I have much choice, Kel. I'm going to accept the offer."

She nodded. "I would, too, if I was you. It's your only chance to lead a decent life."

They sat in silence for a few moments, each considering the implications of that decision. They would have to say goodbye to each other in a matter of days, never to see each other again.

"I'll be in my early 30s when I get there, and you'll be in your late 60s back here on Earth."

"Yeah, that sucks," Kelly said. "But on the positive side, I will have eaten hundreds of bars of chocolate by then, and you won't have had any."

Daniel smiled. "When you put it like that, you've definitely got the better deal." He thought for a moment. "Where do you think you'd like to live?"

"I really don't know," she said, serious again. "I'd prefer somewhere quiet and isolated, somewhere close to nature, but George says it has to be a large city, otherwise I will be too conspicuous as a newcomer."

"You wouldn't be conspicuous on the Longshot mission – we'll all be newcomers there; newcomers to a brand-new world." He looked at her hopefully.

Her face fell. "I know. But the idea of travelling through a deadly vacuum for 38 years – or 7 years or whatever it is – scares the crap out of me. I just don't think I could do it."

Daniel nodded. "I understand. It's a bit of a mind spin for me, too."

They both looked glum, and sat in silence for a while, sipping their coffees. Then Kelly put on a brave face and turned to Daniel.

"But don't think for a second that you're going to get out of taking me to dinner! You owe me a dinner date before you go, and I'm gonna hold you to it. And I expect the full, premium treatment: expensive restaurant, amazing food, classy music, beautiful wine and scintillating conversation. Just because you're about to go galivanting off into the galaxy doesn't mean you get to weasel out of your promises."

"Yes, ma'am," he said with a grin. "Never let it be said that Daniel Newman doesn't keep his promises."

65

Three days later, Daniel and Kelly had been discharged from their hospital rooms in the basement of the JUDAN building in Quito and had been transferred to a secure two-bedroom apartment in the sub-basement level. Most Justice Department buildings in cities around the world had these kinds of secure apartments in their basements, to house people who needed to be kept away from the public eye.

It was mid-afternoon when George dropped in, to finalise details with Daniel, who would be leaving the next day. Kelly sat next to Daniel in the loungeroom as George went through the arrangements.

George addressed Daniel. "At 1:00 pm tomorrow, a flitter will take you directly from our rooftop to a private pad at the tether lift. You will be met by Mission Specialist Lieutenant Olivia Alvarez who will escort you as you ascend the tether lift to Hubble Station. We have ensured that you will have a private pod as you ascend, to minimise security risks. At Hubble Station, you will board a Fast Transit Lunar Shuttle. There are slower shuttles, but the FTLs will get you to the moon in 90 minutes, accelerating at three gravities until half-way and then decelerating at the same rate for the second half of the journey. After you land at Armstrong Base, you will board a Lunar Hopper to make the twenty-minute flight to Longshot Base. Over the following two or three weeks you will be given a crash training course on the base."

"Daniel's already really good at crashing," said Kelly. "I don't think he needs any more help in that area. In fact, I reckon he could probably be an instructor."

"Can you hear an annoying buzzing somewhere in the room, George?" asked Daniel.

George smiled and Daniel rubbed his arm where Kelly had just thumped him.

"In terms of your background story, we have had to think creatively. The problem is that everyone else on board, from the captain down to the lowliest of colonists, all earned a place on the team because they have a skill or a specialty that will be valuable to the mission. There are physicists and farmers, mathematicians and mechanics, lawyers and labourers, and just about anything else you can think of. Because we don't want anyone to know the real reason you are there, we needed to give you a believable cover story that you can reasonably live up to."

Daniel frowned. "I can't think of anything I'm good at – at least nothing I can remember, anyway."

"I think you're selling yourself short. Over these last few days, you've proved yourself to be remarkably resilient and resourceful, and you clearly have an intelligent, analytical mind. That is obvious from the way you ultimately identified Carlos as a traitor and managed to foil his attempt to kidnap you and Kelly."

"By crashing the flitter," added Kelly, enthusiastically. "I'm telling you, that's his primary skill set."

Ignoring her, Daniel asked, "So what did you come up with?"

"We've decided you are a Senior Investigator with JUDAN."

Daniel laughed. "You're kidding me? I'm effectively going on board as a prisoner, and you're making me out to be a law enforcement agent!"

"Yes, there is a certain amount of irony there. But realistically, you have the skill set to back it up and we have already provided the Mission Specialist with all your new documentation. The captain and executive officers have been told that your late arrival to the mission is because your recent role in bringing down a major criminal organisation has placed your life in danger – which is basically the truth."

"Senior Investigator Daniel Newman?" said Kelly. "I like it!"

George continued. "The challenge you will face is that you've missed out on a lot of training. The whole mission team, from executive officers to colonists, have been training for several years on a part time basis, and 18 months intensively. You will have to do your best to catch up in your training prior to launch and in the weeks immediately after. I am told that training will continue on board the starship during the first few weeks of flight, prior to everyone entering cryogenic stasis. Everyone is expected to have some basic proficiency in a second area, apart from their area of specialty, so that there is multiple redundancy. You'll have to decide what your second area of training will be."

"Maybe you could be a hospital janitor," said Kelly, "seeing that you spend so much time in hospitals."

"Very funny."

"I am, aren't I?"

"In terms of tonight ..." George began.

"Your last night on Earth," added Kelly, helpfully.

"... as our way of thanking you," continued George, "we have booked out an exclusive restaurant on the top floor of a building here in Quito. It's the most secure place we could find. We want you to have a night out together without feeling like you're locked up in this dungeon. We'll fly you by flitter from our rooftop to theirs and you'll have the whole place to yourselves for the first sitting. We've booked it from 7:00 pm to 9:00 pm. Have whatever you want – JUDAN is picking up the tab."

"That's very nice of you. Thank you, George," said Daniel.

"I wonder how many lobsters I can eat in one sitting," said Kelly.

~

At 6:45pm, Kelly finally emerged from the bathroom, after having spent more than an hour in there. She walked into the lounge-room where Daniel was waiting. He was dressed in nice casual clothes freshly purchased by the Department. Kelly had taken a lot of time with her makeup and hair. She was wearing high heels and a dress that was skin-tight and very short.

"Wow!" said Daniel, his eyes wide. "What do you call that thing you're wearing?"

"Us girls tend to call this a dress."

"A dress? That's a pitiful excuse for a dress. There's barely enough material there for it to be a pocket handkerchief."

"If you prefer, I could change into something more frumpy."

"No, no! Please keep wearing the pocket handkerchief. It's ... um ... very nice. Actually, it's stunning. And so are you."

"There! That wasn't so hard, was it?" she said with a smile. "Now, are you ready to give a girl a good time?"

"Absolutely." He bowed dramatically. "At your service, ma'am."

They walked into the restaurant shortly after 7:00 pm and were shown to a table beside a window, looking out at the lights of the city below. The lighting was dim, the music was soft and the food and wine, when it arrived, was delightful.

Four security guards had accompanied them in the flitter. One remained on the rooftop with the pilot and three took up positions around the restaurant, staying unobtrusive as much as possible.

A waiter poured their wine and Daniel raised his glass and said, "You are the most beautiful girl in the whole city. It's just as well we've got the restaurant to ourselves tonight because, other-wise, I'd be fighting off every bloke in the joint ..." Then he looked uncomfortable. "I mean ... every girl in the joint ... or something ..."

Now it was Kelly's turn to look uncomfortable, and she started to say, "Daniel, about that ..."

"Would you like to order now, sir and madam?" interrupted a waiter. They spent some time grilling him about the choices, and by the time the orders were placed, their conversation had moved on.

Time seemed to fly for both Kelly and Daniel, as they talked and laughed with the scintillating city skyline in the background. They finished a bottle of wine by the end of their mains and started on their second bottle while they waited for their desserts. Perhaps it was the wine, or the music, or both, but Daniel decided he needed to tell Kelly how he felt.

"Kelly, I don't know how I'm going to cope without you. I don't want to leave you."

"I don't want you to go either," she said, and had to dab her eyes which had suddenly become moist.

"You're the only friend I've got," Daniel continued.

"You'll soon make other friends," she said. "Out of 200 people, there's bound to be at least one who will be prepared to put up with you." She tried to smile bravely, but her eyes gave her away.

"But you're more than just a friend to me. I want you to know that I've grown to have very strong feelings for you, Kelly. You are incredibly special to me. And I need to say something that is probably completely out of order, because I know you're ... um ... you have different inclinations ..."

"Sir, did you order the crème brûlée, or was it madam?" asked a waiter.

"It was me," said Kelly.

"Chef regrets that it is not on the menu tonight. Perhaps madam would like to order something else?" He offered her the dessert menu again and she spent several minutes making another selection. By the time the waiter had departed, the moment had been lost and Kelly did not seem to want to go there again, so Daniel did not press his case any further.

The flight home on the flitter was breathtaking. The air was warm and tropical, and they were allowed to leave the sliding door open. Kelly snuggled up to Daniel and held his hand as they flew between the towering skyscrapers, and Daniel wondered how he was going to be able to leave this beautiful girl tomorrow.

Back in their apartment, once the guard who had accompanied them down in the lift had departed, they stood awkwardly looking at each other in the loungeroom. Again, Daniel felt like he wanted to say something, but he knew he couldn't. She wasn't attracted to men, and he would only make a fool of himself.

"Thank you for a lovely night," she said.

"You are the one who made it lovely," he replied. "I'll remember this night for the rest of my life."

They stood awkwardly for a few more moments, then Kelly said, "Well, I guess this is goodnight."

"Yes. I guess so," he replied.

"Well ... goodnight then."

"Goodnight," said Daniel. He leaned forward to kiss her and there was an awkward moment when he was trying to kiss her cheek and it seemed like she was trying to kiss him on the lips. They fumbled and broke quickly apart.

"Goodnight," said Kelly again, looking flustered. She turned and walked down the hallway, into her bedroom and closed the door, leaving Daniel standing alone in the middle of the room feeling absolutely miserable.

Half an hour later they were both in bed and the apartment was dark and silent. But Daniel couldn't sleep. He couldn't get Kelly out of his mind. Had she just tried to kiss him, and he'd missed his opportunity? Had she started to have feelings for him, too? Surely, the signs were there? She'd been giving off signals all night. In fact, for several days, he had been convinced that she was feeling the same way toward him as he felt for her. He couldn't be misreading it that badly, could he?

He got out of bed. This was his last night on Earth. He would never have another chance to tell her and to see if she felt the same.

He opened the door and crept to her door, putting his ear to the door, wondering if she was already asleep. He heard a vague rustle of sheets and movement, then nothing. He raised his hand to the door, preparing to knock, wanting desperately to believe that he might have a future with this girl. He came within a centimetre of knocking before his hand froze and he came to his senses.

Fool! She's gay! She's already told me that! I'll only offend her and ruin our friendship. He shook his head and walked back to his room.

Meanwhile, Kelly had heard what sounded like soft footfalls outside her door, and her heart had started beating like a hammer. She pulled back her sheets and stood up in her thin nightie and tiptoed to the door. Had he come to take her in his arms? Was he standing outside her door, even now? She stood in silence, listening but heard nothing. She waited as the silence stretched out, then finally summoned the courage to open the door. She cracked it and peeked out. But there was no one there. His door was closed. She closed her own door and lay back down on her bed, but sleep would not come.

66

1:oo pm came all too quickly for Daniel. He and Kelly had shared breakfast and lunch and had chatted happily together all morning, and she had seemed energised and bubbly the whole time. Clearly, she was not feeling the weight of his imminent departure like he was. It was obvious, therefore, that she didn't feel as strongly as he did. He felt relieved that he had not embarrassed them both last night and ruined a good friendship.

George came to collect him shortly before 1:oo pm and he started to say goodbye to Kelly.

"Don't be silly," she said. "I'm not saying goodbye to you here. I'm coming with George to see you off at the tether lift. It's kind of exciting because I've never seen it up close!"

"Oh. Alright. That ... that will be good."

The flight to the Tether Lift Terminal didn't take long. They landed on the rooftop of the three-storey terminal building and caught an ordinary lift down to the ground floor. The building was a doughnut shape and the bottom floor was a massive concourse which ran all the way around, like the concourse behind the tiered seating of a football stadium. The internal curved wall had several entry and exit gates, with security and check-in procedures. Beyond that wall was an open-air tarmac,

100 metres in diameter, open to the air, with the huge tether lift cable itself rising from the centre and disappearing into the sky above.

As the three of them, along with two security guards, walked through the outer concourse of the building, they were greeted by a holographic image of a smiling flight attendant hovering in mid-air, issuing instructions.

"Welcome to Quito Tether Lift Terminal. Entry to the Tether Lift requires appropriate authorisation. Please ensure that your biochip has today's ANSA clearance code. Biochip updaters are located at various points around the terminal. Please update your biochip, if necessary, prior to reaching the scanning gates."

"You don't need to worry about that," said George. "Mission Specialist Alvarez will authorise your chip. Ah, here we are. Gate 2."

George led them to a counter, behind which stood a male attendant in ANSA uniform, which had panels of navy blue and royal blue with the ANSA insignia on the left breast. The signage over the counter read, Alliance of Nations Space Agency, Quito Tether Lift Terminal, Gate 2.

George introduced himself to the attendant who responded, "Welcome, Special Agent Mallard. Lieutenant Alvarez is expecting you. I'll call her immediately." He made a quick comm call and less than a minute later a tall, slender woman in an ANSA officer's uniform stepped out of an adjoining door and greeted them.

As introductions were made, Daniel felt a growing dread at having to say farewell to Kelly. The thought of leaving her was like a dead weight anchoring him to the spot. He couldn't listen properly as introductory small talk was made, so consumed was he with the dreadful task of saying goodbye to the woman he had come to care for so deeply and whom he would never see again.

He realised that Alvarez had just said something to him, and he replayed her words in his mind: "Please show me your wrist, Mr Newman, and I'll authorise you."

He held out his left wrist and Mission Specialist Olivia Alvarez quickly scanned it with her updater. Her portable device gave a satisfied beep and she said, "That's you done. Now you, Dr Rearson."

Daniel watched, dumbfounded, as Alvarez then scanned Kelly's wrist. Kelly was watching him with a sly smile on her face.

"What's happening?" asked Daniel, not quite believing what he was seeing.

"She's authorising me," said Kelly. "I thought that would have been fairly obvious."

"Yes, but ... I thought ..."

"You thought I wasn't coming. Yes. I wasn't. But then I thought I couldn't let you go off and have all the fun and leave me here all alone eating chocolate until I'm the size of a walrus."

"You're coming on the mission?"

"He's not very bright, is he?" said Alvarez to Kelly, with a conspiratorial smile.

"No, he can be a bit thick sometimes. That's why I need to come along; to explain stuff to him."

"When did this happen?" asked Daniel.

"I called George this morning and asked if it was too late to change my mind, and he's been a darling and rushed around all morning getting it organised."

Daniel looked at George and then back to Kelly. "Thank you. Thank you, both of you. This is ... wonderful!"

"In the end, it's the safest option for Kelly as well," George said. "It will be a weight off my mind to know that you are both completely out of harm's way." George reached out and shook Daniel's hand, saying, "I wish you a long and happy life, Daniel. Thank you for everything you've done in recent days."

"You saved my life, George. It's me who should be thanking you."

George turned to Kelly and said, "Take care of yourself, Kelly. You're going to be a great asset to the team."

She reached up and hugged him, saying, "Thank you, George. Thanks for everything."

George stood watching while the three of them walked past the security desk and through the self-opening sliding door onto the central tarmac, with Alvarez in the lead. Daniel had only taken a few steps out onto the tarmac, however, when he heard George call out:

"Daniel! Before you go, can I have a brief word?"

Daniel turned and saw George beckoning him back. Kelly stopped and turned as well.

"Wait here, I'll be back in a second," said Daniel.

Kelly watched Daniel walk back and talk briefly with George then return to her.

"What was that all about?" she asked as they continued walking toward the tether lift.

"I'll tell you later."

67

They walked across the tarmac to the five-metre diameter tether lift cable and tilted their heads back to see it disappear into the sky above. Up close, it became clear that the cable was not one single cable, but many, somehow fused together. At the base of the cable sat one of the two pods that spent the day going up and down to the space station above. As one ascended on one side of the cable, the other descended on the opposite side. The pod was a large, semi-circular conveyance with transparent walls, floor and ceiling.

"Do either of you suffer from vertigo or fear of heights?" asked Alvarez.

They both shook their heads.

"Well, if you start to feel dizzy, I can issue you with contact lenses that will make the walls appear solid."

"I think we'll be alright," said Kelly.

They entered the pod and looked around. Most of the interior was taken up with comfortable seats with harness belts. The perimeter of the pod, nearest to transparent walls, was clear for people to stand or walk around.

As they stood admiring the pod interior, Alvarez explained

what to expect. "When we get to Hubble Space Station, you will weigh about half of your current weight."

"We won't be totally weightless?" said Kelly, somewhat surprised.

"No. To be truly weightless, you would need to be in a stable self-sustained orbit. A self-sustained geosynchronous orbit is at an altitude of 35,786 kilometres, which is where the anchoring asteroid is located, to which the end of the tether cable is attached. If we travelled to that asteroid at the end of the cable, we would be weightless, as we would be in constant freefall around the Earth. But Hubble Station is only a fraction of that distance up the cable; a meagre 1000 kilometres above the Earth. It stays in geosynchronous position above Quito only because it is clinging to the cable. To be weightless at that relatively low altitude you would have to be in a much faster orbit. The upshot is that Hubble Station is travelling much too slowly at that height for us to be in free fall and, therefore, completely weightless. But it is still travelling at a sufficient velocity to cancel out a percentage of Earth's gravitational pull on us. The reason we built Hubble Station so low is so that there would still be partial gravity to make it easier is for people to transit to and from shuttles."

"Easy for us novices?" suggested Daniel.

"Yes. But even in reduced gravity, you will still need to be careful. It will take some getting used to."

"I'm sure we'll be okay," said Daniel, expressing it more confidently than he actually felt.

She gestured to the interior. "We've got the pod to ourselves, so sit anywhere you like. I need to make a couple of calls so, if you don't mind, I'll sit at the back and leave you in peace. There will be plenty of time on the Lunar shuttle flight for me to bring you up to speed and answer your questions. Enjoy the ascent!" She moved to the back, sat down, and started talking softly.

Daniel and Kelly sat in seats in the front row and Daniel was just about to say something when a holograph of a female flight attendant appeared in mid-air in front of them.

"Welcome to Quito Tether Lift. We ask that you keep your

harness fastened during the acceleration and deceleration phases of the ascent. We will be accelerating at 0.25G for approximately two minutes, reaching an ascent speed of 1,140 kilometres per hour. Once acceleration has ceased, a green light on your armrest will indicate that it is safe to move around the pod. The journey to Hubble Station will take 52 minutes. Enjoy your ascent."

She had barely finished speaking when they sensed a soft vibration and felt themselves pushed gently down into their seats. The pod started smoothly and noiselessly ascending the cable. In a matter of only a few moments they had risen higher than the tallest buildings in Quito and the ground began to recede from them at an ever-increasing rate.

"So, are you feeling okay about all this?" asked Daniel. "You told me that the idea of hurtling through a deadly vacuum scared the crap out of you."

"It does," she said. "But the idea of saying goodbye to you was even less appealing." She reached out and took his hand. "Besides, true friends never walk away from each other."

"Is that today's truth?"

"Yep."

"I like that truth."

"So do I," she said, giving his hand a squeeze.

The green light on their arm rests came on, indicating that they could stand up and walk around, but they chose to stay where they were. They watched in fascination as the ground below them shrank and the horizon developed a curve. The sky turned from blue to violet and then, finally to black, and the Earth became a sphere below them.

Eventually, the holograph of the flight attendant appeared before them again. "Deceleration will commence in 30 seconds. Please return to your seat and tighten your harness, ensuring that you have secured all loose items."

Soon after, they felt themselves being forced upward against the restraints of their harnesses as they were decelerated toward the roof of the pod. Finally, the pod slid smoothly into a docking bay on the underside of the space station. A docking tube slid out and attached to the outside of the pod and a loud hissing sound could be heard as the docking tube was pressurised.

A pleasant female voice spoke again, this time without any holographic image. "Welcome to Hubble Station. We hope you enjoyed your ascent. Please make your way through the docking tube. Have a nice day!" The pod door slid open, and they unclipped themselves and stood up.

"How was that?" asked Alvarez as she came to stand beside them.

"Amazing!" said Daniel.

"Stunning!" said Kelly.

Alvarez smiled. "You haven't seen anything yet. Wait until you see our home for the next 12 years. Follow me. We need to catch a shuttle." She walked through to open pod door and turned left into the docking tube, disappearing from view.

Daniel was about to follow, but Kelly grabbed his arm and said, "Wait. There's something I need to do first." She put her arms around him, drew him to her and kissed him. At first it was tentative, but when Daniel responded, she melted into him, and they stayed like that for several seconds. After a few moments Daniel drew back and looked at her in confusion.

"I thought you said you were gay?"

"I lied. It's a defence mechanism I sometimes use."

"It's very effective. It threw me right off the scent. Are you sure?"

She laughed. "Am I sure I'm not gay? Yes, I'm pretty sure. There's not a gay bone in my body."

"Well, what's this, then?" he asked, squeezing something.

"That's my butt."

"Oh. So it is," he said, giving it another squeeze for good measure. "Very nice it is, too."

"Thank you," she said, kissing him again. When she came up for air, she said, "You know, I've always wanted to join the mile high club."

"Umm ... There's a bit more to it than just kissing, if you want to be a fully-fledged club member."

"You don't say? Huh. Do you think you can show me sometime?"

"I don't know, I'm pretty booked up. I'll have to get back to you."

Olivia Alvarez returned to stand in the open doorway, looking on with an expression of mild annoyance. "Are you two coming?"

"Sorry, Lieutenant, just one more thing." She looked at Daniel. "Daniel, what did George say to you as we were leaving?"

Daniel gave her a circumspect look, as if weighing up whether he should say anything. Then he shrugged and said, "George asked me what the square root of 1,081 is."

"Again?"

"Yes."

"He doesn't give up, does he?"

"No."

"And what did you say?"

"I told him the answer."

"Which is what?"

"32.87856444554719."

THE END

... of the beginning.

SCIENCE STUFF

All good science fiction is based on existing science and science that can be reasonably extrapolated into the future. Here are some interesting facts that form the basis for this novel:

QUANTUM COMPUTERS

Quantum computers are already in development and use. IBM current has about 20 quantum computers in operation, but because of the issues I'm about to explain, they aren't exactly portable.

The standard computer that we all use in our current devices, encodes information and carries out computations using 'bits' that exist in a binary state, meaning they are either on or off. They are usually encoded as a 1 or 0. Quantum computers, on the other hand, use particles in the subatomic realm – electrons or photons (as distinct from protons) – for encoding and calculating. The basic units of a quantum computer are called 'qubits' and they have the advantage of being non-binary. This means that as well as being either in an on or off state, they can also be in a third state: on and off simultaneously. They do this via quantum processes called superposition and quantum entanglement.

Okay, all you've probably heard so far is "blah, blah, blah". I get it! But this is a really big deal, because it means that a quantum computer can undertake certain calculations *much* faster than a standard binary computer. Here's an example:

Suppose you wanted to find one item out of a field of one trillion. If you gave that task to a standard computer – even one of today's supercomputers – it would take that computer about one week to find the item you were searching for. (A field of one trillion is a REALLY big field!). But give that same task to a quantum computer, and it would complete it in just one second. That's right! For that kind of computation, a quantum computer is over 600,000 times faster than a standard computer. That is because a quantum computer's non-binary state enables it to examine all one trillion items simultaneously, whereas a standard computer must examine each item in the field individually and consecutively – one at a time.

The major problem with quantum computers is that for qubits to operate in their state of superposition and quantum entanglement (yes, I know, 'blah, blah, blah', but hang in there!), they need to be at extremely cold temperatures – about minus 273 degrees Celsius. This, of course, requires serious refrigeration facilities. That's why you currently don't have a mobile phone or laptop with a quantum operating system.

The push is on, however, to develop a quantum computer that can operate at room temperature. Will it ever happen? I think so. In fact, several scientists are already claiming some success with a room temperature quantum computer of just a few qubits that lasted for a few seconds.

I also believe that a biologically based quantum computer will one day be developed. But inside someone's brain? Maybe not. That's why they call this 'science fiction'. (But who knows? They could have already done it to me and erased my memory!)

GEOSYNCHRONOUS ORBITS

There were several references to geosynchronous orbits in this novel. I have some friends for whom this term was a bit confusing. So here is an attempted explanation.

Geosynchronous orbit refers to an object that orbits the earth and stays permanently above the same point on the Earth's surface. It matches the Earth's rotation. This can only happen at a very precise altitude above the Earth: at an orbital height of 35,786 kilometres (22,236 miles). At this height, the orbital velocity of the object will enable it to precisely match the Earth's rotation, so that an observer on the ground (using a telescope) could see the object as permanently stationed above them. At no other height is this possible because orbital speeds vary with height. An object in a low orbit requires a much faster orbital velocity than an object in a high orbit. This is because the pull of Earth's gravity is stronger the closer an object is to the Earth's surface, therefore requiring a faster lateral (sideways) velocity to counterbalance the force of gravity and keep the object from falling to Earth. An object is in a stable orbit when its lateral velocity perfectly counterbalances the downward pull of Earth's gravity.

Here are the orbital speeds that are required for varying heights:

- Altitude of 200 km = Orbital speed of 7.8 km per second
- Altitude of 20,000 km = Orbital speed of 3.9 km per second
- Altitude of 35,786 km = Orbital speed of 3.1 km per second

The last example is the height and speed of a geosynchronous orbit. An object orbiting the Earth at that precise altitude and velocity, will exactly match the Earth's rotation and will remain stationary over the same point on the Earth's surface. (The Earth is only rotating at 0.465 km per second at its surface but an object in geosynchronous orbit is obviously travelling in a much wider arc and, therefore, at a much higher velocity in order to keep pace with Earth's rotation.)

TETHER LIFTS

I love this idea as a means of travelling into orbit, but whether it will ever be feasible is doubtful. The idea of a structure stretching up into space was proposed as early as 1895 (by a Russian rocket scientist named Konstantin Tsiolkovsky) and has been toyed with ever since. The concept is generally referred to as a 'space elevator', but I have called it a tether lift in my novel. It is an attractive concept, because it does away with the need for expensive rockets which use huge amounts of fuel to boost people and payloads into orbit.

For a tether lift to work, the cable would need to be attached to an object of significant mass in a very high orbit – beyond geosynchronous orbit. This object, perhaps an asteroid, would act as a counterweight, holding the cable up via the centrifugal effect generated by its own orbit. It would be similar to whizzing a tennis ball around your head on the end of a string. The string is held straight and tight by the centrifugal effect generated by the tennis ball's rotation. (The centrifugal effect is really a pseudo-force only made possible by the centripetal force of Earth's gravity. But we don't really need to go into that here.)

In the case of a space elevator or tether lift, the tether cable would be held in tension, allowing an elevator pod to ascend to a space station midway up the cable, in geosynchronous orbit.

The main challenge facing the construction of such a system is that current materials are not strong enough to withstand the tensile forces that would be acting upon the cable. Some scientists, however, have speculated that future advances in carbon nanotubes, boron nitride nanotubes or diamond nanothreads might produce a material that is light enough and strong enough to construct a tether cable.

In this novel, I have utilised the concept of carbon nanotubes mixed with maranium, a new metal mined on Mars. Maranium is a figment of my own imagination. It doesn't actually exist! That's why they call this science fiction. But who knows? We may discover some new metal or mineral in the future that makes the construction of space elevators feasible. Bring it on!

That's enough science stuff for the moment. Keep dreaming, everyone!

"Everything is theoretically impossible, until it is done." – Robert A. Heinlein.

LEAVE A REVIEW

If you enjoyed this book, I would be extremely grateful if you would leave a review on Amazon, Goodreads and other review websites. Reviews are hugely important for me as a self-published author. In Amazon's case, reviews impact Amazon's algorithms, helping the book to climb higher in the charts, thereby making it more visible to potential readers. Every single review really does help!

Leaving a review is very easy. To leave a review, just go to Amazon, search for my book and click on the reviews link next to the stars. A review of 4 or 5 stars is considered to be a positive review and a review of 3 or less stars is considered to be a negative review. (Unfortunately, Amazon only allows reviews from people who have spent at least $50 on Amazon over the preceding 12 months).

Thank you!

GET THE NEXT BOOK IN THE SERIES ...

BOOK 2

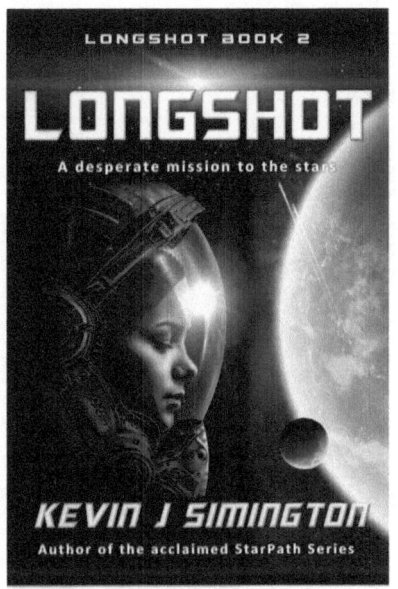

AVAILABLE FROM ALL MAJOR BOOK RETAILERS

The dramatic, action-packed story of mankind's first interstellar voyage.

"A spectacular imagining of the challenges and trials that a colony ship to another planet may face. Even better than the first book! It is one of those rare 'un-put-downable' novels."

BOOK 1 IN THE STARPATH SERIES

In case you haven't read it ...

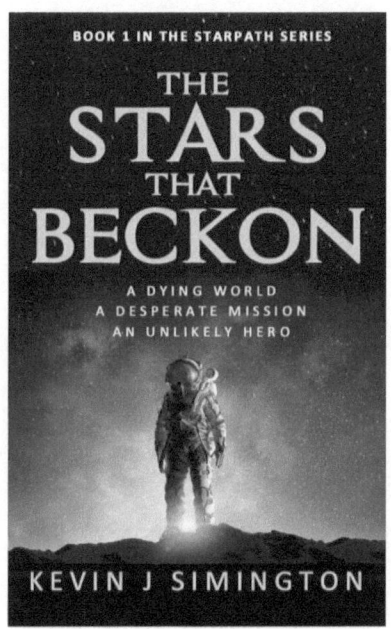

AVAILABLE FROM ALL MAJORE BOOK RETAILERS

A ragged band of desperate survivors flee from a dying world in search of a new home. The first book in the highly acclaimed STARPATH series. Science fiction at its best! You won't be disappointed!

SOMEONE ELSE'S LIFE

KEVIN SIMINGTON'S CRIME THRILLER!

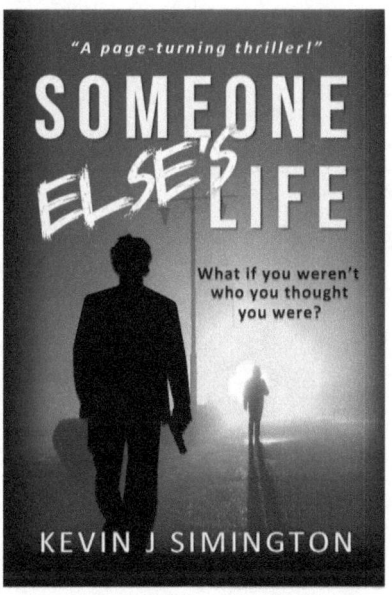

"A page-turning thriller by a master storyteller!"

Much more than a simple detective story, this is a complex portrayal of a good man who is pushed to extraordinary limits.

AVAILABLE FROM ALL MAJOR BOOK RETAILERS

ABOUT THE AUTHOR

Kevin J Simington is an acclaimed fiction and non-fiction author whose books are renowned for their intelligence, clarity and wit. He is a very popular conference speaker on the topics of philosophy, apologetics and science. He also writes for several international magazines.

Website:
https://kevinsimington.com

Amazon Author Page:
amazon.com/author/kevinjsimington

FREE EBOOK!

Join my mailing list and receive a FREE EBOOK. I will email you a complimentary copy of **"Welcome To The Universe: A Pocket Guide For Visitors"**. With stunning photographs and mind-boggling facts, the book provides a fascinating glimpse into the wonders of the universe and the many challenges of space travel. Just visit kevinsimington.com and tell me where to send your free copy!

SEND ME A FREE COPY OF "WELCOME TO THE UNIVERSE"